ADVANCE PRAISE FOR HEALER

Susan Miura's thought-provoking novel, *HEALER* brought out longings in me I've had for years. How I've wanted to have the gift of healing during times when loved ones were suffering, but to no avail. However, Miura's ever-present theme of "be careful what you wish for" is carefully balanced with the supreme message of what faithfulness, acceptance and love do to heal our wounds and bind up our hearts. It doesn't take a special gift to exhibit those, but the resulting miracle is just as powerful. Beautifully rendered. – **Lisa Samson, author of Women of Faith's Novel of the Year, Quaker Summer, The Passion of Mary Margaret, and Summer of Hope.**

Miura pens a unique and moving tale of a young woman's extraordinary spiritual journey amidst all the tangles of being a teenager. Evocative in its possibilities and yet totally relatable, this is a book that will not only keep any reader turning the pages, but also stop and think "What if that happened to me?" -- **Allie Pleiter, award-winning author of over 25 inspirational novels.**

Talented author Susan Miura has crafted an engaging young adult tale of the power of faith, love, family, and friends. I can't wait to read more of what Shilo does next with her amazing gift. –**A.J. Cattapan, award-winning author of Angelhood and Seven Riddles to Nowhere**

Muira's own gift of writing well crafted young adult suspense shines in this page turning story. Shilo's struggle to learn what her gift means for herself and those around her parallels questions many have about their identity and purpose. This diverse, sympathetic cast deals with weighty situations in between soccer practice and normal life in a seamless, enjoyable story. — **Amy Alessio, multipublished author, speaker, and librarian.**

Other Titles by Susan Miura

Show Me a Sign
(Young adult novel)

Pawprints in the Snow
Poems: How God Protects Animals from the Cold
(Non-fiction. Poems and wildlife photos for children.)

"The Perfect Crime"
(A short story in Falling in Love with You)

"Christmas Rainbow"
(A short story in The Spirit of Christmas: With a Foreword by Debbie Macomber)

"The Cotton Candy Man"
(A short story in Missing)

For Gary, my soulmate; for Nico, Kasie and
Dani; and for my grandchildren,
mom, sister, and brothers, who have all
painted my world in the brilliant
colors of love and limitless encouragement

HEALER

SUSAN MIURA

Susan Miura

Vinspire Publishing
www.vinspirepublishing.com

ISBN: 978-1981752034

Published by Vinspire Publishing, LLC

CHAPTER ONE

Shilo, Age Five

Warm, bloody fur oozes through my fingers. "You'll be okay," I whisper, but it doesn't take away the fear in his eyes. "You'll see. You'll be okay."

"Somebody should just shoot the thing." The blue-haired old lady stands by the curb, glaring at Shadow. "Ain't gonna live anyway." Her voice crackles like shoes on gravel. "Dumb dog. What was he doin', runnin' into the street like that? And why's that little girlie kneelin' next to him?"

A truck rumbles by and flings tiny stones that sting my face, but Mommy doesn't notice. She's busy trying to make my baby sister stop fussing. Seems like Julia's *always* fussing.

I lean down until my lips touch Shadow's floppy ear. "Don't die," I whisper. "Please."

Inside my head, I see his broken parts. Inside my soul, I feel his pain. Ba-bum, ba-bum. Our hearts thump together as death creeps closer like a big, hairy spider.

But I know something Shadow doesn't – God can squash death if he wants to.

Please, God, make him better. You have lots of power and lots of love. Please use those things to fix him.

My head gets light and dreamy. All the noises disappear. No more trucks rumbling or babies crying or old lady voices. And the whole world is washed in the color of love. Warmth replaces the tears in my heart. It flows through my body and down my arms like a river of cocoa, sweet and wonderful, then into my hands. Warmer and warmer. I spread my fingers, and they fill with heat. It flows into Shadow from my very own hands, but I can't see my hands; they're covered by bigger, stronger hands like Daddy's, only these glow soft as fireflies.

And I am not afraid.

"Shilo!" Mommy turns away from Julia to look at me. "*Mama mia*, what are you doing?"

The words swirl in a hazy blue mist. Mommy sways in the fog, her face soft and dreamy, but there's worry lines on her forehead. I look down at my red, sticky fingers. "My hands," I whisper. "My hands."

Shadow raises his head. He's not bleeding or jerking like before. He struggles to stand and falls back down but doesn't give up. When he tries again, it works. A warm tongue licks my cheek and makes me smile. He barks a happy bark.

"Would ya look at that," the old lady says. "Simply ain't possible." And all the people start talking at once.

"Oh, no." Mommy shakes her head. "No, no, no." She says it too quiet for the people to hear. But *I* hear. Why isn't she happy like me? I am too sleepy to ask and too sleepy to stand, even though she's telling me we have to go.

By the time we reach home, my jelly legs can hardly

hold me up. I lean against Mommy as she scrubs the rest of the blood off my hands. Julia watches from her stroller, cuddling her bunny blanket.

"So tired."

"I know, Honey. I know." Her voice is calm now, but something in her eyes reminds me of Shadow before he got better. "Come on, I'll tuck you in."

I take one slow step toward my room, then lay down on the cool kitchen tile, and close my eyes. Loving arms wrap around me.

"Please, God." Mommy's voice sounds far away, but her soft kiss brushes my forehead. "Not my daughter, too."

CHAPTER TWO

Shilo, Twelve Years Later

It's been three days since my family got slammed with the news. Cancer. Like a demon it rose from the depths, sinking its ragged claws into the one person who gets me. Really knows me.

On my nightstand, digital numbers glow 12:07 a.m.— nine minutes later than last time I looked. My sluggish brain drifts halfway across town to the hospital bed where Aunt Rita might be lying awake, fearing the future. Powerless over the disease raging through her body. The same body that leapt up to cheer for me at countless soccer games, clapped sixteen times as I blew out last year's birthday candles, and listened to my trials and triumphs since...well, since forever.

Thirst draws me away from the sweet comfort of my bed. I pad down the hall, past the closet where Mom hid my present with the glittery seventeen on top. It is carefully buried beneath an old backpack, where it will have to lie in wait for another month. Not that I care. If auntie's not there, singing off key and insisting I make a wish, what's the point? I tiptoe past Julia's room, where a poster of Yellowstone's prismatic spring covers half the door. She will happily explain, to anyone who will listen, how the colors result from microbes or something in the mineral-rich water. Everyone just nods and says "ohhh" as if they get it.

Before I reach the sink, hushed voices rise faintly from the kitchen, and I stiffen, straining to hear the words. Maybe it's about Aunt Rita.

"Who knows what might happen? I don't want her to find out she's different." Fear edges Mom's voice.

My head says they're talking about Julia again—she's definitely not a normal twelve-year-old—but the prickles on my neck disagree.

"Honey, Annie, look at me." Dad's velvet tone could calm a grizzly. "You can't keep her from going to the hospital."

"But all those sick people. You know what could happen."

The refrigerator door opens and thumps shut. Must be Dad grabbing the last slice of mom's chocolate peanut butter pie. "We've been over this a thousand times. Maybe the dog incident wasn't what you thought."

The prickles creep down my spine as a phantom memory hovers just out of reach.

"You don't know the signs, Nicky," she says. "You don't know what this could do to her life. What child lays her hands on a bloody animal? That dog had three feet in the grave, and to this day it's spry as a puppy." Her tone is laced with a quiet hysteria that unsettles me. Mom is a rock, and it takes nothing short of an earthquake to dislodge her. "Thank goodness she doesn't remember the details."

I stop breathing. No, they're not talking about Julia. My mind struggles to grasp the remnants of something halfway between a dream and reality. A dog. Bloody fur. Eyes crazed with pain and fear.

"Then the sleeping." Mom's words jar me back to the present. "Just like Nonna Marie."

My fingers clench the doorframe as images assault me. Glowing hands. My body warm and peaceful and light as air. Choppy memories that don't make sense but fit together like pieces of an unmarked puzzle.

"And remember what I told you last week? She brushed against the clerk at Target then mumbled something about feeling warm inside."

I gasp, remembering how the lady at the counter handed the gum to me and our hands touched. It was only a moment, but my heart...

"And her eyes, Nick. Her eyes."

"I know." It's the voice Dad uses with Julia when she's all psycho over getting a B on some genius-level test, rare occasion that it is. His sigh is audible even from a distance. "But it's been dormant for over a decade. Why would it surface now?"

"Maybe the dog was just a sign. Maybe she had to get old enough. I don't know." Muffled sobs rise from the kitchen. "And what about Rita?" Mom's voice cracks on her sister's name. "It's possible she could save her, but then the whole world would know."

My throat tightens at Mom's tearful words, but a cloud of confusion shadows the sadness. Who could save Aunt Rita? Certainly not *me*. I'd give anything to save her. Do anything.

And the world would know *what*?

Feet shuffle behind me. I whirl to find Julia standing in the hall, blowing my chance to eavesdrop in peace. "What are you doing up?" I whisper.

"I'm thirsty. Why are you standing here?" Julia's "Geologists Rock!" nightshirt hangs off one shoulder and down to her calves, clearly made for a much larger geology nerd. Dark, layered waves of hair flip crazily around her bed-head.

No need for her to know what I'm doing. "Just heading back to my room."

My sleepyhead little sister shrugs her acceptance, continuing on her way with a yawn. But the bathroom door clicks. Loud.

"Somebody's awake up there." Whispers and footsteps follow Dad's words.

Eavesdropping was tough enough when they were in the kitchen, but words from the family room? Impossible.

Avoiding the creaky floorboards, I sneak back to my room and lay on the carpet, ear pressed against the cool metal of the floor vent. Garbled words and angry tones rise through the air ducts. Puzzled and curious, I return to bed, trying to make sense of it all.

Why are they protecting me? And from what? I search my memories for details about the injured dog, and how it could possibly relate to the color of my eyes - eyes that solicit comments from total strangers who ask where I got the iridescent contacts. But everyone in the family knows I have Nonna Marie's eyes.

"Blue as a summer sky," Dad always says.

So cool to be the only blue-eyed Giannelli. Or as Julia would say, "an enigma." But at the moment, Mom's words, not Julia's, wrap around my brain like the chains of an earthbound ghost.

But then the whole world would know.

Like a mantra, it plays over and over in my mind, until I fade into the darkness of a restless sleep.

"Mom, come *on*! We're hardly going to have any time." I've been ready to visit Aunt Rita for six hours. This is beyond ridiculous. First she had to pay bills, then run to the store for flour and butter, even though she's not teaching her Perfect Pies class until next week. After that, she looked over Julia's homework papers, as if there were any need. Every time I mention going to the hospital, she says "We'll get there; don't worry."

I'm worried. Visiting hours will soon be over. If I had my own car, I'd have been at Chicago Suburban hours ago.

Finally, her bedroom door opens. "Okay." Mom pulls out her keys. "Okay." She repeats the word softer, smooths her skirt. "I'm ready. But remember, we can't stay long. And Shilo, it might be better if we didn't, you know, hug her."

She has officially lost her mind. "Have we stopped being Italian? I didn't get the memo."

"Just a quick hug. Don't linger."

This is the same woman who nearly squeezes the life out of anyone who comes through our door. Even my friends, awkward as it is. On the upside, they don't complain. They just call her Annieconda and, weirdly enough, keep coming back. Now Annieconda has just told me not to touch Aunt Rita. *My* Aunt Rita, who's always seen the best in me, listened to every story, every problem. If I could take her cancer, I would. But all I can do is pray and hug, though the latter is suddenly taboo, according to the stranger beside me.

We ride to the hospital in silence. I wish Dad didn't have to work today or Julia wasn't tied up with homework. Even listening to her drone on about the latest geological discoveries would be better than this. I could ask something about the cooking classes she teaches at the park district or when her article will be published in Chicago Cuisine, but she's clearly not in a talking mood. Stealing a glance at Mom, I search for something in her face that will unravel the mystery of last night's conversation. But it is a blank canvas, void of answers or even a cryptic clue. As we turn into the parking lot, I consider asking her flat out, but her heartbreak over Aunt Rita shadows her face, and I let it go. Instead, I turn to another matter she has uncharacteristically avoided.

"I brought the paper." I open my purse and unfold the parental consent form with the hospital's logo on top. "They did the background check and everything. I'm all set, except for this." Every time I've asked her to sign my hospital volunteer form, she's too busy. A simple signature is all I need. Two seconds of her life.

Mom shakes her head and sighs. "Not now, Shilo. I've got a lot on my mind."

"Two days ago you said you didn't have time. Yesterday you were too tired. Come on, this is the perfect time." I dig a pen out of my purse. "I can drop it off while we're there."

"I don't want to discuss it now."

"*Discuss* it?" My voice rises as I shake my head. "You *do* realize parents normally support this kind of thing."

"Can we just get through this visit? Is that too much to ask?"

I sigh my frustration and decide to drop it, but only because of Aunt Rita. The form returns to its original spot, still void of Mom's elusive signature.

The hands on the old-fashioned lobby clock show we have an hour until visiting time ends. Aunt Rita must be wondering why we abandoned her, and she's not the only one. She and Mom are close, despite the twelve-year age difference, so why are we here so late?

Yellow and purple tulip displays cheerfully decorate the brightly lit lobby, but they cannot erase the tears of the sobbing woman walking past me, or the despair of the man in the wheelchair. Or my fear. Aunt Rita refused to give Mom an update over the phone, saying she wanted to do it in person. We both know "in person" means bad news, plain and simple, but neither of us say it out loud. We simply sign in at the reception desk and head for the elevators that will take us to the fifth floor, where Aunt Rita awaits.

Mom stares at the floor numbers as they light one by one. "Have you heard from Melody?"

The sound of her name nicks my heart. Best friends since second grade, and lately she barely manages to send me a text. I get it. Ballet takes a lot of time and commitment. But so does soccer, and I still make time for my friends. Mom chose the wrong topic if she was trying to break the tension caused by the still-not-signed volunteer form.

"Nope."

The doors part, and I fly out, scanning room numbers until 526 finally appears. I enter first, weighted by fear and anxiety, wondering what the next few minutes will bring. This is a season in our lives, nothing more. A harsh winter with too many gray skies. Soon it will end, and we'll be stronger and happier, knowing spring has arrived. But as the hospital room fills my vision, it becomes clear we are still in the depths of winter.

A bed swallows Aunt Rita.

She lays still, eyes closed, shallow breaths the only indication of life. Her salt and pepper hair, done up every Friday at Curly Cues, lays in limp wisps against the pillow. No Romantic Rose coats her pale lips. No Midnight Black lines those dark Sicilian eyes. Is she sleeping? I look at Mom.

"Maybe we should go." Mom turns toward the door.

I shake my head, determined for this long-awaited visit to take place. Stepping closer, I gently touch Aunt Rita's shoulder. If Mom's going to continue her strange behavior, someone has to step up. "Auntie?" I lean over and whisper. "You awake?"

Eyes open. Thank God.

"Oh." Her forehead crinkles as she squints to clear the sleep from her eyes. Confusion gives way to recognition. "Shilo, it's you. And Annie. It was getting so late, I figured you couldn't make it today."

"Rita." Mom nearly tackles me in her effort to hug her sister, long and hard. "Oh, Rita." Softer now. She can't seem to say anything else.

"It's okay, Honey." Auntie pats Mom's back. "It's not that bad, I swear it. The doctors say I have a good chance. Of course, I have to go through chemotherapy, but a few zaps, and I'll be fine. Don't cry; you'll make me cry."

It's a good effort, I'll give her that, but I'm not buying it.

Mom sits on the edge of the bed. "What stage?"

"Stage, smage. What do numbers mean?" Auntie pastes on a smile as fake as the blue streak in my hair.

I take in the scene, struggling to breathe as I gaze at the skeletal version of my aunt.

"What stage, Rita?" Fear weaves through Mom's words. "I want to know. If you don't tell me, I'll track down that doctor myself."

Silence permeates the room as Aunt Rita's fake smile straightens into a thin line. "Four."

Mom grabs the bed rail. Something about that gesture twists my heart. Stage four. I don't know how many stages cancer has, but I'm guessing it's not a hundred.

"Is it in your liver? Your lymph nodes?" Her words are monotone, controlled.

Auntie nods. "They're not sure where else. I've got all these darn tests to take." She reaches for the water glass on the tray table, takes a sip. "Now enough about all this nonsense. Shilo, where's my hug?"

I steal Mom's spot as she walks to the window. Wrapping my arms around my frail aunt, I imagine her body invaded by the demon cancer. A wave of pain washes through me, blurring the room and seizing my encouraging words for Aunt Rita, whose gaunt face smiles up at me. Thank goodness my grandparents aren't here to see this. It would have killed them…if the helicopter crash hadn't done it first. My grandfather had been so excited about flying over that volcano in Tanzania. He had promised to tell me all about it when he got back. No one ever considered that might not happen.

I can't lose Aunt Rita, too.

"Shhh." Despite her weakness, Aunt Rita remains the comforter. "Shhh. It's okay, Honey." She pushes my arms away so we are face to face. "Now you listen to me, Shilo. You too, Annie. I can beat this, *capish*? I need you to be strong, make me laugh. Have faith—lots of it. Faith and humor and love. That's a mighty powerful combination, don't you think?"

I give her the smile she needs. "Yeah. Sure is."

"Now, Shilo, how did you find time for this with your soccer schedule and a boyfriend? Your mom says you're still with that Japanese boy. Good, I like him. Very personable. Handsome, too." She gives me a thumbs-up. "Not Italian, but these days everything is different. Everyone is with everyone. Kind of crazy, but kind of nice, too."

I lay my hand on her arm. Mom winces. A warning? Maybe shots and blood tests made my aunt's arm tender. I pull away. "Sorry Jules couldn't come. She had to work on a science project, but she'll be here tomorrow."

"Let me guess, a rock project. Or is it astronomy this time?" A weak laugh escapes dry lips.

I nudge and wink. "You'll hear all about it tomorrow."

"Oh, boy. Maybe I'll ask the nurse for extra pills." Aunt Rita laughs weakly at her little joke, then launches into who came to see her today. Uncle Vince left just before we came; he had to go home and take his heart meds. Joey and Charlie visited, too. If we'd just gotten here earlier, I could have seen my uncle and favorite cousins.

"Now, tell me about your next class, Annie. I hear it was standing room only for Summer Salads."

"That's an exaggeration." Mom continues staring out the window.

"They want her to go on cable." I'm eager to maintain a light mood. If only it could make that cancer disappear. If only.

"You do it, Annie. You can cook circles around Rachel Ray. What's next? Marvelous Mexican? Fabulous Fondue?" Auntie grins, and I know what's coming. "Remember when Shilo was little? You made chocolate fondue, and she dipped her hot dog in it?" She is desperately trying to shine a beam of sunlight through the fog, but it's far too thick. Despite the darkness, I laugh. For her.

"There now." Aunt Rita raises her hand to my face, stroking my cheek like it's porcelain. "You look much prettier when you're laughing. Those blue eyes twinkle just like your great Nonna Marie's." She turns her gaze toward my mother's back. "Annie, is it possible?"

Mom whips around. "Not now." Her eyes meet Auntie's and incinerate the rest of her words.

Words I want very much to hear.

"Not now, Ri." Mom's words soften. "Please."

Aunt Rita squeezes my hand. "Shilo, do you think you could go to the cafeteria and get me a coffee?"

I'm getting kicked out, but it's okay. The woman is dying. If she needs to discuss something in private, I'm not going to stand in the way. "Sure, Auntie. Be right back."

As I head down the hallway, familiar music radiates from my purse, and I reach in to grab my cell. Yes! Just the number I want to see. "Hey you."

"How's the hottest girl at Cedarcrest High?"

I grin into my phone, knowing I'm not the hottest by a long shot, but when my boyfriend says it, I can almost believe it. "Thanks, but I think your sister claimed that title."

"Nah. It's you for sure. Hey, I stopped by. Nobody was home. Not even mini Giannelli."

Kenji's teasing drives Julia crazy, and she tells me daily my boyfriend is a "doofus."

"I'm visiting my aunt at Chicago Suburban."

"You want me to call back later?"

"No. Now's good." The task of finding coffee might be slightly less mundane with Kenji's voice to distract me.

"You should stop by and see Miya. She's volunteering over in pediatrics."

Kenji's sister is brains, beauty, and gobs of confidence tied in a pretty pink bow. Normally I'm just fine being who I am, but every time I'm around Miya, I want to be a little more…Miya.

"She's probably there now. She could show you around. Did your mom sign the form?"

"Nope." There's nothing to add. Not a reason that makes sense. Or any reason at all.

"You should go anyway. Seriously. She says you're my best crush since Princess Leia. And that's saying something."

As masked doctors and nurses roll another gurney through the hall, I step aside, searching for a compelling reason to say no. Miya's always nice to me, but we hang in very different circles. On one hand, it would feel awkward, but on the other, I wouldn't mind a glimpse of Pediatrics since I'll soon be volunteering there, too. "Okay. Might as well. Looks like I've got time to kill."

"Not me, I'm heading to practice. But just think,

pretty soon soccer and school will be done, and we'll have the whole summer together. We'll take the train to the city, hit the beaches, Great America. Prepare yourself for the best summer ever."

Happy summer images dance around my head. Hanging out with Kenji, plus soccer camp at Purdue. He's right; it's going to be the best. "I know. Can't wait."

"And the mission trip. Don't forget."

"I won't." As if I could, with his daily reminders. I have to admit, though, his excitement about the trip is contagious.

"Gotta run. Later, Blue."

Blue. His nickname for me always makes me smile, but not today, when the color of my eyes keeps popping into conversations.

Grabbing coffee from a waiting room, I head back, stopping just outside the hospital room for another round of eavesdropping.

"I still haven't told her, Rita. I will soon. You know I want you better. More than anything." Mom's voice echoes the same mysterious tone from last night.

"It's okay, Annie. If it were to be, she would have felt something by now."

If it were to be. Another mysterious phrase to add to the pile.

I walk in and hold out the Styrofoam cup, it's lukewarm contents sloshing inside. "Here you go. Not quite the fresh ground beans you use at home."

Auntie reaffixes her smile, holding out a shaky hand for the coffee cup. "It's fine, Honey. Perfect."

"If you guys don't mind, I'm going to go see a friend who volunteers here."

Mom finally stops pretending to read a tattered People from last January. The actress on the cover has already been in and out of rehab twice since then. "That's fine. I'll meet you at the front door in half an hour."

Rainbows and smiley suns color the halls leading to Pediatrics. Why did I agree to this? We have nothing in common, aside from Kenji. She's all brains and rah-rah; I'm all soccer and music. As I pass the waiting room, my eyes lock onto a girl slumped in a chair. Black waves of hair cascade down to her waist. It's the kind of hair you see on shampoo commercials, and there's only one person I know who possesses it.

"Miya?"

Her tear-streaked face freezes my next step.

Miya Hiyama…crying? In a blink she transforms from Homecoming Queen and Science Club president to just another girl. And her brokenness, whatever it is, crumples my heart. "Oh, I'm sorry. I was just…are you okay?"

She shakes her head. Diluted mascara trickles down one cheek. It's the first time I've ever seen her less than supermodel perfect. I open my purse, fumble past two pens, my cell, and a pack of gum to reach the tissues. "Here."

Miya wipes her nose, then runs her fingers through that thick black mane. "Thanks. I'll be fine. You don't need to stick around."

But I do, because something in her eyes contradicts her words. "I've got time. My mom's visiting my aunt. What happened?"

She sucks in a breath, then another. I wait.

"Today started out fine." Her fingers entwine as if in a prayer. A little girl with meningitis finally got to go home. Life was good for a minute, then bam— everything crashed. People rushed around, shouting orders. Nurses whispered. They brought up a gurney from ER, and all I could see was the face of a little red-headed angel."

I lean forward, already caring about a child I've never met. "Then what?"

"His eyes were glazed. There were fresh stitches on his cheek. The weird thing was, nobody was with him." She shakes her head. "They put him in a room, and the nurses asked me to keep him company. They said his mom's boyfriend beat him. Bad. Broke his arm and three ribs, cut his face. Kicked him so hard it damaged his spleen. His stupid mom stood by and watched. When he went unconscious, she finally called the cops."

Miya continues telling me who said what, but half-way through the story I forget to breathe. What had I expected her to say? Anything but this.

"How can someone beat up a two-year old? Get this—the guy said he did it because the kid spilled soup on the carpet."

What kind of a man brutalizes a child? What mother allows it to happen? The answer comes easily— the kind who doesn't deserve to have kids. Mom and Dad would die to protect me and Julia. If only this little boy had someone in his life to kiss him, laugh with him, and read him happily-ever-after stories.

"Where is he now?"

Miya sniffs. "With a nurse. I told her I needed a minute. I'm supposed to go back."

"I'll go with you." The words slip out before I remember my half hour is nearly half gone. "I mean, if you want."

"Thanks, but they only allow family and volunteers."

"Oh." I slump into my chair, then sit up straight again and dig the form out of my purse. "I'm in the system. Just missing a signature on this. Think they'll notice?"

"Not if you forge it." Soft brown eyes accentuate her hopeful tone.

Desire battles ethics and wins. Mom would have signed it eventually, anyway. "Sure." I pull out my pen and try to imitate my mom's swirly letters, as Miya stands and wipes her cheeks.

"He's right down the hall. We'll have to stop at the nurse's station first, though."

The lone nurse behind the desk is writing on a chart. I give her my name, and she types it, then glances at the screen before reaching out for my form. Avoiding her eyes, I hand it over and hold my breath. Any second now she'll yell for security, who will toss me outside and ban me from the hospital forevermore. Future job interviews will abruptly end with "What? You forged your mother's signature?" Instead, the nurse hands me a peel-off "volunteer" sticker, and my heartbeat plunges toward normal.

Inside the little boy's room, another nurse taps an IV tube, but turns her attention to Miya as we enter.

"Feeling better?"

Cool accent. Possibly from some African country. Her crisp white uniform contrasts sharply with her ebony skin. She finishes with the IV and gently tucks the sheets around Tyler.

"Oh, yeah, I'm fine." Miya manages a smile, exuding confidence mined from somewhere deep inside.

The nurse nods toward the child-sized bulge under the covers. "Are you sure you can handle this? Because if you would prefer not, it is fine. This is difficult."

"Absolutely." Miya straightens her shoulders, keeping her smile intact. "This is my friend, Shilo. She's going to stay for awhile."

My friend. Didn't see that coming, but…okay.

"Hello, Shilo. It is a pleasure to meet you. I am Adanna." Her kind eyes smile at me; eyes that look strangely familiar. "This precious boy is Tyler. We gave him a painkiller and a mild sedative. He should be calm for awhile." She heads out, leaving nothing but silence in her wake. I turn my attention to the bed, so big for one so little.

Copper curls tumble around a face the color of skim milk. I scoot a chair next to his bedrail and gently stroke his hair, so afraid he'll break. My hand lingers in those silky locks as I gaze at the stitches marring his cherub face.

Warmth. Wonderful and sweet. Warmth and peace.

It floods my heart, rippling through me as the room is washed in a dreamy, sky blue mist. The world loses its grasp on me. I float, no longer feeling the burden of flesh and bone, the limitations of time and space. Only my soul exists. My soul…and Tyler's. Our hearts become a muted drum duet, beating out a slow rhythmic ballad. Shades of blue and violet swirl around us in an otherworldly glow.

The child sighs, and I move my hand to the bedrail, worried that I've woken him. The warmth disappears, taking the heavenly music with it. The room is clear again. Bright.

I glance at Miya, wondering if she felt the warmth or saw the heavenly hues. She's pouring a cup of water from a pitcher on the bedside table, saying something about Tyler's injuries. My gaze switches back to the boy. Dull eyes blink open and stare into mine. Did he hear the heartbeat duet?

"Look at him," Miya says, as if nothing happened. "He should be outside playing with friends, running and laughing."

I manage a nod, wondering what just happened and why I don't want to share it. Miya is too focused on Tyler to notice I'm a little out of it. How I hope Tyler felt it, too. Something like that could make his whole world better. If only for a moment.

"My name is Miya." She places his limp hand in

hers. "I'm your friend." Her somber, velvet tone is a far cry from her carefree chatter in Cedarcrest's corridors. "I'm going to stay with you for a while, and I'll visit you after school tomorrow, okay?"

Gone is the flirty cheerleader who walks the halls with her own personal entourage. She continues talking to the groggy boy, and I gaze at the pastel animal border encircling the room, until my eyes land on the clock. "Oh my gosh! My mom." I jump up, grabbing my purse. "I forgot I was supposed to meet her in the lobby. Miya, I'm *so* sorry. Do you think I could come back and visit him, too?"

"Sure. And hey, thanks for staying with me. Just please don't tell anyone at school about this. It's like…my separate world. I don't want them coming here or asking me about it."

Interesting. Her separate world. A secret between us, and another that's all mine. Truth is…I wouldn't know how to explain it if I tried.

"I won't, I promise." My fingers brush Tyler's arm as I stand to leave. The warmth emits from my heart again, but only for a couple of beats, then disappears.

Maybe I'm coming down with something.

CHAPTER THREE

Misty

What are they doin', keeping me in this police station? Has everybody gone crazy? Don't they get it? I have to get back to my son. My Tyler. He needs me. Inside my head, I'm screamin' for them to let me go, but I don't let on cuz that'll just give them a reason to keep me longer. At least they told me he's got a great doc working on him. It's the only thing givin' me a shred of sanity.

"Where were you when the beating occurred? You can take your time if you need to think about it."

This syrupy-sweet social worker is makin' me nuts. I've already given this answer to the police and paramedics, but if it gets me outta here faster, I'll give it *again*.

"The library. Two blocks away. My books were due, and I just had to drop them off real quick."

I don't bother telling her I ran the whole way there and back. Even though everything seemed fine when I left, somethin' pushed me to run. The air felt heavy, and my blood raced through my veins.

She nods and jots down a note, then asks more questions I've answered a million times in the past hours. I need to go. Now. Images of Tyler lyin' on a stretcher looking half dead rip through my soul. My fists clench in my lap. Somebody *please* help me.

"Alrighty, then." She gazes at me with those sympathy eyes I've seen my whole life. "I'll be in touch within forty-eight hours for a follow-up. In the meantime, you call me if you need anything, okay?" She hands over her card, and I shove it in my pocket, where it will still be the next time my jeans hit the wash.

As she disappears out the door, two cops walk out of a room with a handcuffed Neanderthal sandwiched between them. A snake tattoo runs the length of his arm. As they approach, he leers at me through greasy strands of hair. "Hey sweet thing, you free tonight?"

One of the cops jerks his arm. "Shut up."

What am I doin' in this place? So unfair. The thought almost makes me laugh. In my eighteen years on this planet, when has life ever been fair? *Any* of it. But I did the right thing. Called 911 and did everything the lady on the phone told me while I was waitin' for the cops to come. Told them where to find Jake. How humiliating, havin' to admit he was my boyfriend...and Tyler's daddy. I knew that idiot would run to his mom's place. Real tough guy, beating up my baby, but when his brain kicks in and he realizes he's in trouble big time, he runs to mama.

A man heads my way—the only one with a white shirt. Must be the boss. He grabs a file off a desk and starts walking back the way he came. No. I *have* to get out of here.

"Sir?"

It works. He hears me and turns back. "Yes?"

Dark wavy hair. Brown, confident eyes—good eyes, like maybe he's nice when he's not doin' his cop thing.

"Please, I've answered everybody's questions. Can I go to the hospital and be with my boy? He's alone over there." The sergeant's face blurs, but I force myself to keep it together; to keep my tears inside. "He's just two."

"You wait right here, ma'am. Let me see if we can get you over to the hospital."

Nice voice. Kinda reminds me of warm gravy. No one ever called me "ma'am" before, that's for sure.

"Hey, Hutchins! Where are you on the Tyler Morning case? His mother's waiting."

See? I can always tell good eyes.

"Almost done, boss." Hutchins walks over with some papers, and the sergeant signs them. Next he turns to me. "You're free to go, ma'am. I may be in touch, though, if I have more questions."

"Okay." I pick up my purse and stand, but now what? My feet want to fly to that hospital. My arms ache to hold my precious boy and tell him everything's going to be all right. Is it? My throat thickens as the possibilities fill my head. No, I need to push away those stupid thoughts and focus. I came here in a squad, so Jake's car is still at the apartment. I've got six bucks and change, which sure ain't gonna cover a cab.

"You all right, ma'am?" The sergeant's cocoa eyes look right into mine, instead of past me or over me, like most eyes do.

The last thing I want is to ask these guys for help. If there's one thing I've learned, it's every girl for herself. Dependin' on anyone else just ends in disaster. But I'm desperate. *Beyond* desperate. "I don't know where the hospital is." Might as well just spit out the rest. "I don't actually have a way of gettin' there, either."

He signals Hutchins back over. "Seeing as how we brought you here, I think it's only fair we get you to your son. Sound good to you?"

Better than good. I let out a breath I didn't even

know I was holdin'. "Yes, sir. Thank you. I'm grateful."
Mrs. Howell said always show your appreciation when
someone does something nice. I hope he can see how
much this means to me. Maybe I shoulda showed more
appreciation to the Howells. Maybe they would've
adopted me.

Stop. Don't go there. Don't imagine the birthday
parties or trips to the beach. Forget the scent of cookies
baking in the oven or the piney fragrance of a real
Christmas tree. In the end, it was just another heartbreak. And those days are gone. The only one who can
touch my heart now is waitin' for me at the hospital.

The sergeant tells Hutchins I need an escort to the
hospital and even up to Tyler's room. Man, this guy is
somethin' else. My eyes dart to his name tag. Giannelli. I
never met a cop so nice before. Then again, whenever I
met any it was cuz Jake was mouthin' off to them, usually wasted and causing trouble. Guess I can't blame
them for a little attitude.

Hutchins lets me sit in the front seat of the squad
as we drive to the hospital. If I wasn't so scared for my
baby, I'd think it was the coolest thing ever. But no matter how fast we go, it just ain't fast enough. All these
scenes keep playin' in my head, but the worst is when I
picture nurses covering Tyler's face with a sheet, like
they do when someone dies on those hospital shows. I
try to push that image right out of my head, but I keep
seeing it over and over. If he's not okay…if my sweet
little boy is not all right…well, that's it for me, then. I'm
done. He's the only light I've got in this murky old
world.

"Almost there, ma'am."

"Thank you." I've got to be strong, like that girl in
Hunger Games. She kept doin' whatever she needed to
survive, to protect her family. That's just what I've got
to do.

Hutchins glances at me in the rear-view mirror. "Sorry if I was a little hard on you earlier. We didn't know what your role was, whether you had something to do with it. Know what I mean?"

I swallow a smart comment. Who could blame them for thinkin' that way? "Yeah. It's okay."

"I hope your son'll heal up fast. They've got some great doctors over there."

They better. My baby needs a miracle.

CHAPTER FOUR

Shilo

Walking toward class, I feel older and wiser than just twenty-four hours ago. I'd read about child abuse, even discussed it in classes, but now it had a name and a sweet little face. Wounds that may never heal. It had reached out from the headlines and grabbed hold of my heart. I plop down at my desk, wondering how I'll concentrate on U.S. History when my mind is zeroed in on getting back to little Tyler.

"Why was the Peace Corps established, who established it, and when?" Mr. Myners' monotone voice drifts in hazy circles around my thoughts, which are far from this classroom. I contemplate ways to get to the hospital after soccer—only fifteen minutes by car, but too far to walk or bike. Maybe Mom. No, she's got an instructor's meeting at the park district. A cab? Somehow it *has* to happen.

"Shilo, can you tell me? Shilo?"

Kelly nudges me from behind. "He's talking to *you*,

Shi."

"Oh."

"Miss Giannelli, will you be joining us today?"

Snickers launch a heat wave that begins at the base of my neck and rises to my ears. There is no saving the moment. "Sorry. I didn't hear the question."

"The Peace Corps—who, when, and why?"

"The Peace Corps." Repeating is my lame attempt to buy some time. Between the hospital visit and soccer practice, I was wiped out last night. Never got to that particular chapter. But if there's one thing I know about, it's the Peace Corps. Mom and her best friend, Shannon, signed up and spent three years teaching English in some rural area of Thailand. I've heard enough Peace Corps stories over the years to answer those questions in my sleep.

"Umm, President Kennedy, when he was still a senator. He met with students in Wisconsin. No, Michigan. They said they could serve their country by helping people overseas. His idea led to the Peace Corps."

"Not bad for someone lost in a daydream. When did this occur?"

Apparently, I didn't absorb as much as I thought. 1969? No, that was the first moon landing. I glance at Kenji. His eyes are on Mr. Myners, but his hand holds a little piece of paper with writing. I squint to see the numbers. "1960."

"Very good."

I can't suppress my smile. Mr. Myners can think it's a response to his compliment, but it's all for Kenji.

Six classes later, the final bell rings, and I'm swept in a sea of students heading toward the double doors.

"Shilo!"

I stop in mid stride at the now familiar voice. The boy behind me does not. Our bodies crash, books hit the floor, and papers scatter.

"Hey!" The single word brims with anger and embarrassment. He seems unsure of which to choose.

"Sorry." I bend and scoop up papers before hurried feet trample them.

"No problem. I've crashed into worse things than you."

"Here." I hand over the papers. "These are yours."

He reaches out and looks at me. And keeps on looking. Here we go. I'd like to just answer the question before he asks it, but that would probably sound cocky.

"Your eyes. Wow. Are those contacts?"

"No."

"You sure?"

"Pretty sure."

"Huh. Cool." His eyes linger on mine, then he shoves his stuff into a backpack and takes off just as Miya motions me over.

"Listen, I can't go to the hospital after school." She talks like she's guzzled six cups of coffee. "I was going to skip cheerleading, but there's a new routine. Captain's gotta be there, know what I mean?"

I nod as if I actually have a clue what it feels like to be cheerleader captain.

"Now I can't see Tyler 'til after dinner. Can *you* go?"

Everything inside me wants to say "yes." Everything but the soccer part. Skipping practice is a good way to spend the next game benched, especially in club soccer. And then…images of little Tyler float into my mind. His sweet face. The ugly gash. "Yeah, if I can find a way to get there. No car." So I sit out a game. It suddenly doesn't seem terribly important.

"Kenji can take you, but you'll need a way home. He was gonna take me."

I nod. "That should work. My mom can get me back." I cringe, wishing I'd left out the mom part.

"He'll be at your house in twenty. I gotta go."

With a flip of her hair, she struts down the hall like she owns it. Guys huddled by the lockers nearly break their necks to catch every curve and sway before she turns the corner. Watching them watch her is pure entertainment.

Outside, I resist the urge to talk with my friends, determined to cover the walk home before Kenji gets there. Thoughts of Tyler swirl through my mind as I pass manicured lawns and spring landscaping. Trying to find the logic in a man beating a child hurts my brain, and produces no answers that make sense. Likewise, there is no explanation for the crazy wonderful feeling that washed over me when I touched him—a sensation so out-of-this-world awesome that I long to feel it again. In that moment, there was nothing holding me down. No gravity, no fear, no stress. Love became a place, instead of an emotion. It simultaneously surrounded and permeated me. And it made me feel complete. Lost in thought, I nearly collide with a little boy pumping his tricycle pedals like a Tour de France contender.

Almost there.

I hurry past the corner house, where strands of toilet paper hang from trees and bushes. That's going to be a pain for someone to clean up. Did it twice last year.

Finally home, I punch in the garage code, fly inside, and scrawl a note to Mom. A quick fix with the comb and lip gloss, then out to the porch where there's no sign of Kenji. I wait, drifting back to that day—that *perfect* day—just after Christmas, when the church teen group went bowling. Pastor Frank assigned teams so we wouldn't just hang with our friends. He said we should meet new people, but I'd come with Brittany and Lauren, and we wanted to bowl *together*. So there I was, wishing I hadn't come and easing my feet into scratched up rental shoes, when Kenji plopped down next to me.

"Nice shoes." He grinned as he tied his laces.

"Bloomingdales or Nordstrom's?"

I'd seen him before, laughing with friends, playing soccer, sitting across the room in history, but never close enough to smell his cologne. Never close enough for him to hear the bass drum beating in my heart.

"Actually, they're from a private collection, hand-made in Brazil." I stretched out my leg, as though admiring the beauty of the green and orange stitched leather. "You can't purchase quality footwear like this from just *any* store."

We were bench partners and fierce competitors until the last ball rolled down the lane. He teased me during each throw; a strategy that worked perfectly. I'd laugh and mess up, then shoot my best fiery glare. When he beat me by fourteen points, I accused him of "verbal cheating" and demanded a rematch.

"There's no such thing as verbal cheating." He waved the score sheet in front of my face. "Admit it;, your bowling needs more polish than those shoes."

"Hey, these are designer—..."

"Anyway," he jumped in, espresso eyes smiling, "it happens to be winner-buys-pizza night." He shook his head. "Just my luck."

Brittany and Lauren sat across from us at Pizza Pete's, failing in their lame attempt at discretion. I caught their glances again and again, knowing they'd expect a full report later. But I didn't want to think about later. I'd hung onto the moment until people stood to leave, wishing I could sit in that booth with Kenji until sunrise. Or longer.

Kenji pulls into the driveway, windows rolled down, shaggy hair tousled like a little boy's.

"Hi, Blue." He hands me a bag of M&Ms as I slide in next to him. "Stopped at Seven-Eleven and heard these calling your name."

Five months into the relationship, he still pours into my heart like warm maple syrup. That velvet voice, the floppy hair, and my favorite—: his laid back, life-is-good smile.

"To the hospital, James."

Kenji laughs at my pathetic imitation of an English accent. "All I said was 'go say hi to my sister.' I didn't know she'd recruit you."

"You know I was signing up, anyway. Then yesterday…" I give him the Reader's Digest version of meeting Tyler.

"Wow. Heavy stuff. Miya said she was glad you were there, but she didn't give me the whole scoop. Wish I could go in with you, but my mom wants me to pick up dinner."

"Having something Japanesy?"

"Yeah, tacos." He grins. "Hey, did you ask about the mission trip yet? Pastor Frank said it's the week after school lets out. Can you go?"

I tear into my bag and munch a few M&Ms, the perfect candy. Crunchy outside, pure chocolaty deliciousness inside. "Probably. A little more info would help." It isn't actually me who needs the info, but it sounds better than telling him my parents want all the details before they'll consider it.

"Ten days, eastern Kentucky. It'll be so cool. The last day, we get to go whitewater rafting."

"And the first nine?"

"Work. A lot. Repair the school, build things, all that stuff. We teach a Sunday school class, too." He flashes the magic Kenji smile that makes all my insides sigh. "You'll love it. The kids are great."

"I really want to go. Let me talk to my parents." Everything seems to be a battle lately, even volunteering at the hospital. I better not have to justify a mission trip.

"Pastor Frank said he'd fill us in at Saturday's meeting. Don't worry; it's better than it sounds. The people are really cool."

We cruise past McDonalds, where the after-school crowd is getting their French fry fix. Coming up next is the all-too familiar blue and white sign of Digs, Julia's favorite rock shop. About once a month I take her there and hang around while she ogles everything and drives herself crazy trying to decide the best use of her allowance.

"They don't have much, so we bring stuff," Kenji continues, one hand on the wheel, the other holding mine. "Bibles, snacks, soap, toothbrushes, and oh, yeah, bubbles. Man, Shi, you should have seen them. They thought it was the greatest thing ever."

"I bet you felt like a hero."

"No, not really." His smile fades. "It's hard to explain. It just hits you, like, look what *they've* got, look what *I've* got. And here they are, bursting with excitement over a stupid bottle of bubbles. You'll see what I mean, if you go."

We drive past the strip mall, its line of stores and restaurants a perfect reflection of the Cedarcrest melting pot. At the north end stands El Meson, best Mexican restaurant in the U.S. At the opposite end is an Indian banquet hall, and filling in the middle is Yong's Dry Cleaner, Frosty Freeze, and a tutoring place. The beige buildings of the hospital campus loom ahead. Inside, the aunt I've loved since I could breathe battles a microscopic killer, and a little boy still new to this world lies broken.

And here am I, useless to them both. And hating it.

"There it is." I point, knowing full well Kenji sees it. "Turn in at the second driveway and follow it around to the front door." My grip tightens on Kenji's hand. "Not really sure what do to once I get there."

"Miya plays with them, reads books, that kind of

stuff. Sometimes they just want someone to listen. Don't worry. Y, you'll be great, and he'll love you. Who wouldn't?" He parks and leans over. Warm lips touch mine. His arm encircles me, pulls me closer, but it is never close enough. One more kiss, then another and another. Nothing matters but the kisses. I float away from the hospital, into cotton candy clouds, feeling the heat from his hand against the back of my neck. A faint siren sounds in the distance, its irritating blare dragging me back to Earth, the car...and the reason I'm here.

I pull back. "I better go," I force myself to say.

"What? This isn't the perfect makeout spot?" He smiles, eyes twinkling.

"Sorry, dude, I have another man waiting for me."

Kenji laughs. "Man, you're hot property. I'm jealous."

"You should be. He's way cuter than you, even if he is only three feet tall. Anyway, your sister would kill me if I didn't show up." But it isn't Miya propelling me toward that little boy. It is a need too powerful to explain. And suddenly, it can't happen fast enough.

"Miya's not as tough as you think. Anyway, I know you gotta go. Take care, Blue. I'll call you tonight."

"Okay. Thanks for the ride." Translation: I love you, Kenji. But I don't dare say it. Not here, not now. Soon, though, when the time is right.

At the Pediatrics Desk, four nurses huddle around a schedule, but glance up in unison as I walk in. Seconds later, I'm wearing my "volunteer" sticker and strolling into Tyler's room.

And hit a brick wall.

The girl sitting at the edge of his bed sniffs softly, her blue jean purse and car keys tossed carelessly on the floor beside her feet. A rubber band holds greasy blond hair. Red-rimmed eyes, one smeared with blue eyeliner, clash with pasty skin. The half-faded name of some band is scrawled across her baggy tee shirt. It drapes a body Aunt Rita would call "nothin' but skin and bones."

I've seen more flesh on chicken wings.

Tyler sleeps, his little hand hidden by hers. Swiping tears off her cheeks, she turns toward me. "You've got the wrong room," she whispers, glancing at the sleeping boy.

Awkward.

"No. I'm here to visit Tyler."

Eyebrows arch. "How do you know my son?"

She's got to be kidding. She's too young, too scraggly. All wrong. She *can't* be his mother. Miya said she stood by and let it happen. My teeth clench. Tiny hairs bristle along my arm. "I met him yesterday." I strain to cool the anger heating up inside. "I volunteer here."

She sighs like I'm an annoying fly she wants to swat. "Great."

Her "great" means anything but. She let her son get beaten half to death, and she's got attitude? She should be behind bars. Better yet, she should be lynched, and I'm not even sure what that means. "Excuse me?"

"Great. As in, great that you know what happened, and you're probably judgin' me like everybody else in this place."

"It's not my place to judge you." Canned words emerge from clenched teeth.

"Whatever."

Silence. I press clammy hands against my jeans. Now what? I'm not leaving him alone with her. Too dangerous. I search my mind, my heart, tuck my hair behind my ears, but no words come.

Mother of the Year breaks the silence. "Judge away. Whatever. It's all my fault. I left him with Jake, his daddy, just for a few minutes." Tears slide from ashen cheeks onto the sheet. "When I saw what happened, I went nuts. But it didn't matter. Didn't change anything."

My jaw relaxes as the bristles disappear. Her tears remind me of something I shouldn't have forgotten because I've heard a lifetime of Dad's crime stories. There's always another side. "I'm sorry. He's such a sweetheart."

The girl covers her face with both hands. What do I say now? I still don't trust her and don't especially like her. But she's hurting, and I'm the only one here. "So…you need anything?"

She lowers her hands. "I'm fine."

I twist my necklace, fingering the familiar pendant. My hands don't know what else to do, just like the rest of me.

The girl looks up at me, squints, and shakes her head. "Weird."

Really? *She's* judging *me* now? "What?"

She tugs at a thin strap around her neck. From beneath her t-shirt emerges a necklace—a mirror-image of the cross I've worn for four years. Dark, polished wood, suspended by a thin braid of brown leather. Aunt Rita got it for me from the Harvest Craft Fair. She said it was more "me" than anything silver or gold. I've never seen one on anyone else.

And I liked it that way.

She points to mine. "Where'd you get it?"

"My aunt. You?"

"Foster mom."

The conversation dies. Think, think, think. We have something in common. It doesn't exactly thrill me, but I can use it. "So what church do you go to?"

Her sad smile adds twenty years to her age. "It's just a necklace, that's all. Not into the God thing."

"Oh."

"It's just not somethin' I need, you know? Jake says believin' in God is stupid. Jake's my boyfriend. Well, he was…'till this happened."

Stupid? This from the guy who beats up little boys. No wonder she's a mess. Her boyfriend is a monster, her son is lying in the hospital, and she looks like she hasn't eaten since last Thursday.

The girl leans over to kiss Tyler's head. Love and pain pool in her eyes, condensing in a tear that rolls off her face. Then I see it, peeking out from the edge of her sleeve—a purple bruise. My eyes dart to that bluish smudge around her eye, and I realize it isn't make-up at all. Part of me wants to fly out the door and head back to my comfort zone, where brainiac Julia labels her rocks, Mom concocts outrageous foods, and Sergeant Dad arrests bad guys. But a bigger part of me wants to shield her from the monster, make her world shiny and new. Flee or stay? My feet remain hot-glued to the floor as I stare at the frail boy.

"I'm Shilo, by the way." I set my purse on the floor and plop down in the chair against the wall.

"Misty."

Cool name, like *Misty of Chincoteague*, my favorite childhood book. But I don't say it. Instead I point to Tyler. "So how's he doing?"

"Not so great. Doc said the kick ruptured his spleen. The only good thing is it ain't bad enough for an operation. Still...it's gonna take awhile to heal." She brushes a stray curl from his forehead. "This sucks. I wanted him to have better. Better than me."

Not sure if she means a better life than the one she had, or a better mom than herself, but either way, her words derail me. The wall of anger I conjured upon seeing her begins to crumble with each tick of the Winnie the Pooh clock above Tyler's head.

"Better?" The question may have crossed one of those socially appropriate lines, but I can't help it. I want to know what she's talking about.

Misty shifts, crosses her legs. "Nothing very original. Never knew Dad. Mom was a…well, let's just say the drugs got her in the end."

"I'm sorry." I focus on a drip sliding down the outside of the water pitcher. "You have Tyler, right? That's a good thing."

"Yeah. Too bad his daddy is an idiot meth-head."

The perfect boyfriend.

"I know it's none of my business, but why do you…"

"Stay with him? Not much choice. I'm eighteen with a two-year-old kid. No money, no family. Dropped outta high school." Misty's shrug fails to convince me it's all no big deal. "At least with Jake, me and Tyler were off the streets. K, know what I mean?"

As much as I do about being a cheerleader captain.

"But now I'm thinkin' Jake's gonna kill one of us sooner or later. Maybe after Tyler gets better, *if* he gets better, we'll hang out at the women's shelter. 'Course, they might put him in foster care after this." She pauses, smoothing the covers around her son. "I should just let some nice people adopt him."

Mom says sometimes the bruised fruit is the sweetest. The phrase comes to me as Misty covers her face with her hands again. Somewhere inside her is a sugarsweet heart that might stop beating if anyone takes away her little boy.

I lean forward. "There's people who can help you, you know. People from my church help single moms all the time. There's a food pantry and …"

"Don't need help." Again, she cuts me off. "I'll figure it out." Voices in the hall grow louder as they near Tyler's room. We both glance at the door. An old couple shuffles past and into the room next to us. Misty turns her attention back to me. "So what are you? A preacher's daughter or somethin'? Seems like it."

"No. My Dad's a police sergeant. Mom's a chef."

"Figures. Fairytale perfect. Coulda guessed."

Perfect? *My* life? But then, I never compared it to living on the street, or living with violence. Or being a teen mom. We avoid each other by staring at Tyler. Strips of white tape secure a long, thin needle to the back of his hand. A bottle of clear liquid suspends from a metal pole, its contents dripping down a plastic tube connected to the needle. Stitches crisscross his cheek—black thread whipped against the raw red wound. Eyes closed, breaths soft and slow, he appears oblivious to his injuries. Oblivious to the fact that he's been beaten by a man who fathered him, but is not a father.

"Would you pray for him?"

I replay her words, feeling my eyebrows rise before I can stop them. "Um, what?"

"Would you pray for Tyler? God might listen to someone like you."

I'm not even sure what that means, but the glimmer of hope in her voice is incentive enough to comply. "Sure. Yeah." I could do it right here in my chair, but something draws me toward the boy. Knees hit tile—not a pleasant sensation, but I try to ignore it, focusing instead on the child beneath the sheets. Misty still has a firm grip on his left hand, so I hold his right one, which peeks out from the stiff cast encasing his broken arm.

Warmth, just like yesterday. It begins in my heart, tepid at first, but warmer with every beat. Weird, but nice. I close my eyes and speak to God in the silence of my mind.

Lord, please heal this little boy. Repair his bones; heal his cuts and bruises. Save him from the fear and heartache of living with abuse.

Like a wave of tranquility, the heat spreads through my chest as the hums and clicks of hospital machines fade into silence. Warm shoulders, warm arms. The sensation journeys toward my hands, transporting me to a time when the world was new. Before evil or fear or hardship. Before sickness. I am weightless in a dreamy blue world, where an invisible power guides the heat into my fingers. It gathers and intensifies until all I can see are big, strong hands enveloping mine. They radiate with light, like rays from the sun. The glowing hands from that long-ago day.

Our hands glide to his sunken stomach, and I pray for the healing of his spleen. Somehow, I know exactly where to touch him next. I ask God to mend his broken ribs and gashed cheek. In response, the divine warmth radiates from my fingers into Tyler, riding on the invisible waves of my energy.

Please help his mother, too. Heal her heart. Give her friends who will care about her. Amen.

The last trace of warmth leaves my fingertips, replaced by pure exhaustion. I try to blink away the fogginess. Where am I? Where was I? It doesn't matter, because God's spirit burned inside me like a holy fire…and it was beyond wonderful.

Misty stares at me, mouth open, eyes big as dinner plates. I'm too tired to question it, though. Too dreamy. If I can just crawl forward to that empty bed across the room. But it is so very far away.

CHAPTER FIVE

Misty

I turn toward the sleeping girl on the next bed. Strange bird, but not so bad. That prayer thing was bizarre, though. Hands gliding over Tyler's body, lips moving, no words comin' out. And her skin…all glowy, like she was sweating or somethin'. When Tyler's hand got warm, I almost called the nurse. But the warmth flowed from his hand into mine and filled me like beams of love. How corny is that? I close my eyes and try to get the feelin' back, but the best I can do is hang onto that memory like my life depends on it. Not sure what it was, but I'm sure of one thing: somethin' filled this room. Somethin' big and kinda ghostly. Powerful, but real peaceful, too. I'm not telling a soul. They'll think I'm crazy and take Tyler away for sure.

But it was here.

Footsteps click-clack down the hall and stop at the nurses' station. "Excuse me, my name is Anne Giannelli. I'm looking for my daughter, Shilo. My height. Dark, wavy hair. She was visiting a boy in this ward."

Giannelli? Same as the sergeant? Nah, probably heard wrong. More talking follows. I can't hear it all, but there's somethin' about an ID and signin' in. Two sets of footsteps head this way, then the nurse walks in with a lady who shoots me a polite smile. I give her one back. Bet she didn't expect someone like me in here. Look at her, with her pretty purple pants and little spring sweater. Purple shoes, too. It figures. Her sweet little smile fades real fast when she sees Shilo lyin' on the bed.

I glance at my grungy t-shirt, then at the faded white knees on my jeans. Jake said we had to keep the water bill down, so I ain't showered or done laundry in three days. I twist the strands in my ponytail, hoping I won't scare the woman.

"What happened?" She turns to me. Probably figures I did somethin' to her. "Is she okay?"

My stomach burns inside, like when Jake gets that sneer on his face. If they think I did somethin' to Shilo, they might bring me back to the police station. Maybe put me in jail. "I think so. She fell asleep, just a few minutes ago. Seemed real tired."

The woman whispers to Shilo, gently stroking her hair. Her clean, shiny, combed hair.

The nurse ignores me, as usual, and turns to the woman. "Is she all right, Mrs. Giannelli? Would you like Dr. Shurden to look at her?"

So it *is* Giannelli. Could there be a connection? After what just happened in this room, anything's possible. And I don't even know what happened. Worry darkens the woman's eyes as she looks from the nurse to her daughter. I know the feelin'.

"No, I'm sure she's fine." She gives the nurse a fakey smile. "My daughter's been so busy lately. I'll let her rest a moment before we go."

The nurse hesitates. "If you are sure."

"Oh, yes. She's fine." She says it real quick, with another smile to hide whatever she's thinkin'. "Thank you."

Soon as the nurse walks out, Shilo's mom sits down on the bed and takes her daughter's hand. Somethin' about the gesture kinda smacks my heart, bringing back images I've been fighting to forget. Twelve-year-old me, lyin' in bed with the stomach flu, surrounded by my "menagerie" of fluffy stuffed animals. That's what Mrs. Howell used to call 'em. My menagerie. But she always said it with smiling eyes. Bought all of 'em, too. She was the only foster mom I ever loved. Used to hold my hand that same way when I was sick. But it was a lifetime ago, and now I'm more like that girl in *The Glass Menagerie*, Laura, stuck inside my messed-up world with no clue how to get out. Not like those two, over on the next bed.

Shilo's mom doesn't know I'm spyin'. She's too focused on her sleeping daughter to notice me watching her. She closes her eyes. When she opens them, a tear trickles down her cheek. "*La mia bella figlia.*" Lullaby words. Wish I could talk to my little guy that way. He's all broken and bruised, thanks to stupid Jake. I turn back to Tyler, and twinklin' hazel eyes smile back at me.

"Hi, Mommy."

His face glimmers with a joy I've never seen before. But that's not all. Not by a long shot. I stare and stare, my heart beating like it's gonna fly right outta me. It can't be. I shake my head and look at Shilo, then back to Tyler. The ugly gash on his cheek…

It's gone.

CHAPTER SIX

Shilo

Words drift in and out on invisible currents, but I lack the energy to respond or even open my eyes as I lay on the hospital bed.

"Misty, please listen to me." Urgency quivers Mom's voice, but I don't move, don't understand. Strangely, don't care. "We just have a few minutes before the Dr. Shurden gets back. Thank you for telling me about the prayer. I know you're shocked by Tyler's sudden recovery."

"No kiddin'."

The second voice comes from across the room. It's familiar...but why?

"Doc seems pretty blown away, too. Did you see his face?"

Mom's sigh floats my way. "Yes. The thing is..."

"Do you think his spleen's better, too? He didn't even wince when the doctor pressed his tummy. It's like a miracle or somethin'."

Nothing about this conversation makes sense. It's okay, though. So relaxed. My body sinks into the mattress. Must be a dream. That's why I can hear and not move. But it feels different than a dream. Hazy and happy. I'll just stay here forever. The muted voices fade into nothingness, and so do I, until Mom's voice drifts back into my head.

"So will you help me get her out before they come back?"

"I'll try."

I know that second voice. My brain strains to remember. It was the last one I heard before everything went dark. Misty.

Soft lips kiss my forehead. "Wake up, Honey." Mom's words caress me. "Please wake up."

"Here, Annie. Try this."

A cool, wet cloth slips across my face. Mmm, feels nice. My foggy head begins to clear.

"Wake up, Shilo. You have to wake up. Open your eyes." Worry laces through each whispered word. "Please...for me."

I concentrate on my eyelids. They seem to weigh a hundred pounds. The cloth softly swipes my forehead again, giving me the strength to open them. Mom's eyes peer into mine.

"Thank Heaven." She smiles. "Let's get you out of here."

My mind strains to remember where "here" might be. Machines hum and beep. Across the room, a little boy lies in a bed edged with guardrails. "Hospital?"

"Yes. We're in the hospital. Focus, Honey." She scrunches down so her eyes are level with mine. "We have to go."

"So tired. Just five more minutes."

"No, Shilo, now. We have to go. You have to try."

I slide my legs off the bed and, wedged between

Mom and Misty, I manage to stand. If either one let's go, I'm hitting the ground. The two of them take a step, still holding my arms. I do the same.

"Good. Keep going. One more. Another. That's it."

We pass Tyler's bed, where he lays quietly with eyes closed. But something's different. Cherub cheeks emanate a healthy pink glow. Even the one with the stitches looks...

I stop. And gasp. The stitches are still there, but the skin beneath is fine. Normal. The nasty wound is completely gone.

"Where's his stitches?" My words slur.

"We'll talk later. See if you can walk without Misty holding on."

Misty let's go, and I wobble, but remain upright. Mom reaches into her purse with her free hand and pulls out a business card. The words *Chef Annie Giannelli* stand out in bold blue letters next to her photo. I would know; I designed it.

"Call me." She holds the card out to Misty.

Like a shy puppy, Misty hesitates, then grabs it. "Okay."

"I'm not kidding." Mom's eyes and tone confirm her words. "You and me, we're going to do something about your life."

She nods, then tucks the card beneath the frayed flaps of her purse. "Bye, Shilo." Her voice cracks on my name. "I'll never forget this. What you did—it was the most amazing thing ever."

Man, I must have missed a lot while I was sleeping.

CHAPTER SEVEN

Misty

So good to be back home. No more doctors and nurses and endless tests. No more Jake, at least for now. Tyler pulls the tab on his dinosaur book, and a T-Rex opens his mouth to bare pointy teeth. He bounces on my lap, causin' the due date card to slip from its pocket and peek out. Cedarcrest Public Library—our home away from home. Our peaceful island. The place where I was when Jake went crazy on Tyler. Fifteen minutes was all it took.

Tyler points at the dino. "Big teef, Mommy. Big, big teef."

There's no reason those words oughtta make me teary, but they do. Because sittin' on our ratty old couch with Tyler bouncing on my lap is nothin' short of a miracle. And maybe I've never seen one before, but there ain't no question. They can't tell me what happened in that hospital room was a coincidence.

He snuggles closer, with the warmth of his body,

just the smell of him, filling me up inside, making me feel like I could do anything to protect him. To keep him. And I will, just like I told the social worker this morning. He's *mine,* and he's going to stay mine. I'm gonna find a way to be the best mom ever. The mom he deserves. 'Course, that means getting us away from the dad who doesn't deserve him. Me and Tyler should have run off years ago, but Jake, he had a hold on me from the start, and I was so afraid to face the world on my own. Not anymore, though. I'm not that scaredy cat pregnant sixteen-year-old.

Footsteps in the outside hallway jerk my head toward the apartment door. No! It can't be him. He's in jail, and they said we had time, that he would be there for awhile. Weeks. Maybe longer. Chewed fingernails dig into my wet palms. Fear steals my breath, swarmin' through my head and freezing my body to the couch.

Please, God, don't let it be Jake.

Did I just pray? It's been a lifetime, but it slipped out as natural as breathin'.

"Mommy!" Tyler grabs my arm, wrapped tight around his waist, and pulls at it. "Mommy!"

I loosen up. "Sorry, Tiger. Didn't mean to squeeze so hard."

"Daddy home?" Little fingers wrap around my wrist. "Daddy hurt me."

Three simple words, yet they smack me like a tidal wave, flooding my heart with a crazy mixture of love and anger. "I know. That's not gonna happen again, I promise." I don't know how I'm gonna keep that promise, but somehow I have to. I know how broken promises feel, and it doesn't matter if the person makin' them really means to keep them. All that matters is they don't. And then you end up in foster homes again and again, thinkin' each time you come home it's for good. Until one day you're standing at a grave knowin' you won't be going home ever again.

Tyler shuffles around to face me, kneelin' on my thighs. Cherub arms enfold my neck. "I wuv you, Mommy."

A salty tear drizzles into the corner of my mouth. Those were the last words I said to my Mom, but she never heard me. The drugs had already stopped her heart. "Love you, too, Tiger. Love you lots."

Tyler unwraps one arm to touch my tear. "Don't be sad, 'kay?"

A two-year old boy shouldn't have so much worry in his eyes. I smile, and we rub noses. "Okay."

The footsteps continue down the hall, and an apartment door opens and clicks shut. I sigh, feeling a truckload of relief escaping with my breath, and lean back against the couch. Just a neighbor. Probably one of the college guys, Jimmy or Kyle. They're both juniors at the university across town. Next year they'll be graduating and gettin' cool jobs and who knows what. They have all kinds of possibilities ahead of them. Jake calls them "the nerds" or "the idiots," but I think they're real nice. Sometimes I hear 'em in the hall, talking about classes, and I pretend I'm goin' to college, too. Taking classes, draggin' a backpack around. Staying up late to study for a big, important test.

Another silly fantasy. I have too many to count, but right now I have to focus on those options the social worker told me to think about. Like getting a job and findin' a safe place for my Tiger while I'm at work. And makin' sure we have a place to live. At least I already got my GED—*that* surprised her. My head's swimming with all these possibilities. Soon as Ty takes a nap, I'll look at the papers she gave me and try to figure stuff out.

If I can just keep my mind off that Shilo girl and what happened at the hospital.

CHAPTER EIGHT

Shilo

Blue eyes stare into mine from the worn pages of an old photo album. I lay on my velvety comforter, still groggy after a two-hour nap, and peer back at Nonna Marie. She never leaves Sicily to visit us, but her name comes up every time relatives comment on my eyes. My gut tells me there's more to the story than color. Much more. I see it in the glances they exchange; hear it in the whispers when I step into a room. Clues elude me as I gaze at the photos, unsure of what to look for, and hoping I'll know it when I see it.

Low music emanates from my backpack. I reach over and grab my cell.

"Hey, Blue. Miss me?"

I smile to myself, picturing those teasing eyes. "Didn't I see you four hours ago?"

"Yeah, but you can never get enough of Kenji Hiyama."

"Pretty sure I can."

"Your words are a dagger to my heart."

I laugh at the drama. "You'll survive. What are you doing?"

"You're my study break. I can't read one more word about genetics, or my brain will explode and cover my room with slimy bits of gray matter."

Ugh! The genetics test. Totally forgot with everything else going on. "Somebody's watched one too many episodes of CSI. And worse, you're using me as a mere study distraction."

"On the bright side, you're my favorite distraction. Want to compare notes?"

Normally that would be a big "yes." Studying with Kenji, *any* chance to be with Kenji, is what I'd rather be doing than anything else. Normally. But today...

"I don't think so. Kinda tired. I'll probably just study later." I flip to the next page of the album. There she is again, my great grandmother. Leaning in for a closer look reveals no answers or clues. Nothing.

"Oh. Yeah, no problem." The smile fades from Kenji's voice.

Sounds like a problem.

"So," he continues, "everything okay?"

A little red flag shoots up in my head. Why would he ask that? "Definitely. I just don't feel like studying right now. I have some things to figure out."

Kenji pauses. "Are *we* okay? I mean, you didn't even answer my calls or texts for four hours."

So that's it. A tinge of insecurity, which is ironic considering he's by far the more popular of the two of us. "*We* are fine. I was sleeping, and now I've got some family stuff to deal with. Really. Please understand."

"I can't understand what I don't know."

"There's nothing to know. Seriously, don't take it personally. I need a little time to myself, nothing more."

That probably sounded worse than how I meant it.

I push aside the album and pace the length of my room. Seconds tick by like hours. What's whirling around beneath his floppy black hair? "Kenji, I'm sorry. I'm so tired, and I've got this family thing, and none of this has anything to do with us. Honestly, I'd rather be with you."

"Okay, no problem." His tone betrays his words. "Everybody needs space sometimes."

He's disappointed. So am I, but there's something's gnawing my insides, stealing my focus. Something just out of reach.

"Guess I'll go, then. Hope you get everything figured out."

"Thanks. Me, too." I wait for a sweet ending, but nothing comes except "goodbye."

How am I supposed to study for a test? Who cares about genetics? I'm not planning to be a doctor, and I can live a satisfying life without fully understanding the causes of deformities or freckles or blue eyes.

It can wait. I return to the friendly pages of my family photo album, where the next picture transports me back to last summer and that awesome beach at Aunt Rita's Michigan lake house. There's me, sitting on the sand with Mom, Dad, Julia, and my cousins, Charlie and Joey. Next up, Mom, sitting in the canoe looking tan and happy, those Mediterranean eyes sparkling with vacation joy.

Genetics. I grab the science book from my backpack, flip to pigmentation. "Eye color is a physical trait that is genetically determined …eye color is determined by the amount of a pigment called melanin in the iris of the eye." Brown eyes have lots of pigment. Brown eyes are dominant. And yet, mine are blue like Nonna's.

No answers come to me from the album, and certainly not from my minimal genetics knowledge. So much for sleuthing. This may actually require a conversation—the kind where parents are involved.

Mom's words from the previous night echo in my head. "I don't want her to find out she's different."

Talking with them will have to wait until Julia goes to bed, unless I want a detailed lecture on the science of pigmentation. Which I don't. To kill time, I hang up the clothes tossed across my desk chair, then clear off the top of my bookcase and dust it, which doesn't look half bad. I glance at the clock, sure the battery is dying. Maybe I can do something with my closet.

"Dinnertime, girls!"

Julia's bedroom door flies open, followed by her feet tromping down the stairs like it's Christmas morning. No one loves meals like skinny little Julia. Maybe all that brain activity burns up tons of calories.

Pot roast, gravy, and vegetables take center stage on the table, a sight that usually has me anxious to grab a fork. But tonight...not so much. Too many thoughts are churning in my stomach. At least Dad's here. With his cop schedule, that only happens once or twice a week. Five minutes into dinner, the phone rings. Julia, as usual, jumps up to answer it. Mom, as usual, says "Remember our phone call rule during dinner."

"I know, Mom."

Seconds later Julia hands the phone to Mom, whispering "phone call rule, Mom."

Dad gazes at his chunk of gravy-smothered meat like he wants to marry it. "Mmm. This sure beats eating a sub sandwich in the squad. Who's on the phone?"

"I don't know." Julia goes for the salad and scalloped apples. She went all vegetarian on us about two years ago. Something about antibiotics and animal rights. "Some girl."

Mom takes the phone. "Hello? Yes, this is Annie." She pauses, sets down her fork. Happiness glimmers her eyes. "Oh! I'm so glad you called. Hold on just a moment." Covering the receiver, she stands. "I have to take this. You guys go ahead." She offers no further explanation as she walks into her room and closes the door.

"Well, that's interesting." Julia stabs at the giant mound of salad on her plate, carefully separated from the apples so they don't contaminate each other.

So not like Mom to leave the table. "She didn't give you a name?"

"No. I thought it was Melody for a sec, but then she asked for Mom. How come Mel never comes around anymore? I miss her."

Me, too, kiddo. "Oh, you know. Busy with ballet and stuff."

Dinner nearly over, Mom returns to the kitchen and microwaves her plate while Dad ladles gravy on his last bite of meat. "Can't leave out the gravy;, otherwise it would just sit there naked."

I roll my eyes, knowing gravy is his favorite food group, and Dad asks mom about the call.

"Believe it or not, it was Misty. The girl from the hospital. She said Tyler is feeling much better."

"Misty. Whoa, hold on. Is she a skinny little thing like our Jules? Baby got beat up by the boyfriend?"

Mom nods, and Dad says he met her the same day we did. He tells Mom she didn't have any friends or family to call. They're still talking about her as I slide the last clean plate into the cupboard and head upstairs. Julia drags me into her room to see her latest acquisitions from Digs, and there goes ten minutes of my life. I could have left sooner, but no, I just had to ask a question. Maybe I'm a sucker for the way her face lights up every time I do that.

Two hours later, I stare at my unopened science book, listening for shuffles and bumps from Julia's room.

Silence. Time to have the talk.

Thoughts whirl and spin in a desperate attempt to be heard. How do I explain that something is haunting me? Not ghost haunting, just...haunting. Like everyone but me knows what lies behind Door Number Three. It's somehow connected to my blue eyes, the bloody dog, Nonna Marie, and the warmth I felt with Tyler. But that's crazy, because how can all of those things go together? Yet, I know there's a mystery. A secret. And somehow I'm at the heart of it.

I stop at the bottom of the stairs, holding tight to the smooth, wooden railing. Solid and sturdy, it feels comforting under my hand, which is threatening to shake like an old lady's if I let go. Yet letting go is critical to my plan, since I can't talk to them from here. I force my fingers to release, then head through the kitchen to the family room stairs. The faint aroma of pot roast still hangs in the air. Mom and Dad snuggle on the couch, focused on a TV reporter, oblivious to my gaze.

Mom looks up first. "Hey, how come you're still up? Tomorrow's a school..." She stops. "Honey, what's wrong?"

My fingers squeeze another banister. Deep in my soul, I know this conversation will change everything.

"What is it? My goodness, you look as if someone died."

"We need to talk." I step down, wondering where my head and heart will be on the return trip.

"This looks serious." Dad clicks off the television. "Come, sit down."

They make a space on the couch between them, and suddenly the questions I've held captive all evening can no longer be contained. No matter the outcome.

"You said I'm different. I heard you last night. Maybe I've always known, but just kept it buried." The last few words get squeezed out as my throat thickens. This could all be nothing, settled by a simple, silly explanation, followed by life as usual. My gut, however, says otherwise. "Whatever it is, it's time I knew."

No one speaks. No one moves. My suspicions are painfully verified in that thundering sound of silence.

Mom's dark eyes turn to Dad for support. He squeezes my hand. "No point pretending it's your imagination. Not after today. But no matter what, Shi girl, we're all in this together. Don't ever forget that."

I stare at him, studying the familiar details of his face—crescent laugh lines, salt and pepper stubble. But those milk chocolate eyes reveal a sadness I saw years ago, when Mom had her miscarriage, and a few weeks ago, when we got the news about Aunt Rita.

"Tell me before I go crazy."

Mom's eyes drop to her hands, which definitely seem to need a banister's sturdy support.

"Annie." Dad tenderly rubs Mom's shoulder. "You were planning to tell her anyway. It might as well be now. She deserves to know.... about everything."

"It's going to be a long night." Mom sighs. "I better go make us some coffee."

Minutes later, hands cupped around a warm mug of decaf, I wait for answers that are sure to change my world. Something weird happened today in that hospital room—something big. And whether its good, bad, or just plain freaky, I want to know.

"It's a long story, Honey. I have to start at the beginning. At least, what I remember of it, since I was just a child. In the end, you'll have your answers. But know this, Shilo. you will also have more questions than you could have imagined."

Mom sits back and begins unraveling a tale set in a Chicago Italian neighborhood, where she lived with her parents and Nonna Marie. A handful of people had witnessed a miracle. My great-grandmother had prayed for a priest suffering from brain cancer. She had knelt by his hospital bed and, according to witnesses, went into a trance. Her hands glided over his body and rested on his head. When she opened her eyes, she appeared disoriented and collapsed on the carpet, then slept soundly for several hours. In the morning, the priest told the nurse he didn't need any pain medication. Doctors were amazed at his increased energy and appetite.

"Within days, he left the hospital and returned to the rectory, completely cured. Word spread quickly. Naturally, many were skeptical." Mom stops for a sip of coffee.

"What happened?" I can't help jumping in. "How was he cured? Was it Nonna?"

"Even Nonna Marie wasn't sure what happened. She remembered feeling warm when she touched him. Said it was like nothing she ever felt before."

Prickles ice my neck. That warmth…it is indescribable. It is peace. Love. Grace. It is a fortress, where no harm can come to me. It is real…and surreal. "I felt that today. Yesterday, too." I stand up, pace the room. "I know that warmth. It was in me. Around me."

Dad motions me back to the couch. "Just listen, Honey." His words are soft. Love fills every crevice of his face. I sit.

"The following week, a young mother came to the door. As usual, I stayed hidden, listening to every word. She told Nonna Marie her baby had a high fever and rash. She asked Nonna to heal her baby, like she healed the priest. Nonna left with her. She didn't come back until late that night."

I look at her, aching to know. "Was the baby cured?"

"Yes. The woman's husband came over with roses the next day. Said Nonna was an angel from Heaven." Mom stops for another sip. "That was the beginning; the trigger that turned our lives inside out."

My stomach tightens. "What do you mean?"

She tells me more people came each day, even late at night, to seek Nonna Marie's gift. Sick people, doctors, reporters. Their lives spiraled after that. It got so bad they all moved to New Mexico and stayed with relatives...until life got crazy there, too. Mom says they snuck away on a midnight flight to Sicily, where they left my great grandmother in the care of cousins.

"Where was Aunt Rita during all this?"

"In college, mostly. Then she married Uncle Vince."

"Did Nonna Marie ever come back?" The story is fascinating, but my mind can't tear away from the warmth. *Like nothing she ever felt before.*

"Only once, just over seventeen years ago, because someone she loved desperately needed a miracle."

"Who? What?"

Chills crawl up my arms during the silence that follows. Mom glances at Dad, who nods, entwining his fingers with hers. She turns her gaze on me and forces a smile. "Me."

"What happened? Were you sick?"

"I couldn't get pregnant." She pauses again, a faraway look in her eyes. "Nothing worked. Nonna Marie prayed with her hands on my stomach." Mom strokes my hair, her dark eyes boring deep into mine, right into my heart. "The miracle was *you.*"

The words echo in my head. I struggle to comprehend and replay them. "The miracle was *you.*"

You, you, you.

A heat wave pulsates through my body, but not like what happened in the hospital. This is the kind that accompanies a panic attack. It offers no promise of tranquility. I press clammy palms against the couch cushion while my brain swells with more questions than it can process.

"I'm here because of Nonna Marie?" Images of the hospital visit swirl through my head. Tyler, pasty white, the red gash. Praying for him while the wonderful warmth spread through my body. Feeling the presence of a love so pure and powerful, it left me weak. Is that why I felt it? Because I'm the result of Nonna's prayer? That alone is amazing, but there are still pieces missing in this puzzle.

"It's true, Shi girl." Dad's eyes confirm his words. "You were born nine months after her visit. Mom and I had been trying for two years. Doctors couldn't find anything wrong. Fertility drugs didn't work. Nonna Marie prayed, and five weeks later, we found out your mother she was pregnant. Of course," he adds with a grin, "I had something to do with it, too."

Must he? "Thanks, Dad, but I can do without that image."

Dad laughs. "See, you're a smart aleck. That part came from me."

I turn back toward Mom. "A great grandmother with the power to heal people. That's incredible."

"That's only part of the story." Mom's eyes darken, and the chills return. It's coming. The thing I most want to know. The thing a tiny part of me doesn't want to hear. "First of all, Shilo, and you must *always* remember this, Nonna Marie did not have the power."

"But you just said…"

"What she had was a God-given gift. It was God's power, not hers. He blessed her with this gift. He also took it away."

"You mean she can't heal people anymore? Why not?"

"She misused it. At first, she was amazed. Awestruck. Prayed daily for guidance and tried to use it discreetly. People offered money and presents, but she always refused. Then after a few years in Sicily, she got

…. I don't know, full of herself, I guess. Arrogant." Dad nods as she continues. "She acted as though the power was *hers*, and started welcoming, even pursuing the fame, instead of shunning it. She wasn't serving God anymore, just her ego. At least, that's what my parents told me after I'd grown up. After awhile, the healing just stopped happening."

The thing that has haunted me draws closer. It hangs in the air, taunting me, like it's just a whisper away. I sip cold coffee without even tasting it. "So what happened?"

"We lost touch, and I blame myself. It cost too much for us to visit, and she doesn't use a computer, so no email. And we didn't have cell phones back then." Mom shifts, tucking her legs beneath her. "Years later, I talked about it with my mother and learned that Nonna Marie had been devastated when she lost The Gift. People called her a fraud and shunned her. She went into a deep depression. Even tried to commit suicide."

"Seriously?" A movie plays in my mind, starring the young Nonna Marie I've seen in pictures, eyes cast down, people pointing at her. Laughing. The images hurt my heart.

"Oh, yes. After that, a cousin took her to a convent. It was supposed to be temporary, but she still lives there."

"And?"

"She eventually realized her mistake and grew stronger in her faith, but The Gift never returned."

"I don't get it. Why doesn't she visit us? Why don't we go there?" I wouldn't mind a trip to Sicily. Mountains, beaches, Italian guys.

"Partly because she felt she'd shamed the family, and partly because of *you*, Sweetheart. She must have known from the moment you were born, and feared you would suffer the same fate she did."

My breath catches in my throat. Here we go. "Okay, Mom, you've got my attention." The mantle clock above the fireplace ticks a mantra. *She must have known.* I should wait until she's ready to speak again, but I'm near exploding. "Known what?"

"Do you want me to say it, Annie?" Always the protector, Dad offers to step in.

"No, Nick. I can do this."

A chill shudders through me as the point of this story becomes too clear to ignore. I fear her next words, but crave them even more. "Just tell me. *Please.*"

But there's really no need, because I already know.

CHAPTER NINE

Shilo

"You're a healer, Sweetheart." Mom's trembling hands hold mine. "You have The Gift, just like Nonna Marie."

The churning brew will not stay down. I run into the bathroom and vomit, then slump against the wall wondering what just happened. How does a person's life go from normal to light speed in three-point-two seconds? This can't be real. Reflected in the mirror is the same face I see everyday. No halo, no luminous glow in my eyes. Just me. Suburban girl. Soccer player. High school nobody. I rinse my mouth and return to the couch.

Dad wraps Nonna's handmade afghan around my trembling shoulders. "You need anything?"

I almost laugh. Like what? An aspirin? "I'm fine."

"No, you're not. But listen." His hand cups my chin. Brown eyes meet mine. "You *will* be fine. You are strong. I told you earlier we are all in this together, and I meant it."

But I'm the freak, not him. At the end of the day—
every day—it's me that has to lay my head on my pillow
knowing I'm no longer the person I was for nearly seventeen years. The Gift is hands-down the most phenomenal thing I could imagine, but it means goodbye to
my life. And yeah, it has a few problems, but it's *my* life,
and I kinda like it as is. Except for Aunt...

"Aunt Rita!" The revelation surges through me on a
wave of hope. "We have to go there. When does the
hospital open? Never mind. We'll sneak in. Mom...Aunt
Rita!" I can't get the words out fast enough. No matter
how scary this gift, or what challenges lay ahead, healing
Aunt Rita will make it all worthwhile. I fling off the
blanket and leap from the couch, ready to see her right
now.

But Mom isn't leaping, or even smiling. Worse, she
shakes her head. "I don't think so. It's worth a try, of
course, but not likely. Not likely at all."

Why would she suck all the joy out of this moment? Maybe she misunderstood. Maybe, for reasons I
can't begin to fathom, she's not making the connection
between my ability to heal and Aunt Rita's cancer. "How
can you say that?"

"Because you already healed Tyler, just like you
healed that dog twelve years ago. Both times you felt it
on the first touch, just like Nonna. With all the time
you've spent around Aunt Rita, you would have felt
something by now."

"Tyler's healed? Completely?"

Mom nods. "Completely. Misty said there's no
blood leaking out of his spleen, and his arm is almost
good as new."

Dad smiles at me. "Really something, isn't it? Do
you remember what you felt?"

I have to remember. Have to make it happen again

so I can purge the cancer from my aunt. I close my eyes and see Tyler's innocent, pale face. Red curls framing freckled cheeks marred by a horrid red slash. My knees hitting tile, my hands on his broken arm. One touch sent a current of warmth flowing through my heart, down my arms, into my palms. It intensified in my fingers til they nearly burned, then streamed into Tyler. I couldn't see him. Couldn't see my hands. But I could *feel*, and what I felt was far beyond the limitations of mere words. Because that heat set my soul on fire, and in the midst of that holy blaze, God's spirit filled the room so powerfully it left me weak.

I journey back further to the day of the dog and can almost smell the burnt rubber, feel the sticky fur, and hear my little girl voice. *Please, God, make him well.* And then the warmth. I share the memories with my parents.

"You never felt it with Auntie, did you?" Mom pats my leg. She knows the answer.

There's no memory of feeling it with Aunt Rita. Despite all the hugs and hand-holding, the Heaven-sent warmth hasn't come. I shake my head. "But I have to try. Maybe now it will be different. I can concentrate on healing her."

"If only it were that easy. Remember what I said? It is His power, not yours. God has His own plans, His own timing. You'll have to trust Him, no matter how much it hurts."

Is it possible to have this incredible power and not be able to heal Aunt Rita? That's insane. It has to work.

Has to.

And here I am, five minutes into finding out I've been blessed with an awesome power, and already wanting to control it. I'm worse than Nonna Marie.

"Your eyes are full of questions." Dad loops an arm around me.

"Yeah, about a million, starting with what do I do now?"

Mom takes my hands in hers, an unexpected gesture, even for Annieconda. Her eyes lock onto mine. "Nothing. You don't tell anyone, not a soul, and you definitely don't heal anyone."

The shock-and-awe of this whole thing must be getting to me, because my mother's words make no sense. A heartbeat ago she told me to trust in God. I have an out-of-this-world gift that can save lives. She couldn't have told me to hide it. No way. I misunderstood her;, that's all. "What?"

She squeezes my hands, eyes glistening. "You needed to know, so we told you. That's where it ends." Her words are soft, but firm. They cloud my mind, and I strain to overcome the haze, hoping whatever she says next will clarify the meaning of "that's where it ends."

"The story I told you about Nonna Marie is just a snapshot," she continues. "The bigger picture is this. A: a lifetime of living on the run, getting hounded by the media, constantly pursued by the sick and injured. Scientists will want to experiment on you;, talk show hosts will mock you. There will be nowhere for you to escape." A tear slips down her cheek. "That is not the life we want for our girl."

A miracle…to be buried like a curse? I look at Dad, expecting him to laugh and say she's joking. But he stares at the carpet as though searching for gems among the teal fibers.

"Promise me, Sweetheart." Mom places her hand under my chin. Fear darkens ebony eyes. "Promise me you will take this secret to your grave. You will ignore the signs and keep your normal life."

I look at the woman who makes meals for the homebound and tutors people learning English. The same woman who sponsors two Nigerian children so they can get medical care and go to school. These words could not have come from her. Not my mom.

"Promise me, Shilo Marie."

My soul cringes. My whole life, she has taught me to do what's right. I've trusted her to guide me through murky waters, and keep me afloat when those waters got rough. But now…now she is pushing me under. My breath catches in my throat. I may not know much about this gift, or what the future holds, but there is one thing of which I am certain.

I can not, *will* not, make that promise.

Sunlight filters through my eyelids. Soft footsteps and slamming dresser drawers tell me Julia is awake. The bathroom faucet squeaks and whooshes. Fluffy bunny slippers traipse downstairs for Mini Wheats and juice.

School! Why didn't anybody wake me? Sitting up fast makes me woozy, so I keep still until the room stops swirling, then stand with the intention of sprinting to my closet.

Until last night's memory slams me back onto the bed.

The dog, Tyler, Nonna Marie.

The Gift.

Dad saying I can stay home today. It wasn't a dream. I look down at my hands, palms up, palms down. A random freckle on the right, a measles scar on the left, and a couple of broken nails. Normal hands. N; nothing miraculous. They play guitar and mold clay into pots. They type out papers that get As in English and Bs and Cs in pretty much everything else. They help Mom cook, hold other hands—mostly Kenji's these days—and have examined every one of Julia's two-hundred and twelve rocks and minerals. And once they accidentally set fire to the bush in our backyard. But despite all they do, and how well they've served me, I've never really given my hands much thought. Until now. Because now, they have healed a dying dog and a broken child.

Toast pops in the kitchen. I lay in bed, searching the winding catacombs of my mind to find the memory of what happened during that prayer. What was I doing? How does the miracle happen? All I know is how I felt.

From the living room comes sounds of Julia stuffing books into her backpack and heading out the door with a "Bye, Mom. Love you." It thumps shut, and another sound reaches my ears, one I shouldn't be hearing at seven-thirty in the morning. The telephone.

Mom grabs it on the first ring, probably hoping to catch it before it wakes me and Dad. Curiosity pulls me toward the door, which I crack open just enough to eavesdrop.

"Hello? No, I'm afraid she's still sleeping. May I ask who's calling?"

It's for me?

"I don't understand. Why do you want to talk to my daughter?" A pause, then, "Well, you know she's still a minor. If you have questions about that, you can talk to me."

My mouth opens. What? Why doesn't Mom want this person talking to me?

"I see. Well, I don't think she can tell you much. The boy's mom simply asked her to say a prayer for her son. That's really all that happened." Mom is quiet. Listening?

"I'm certainly glad he's better," she finally says. "There have been studies linking recovery to prayer, but being a doctor, you probably know that. There's really no purpose in your speaking with her. Thank you for calling. Goodbye."

It's true, then. Tyler got better. Now the doctor is figuring maybe I had something to do with it, and Mom is protecting me, the way everyone tried to protect Nonna Marie. Which didn't work so well. Last night's nausea returns, but there's nothing inside to throw up.

I lay back down, staring at the ceiling. Now what? There's no denying it's true. No pretending it was a crazy dream. Emotions battle inside my head, where Team Courage charges forward on white horses to save the world, and Team Wuss retreats in fear of ending up like Nonna Marie. I don't want to stop playing soccer or hanging with my friends. Don't want to lose the Frosty Freeze job before I even start. And Kenji. My heart winces at the thought. Not Kenji. The ceiling blurs. My throat thickens.

Not Kenji.

He can't find out about this. Not ever. I lay there mulling the whole thing over until I just can't mull a minute more. Blowing a rare opportunity to sleep in on a school day, I get up and plod downstairs.

A late May breeze ruffles the kitchen curtains as Mom sits at the table, drinking coffee and flipping through *Bon Appetit*. She looks up with a smile, but it's muted by compassion and something else. Fear?

"I didn't think I'd see you this early."

"Couldn't sleep. Too many thoughts. Too many questions."

She nods her understanding, pushing the magazine aside. "Why don't you make yourself a cup of tea? Then we'll talk."

While the water heats, she says Dad got called in to work around six, due to a break-in at the elementary school. "That poor janitor. The place was really trashed."

"Man, Dad didn't get much sleep. Does he still have to work 'till late?"

"Unfortunately, yes." She sips her coffee. The scent of hazelnut steams my way. Her favorite from the fair-trade store. "He's going to be one very tired guy."

The teapot whistles, and in minutes I join her at the table, cupping my own steaming mug, breathing in the exotic scents of citrus and cloves, with a shot of honey. The sweet, hot tea flows through me like liquid bliss, settling my stomach. Calming me.

"How early can we visit Aunt Rita?"

Mom shakes her head. "Uncle Vince sent everyone a text this morning. No visitors. She's not up to it."

"But I ..."

"When the time is right, Shilo. Not today. Now tell me what's going on inside that head of yours."

Where to begin? There's the five hundred questions about how this thing works, the whole Team Courage-Team Wuss battle, and the absolute weirdness of it all. And the absolute awesomeness. And the guilt of not assuring my mother I won't use it. "I get why you wanted me to make that promise, but…"

She stops me with an upraised palm. "No, Shilo. You don't. You heard *one* story. It doesn't begin to reflect the years of hiding, and moving Nonna Marie from place to place. Reporters and photographers sneaking around our house. People at our door, stalking us, begging, bribing. It would be a thousand times worse with today's technology." She gazes into her cup. I wait. "There were two kidnapping attempts. I can't bear to think about that happening to you."

Her words radiate with love and dread. Funny how often those two emotions are entwined. "It won't."

"Don't say it. You don't know, and you can't promise."

I understand her pain. Her apprehension. It's really not something I can ease, but maybe I can use her own heroes to show her this is bigger than us. "Remember when you first told me about Mother Theresa, how she gave up her normal life to serve the poor and sick in the slums of India? And all the times you've said the world needs another Martin Luther King? They were brave. I bet they were scared a lot of times, but they did what they were meant to do. And they made a difference."

"Martin Luther King was brutally assassinated."

"But he *made a difference*, Mom. Maybe I'm supposed to make a difference, too. How can I say 'no' to that?"

She sighs emphatically, which tells me her Italian is about to emerge. Hands thrust out like she's guiding me down a runway. Maybe she is. "Shilo, those people weren't my daughter!"

"You told me God uses people to help other people." I force my voice to stay calm, hoping it will diminish her fear. "Your words, Mom. Remember? If God trusts me to handle this, why can't *you*?"

She sighs and rests her head in her hands. "All right, all right. That's enough for now. This is already wearing me out, and Dad needs to be part of this conversation. Let's switch gears. Talk about something else for now."

In a silent time out, we both lift mugs to lips. The abrupt end to our conversation is fine with me, though. I need to think about it more on my own before the next talk.

"Sooo, what's the deal with Misty?" This should be a safe topic. "What else did she say last night?"

Mom says she invited Misty and Tyler to come for dinner tonight. By that time, she hopes to have a plan in place for helping them. No one knows for sure how long Jake will be in jail, and Misty does *not* want to be around when he gets out.

"She's already packing her things, which won't take long seeing as how the poor girl has nothing. I have some ideas, but I need to make a few phone calls and see what's what."

Little does Misty know she's on Mom's radar, which means crashing is not an option. Faith and tenacity make powerful allies. "Sounds like a challenge."

"I guess so, but I believe in this girl. She's got a good heart. I can see it in her eyes. Brains, too. She's been battered every which way, but through it all, there's a mountain of love for her little boy. And love…well, love conquers all."

What's life like in Misty's shoes? Focusing on her problems might get my mind off this faith healer thing. I was drawn to her, too, and that beautiful little boy.

My stomach rumbles, ready for more than tea. I toss pita bread in the toaster and search for the raspberry preserves. "Maybe we could buy Misty and Tyler some clothes."

"Great idea! And let's get a toy or two. I bet he doesn't have any."

Mom spends the next couple of hours on the phone and Internet. She repeats Misty's story several times, apparently being transferred from one desk to another. Bits and pieces float up to my room, her tone rising and falling in a medley of progress and setbacks.

Outside, Cedarcrest is looking a little duller and grayer than it was this morning. I open my window and inhale the scent of spring rain. All around me are houses where normal people live, play, work, love, and argue. I used to be one of them, but one night, one conversation, changed everything. And no matter how challenging the future may be, there's no turning back.

Ten o'clock chimes bong from the Town Square clock tower two miles away. Kenji's probably wondering…oh, man! Never checked my phone. I grab it and see three texts. "Where are you?" then, "You OK?" and finally, "Call me." I shoot him a text about taking the day off to help my mom with something, and promise to call him later.

Kenji, with those smoky eyes that blind me to every other guy. *My* Kenji. But for how much longer? If my secret gets out, we're done. I have no doubt. This is way beyond what anyone signs up for in a relationship. We've had five incredible months, walked a million miles along the river path, and talked about everything— school, sports, parents, college, plans for the future.

But the future never included *this*.

My brain swells with a lethal combination of emotions, questions, and fear of the unknown. I need to stay busy while Mom finishes working on Project Misty. Poor girl, with her messed up life and ragged clothes. My open closet mocks me from across the room. Stuffed with more clothes than I wear, it must have some hidden treasures for Misty. Dangling from a hanger is the purple shirt that shrunk a little the first time I washed it. Still looks new, and it would fit her perfectly. I dig through the rest of my closet and dresser drawers. Three shirts, a pair of jeans, and a skirt get added to the pile. I fold them neater than I've ever folded my own stuff and imagine handing them to Misty, liking the feeling that washes through me.

I run downstairs as Mom is saying "goodbye" and setting down her cell. "You done?"

"For now. I may need to meet with someone later."

"We should get going. And how about lunch? We haven't done that in ages." Might as well take full advantage of a day off. "There's a salad bar place by the toy store. We could shop for Tyler after lunch."

"Slow down, girl." Mom smiles. "I'm glad you're excited, but I need another five minutes. Believe it or not, I may have worked something out. I'll tell you all about it in the car."

Despite blossoming trees and balmy temperatures, our shopping trip feels like Christmas. We pick up gray jeans and a t-shirt for Misty, along with two outfits for Tyler. Bags in hand, we head to lunch before hitting the toy store. Inside The Plump Tomato, Mom relays her morning phone conversations.

"The first couple of women's shelters I called weren't much help." She stops to crunch a cucumber. "They're fine as a temporary safe haven, but Misty needs more. So I called church and found out about Sonrise House. Women who stay there can attend classes, and even get free daycare. Want to check it out with me?"

"Definitely. But let's get Tyler's toys first."

"It's a deal. So do you know who runs Sonrise?"

I shake my head with a mouth full of salad.

"The Nicholls Travel people."

"Who?" I manage to mumble.

"Everyone knows Nicholls Travel. They have those great commercials that make you want to jump on a plane bound for anywhere."

"Huh. Rich and nice. Good combo."

I hadn't been paying attention to the background music, but familiar words fill the pause in our conversation, and we grin simultaneously.

Shilo is my song. I know every word, every pitch and tone in Neil Diamond's voice, even though it dates back to the sixties. We stop eating and listen.

"Oh, that man had the sexiest voice ever! Don't you think?"

I like the song because it's the source of my name, but that doesn't change the fact the singer is even older than my parents. Sexy? Maybe once upon a time, but...

"Um, well."

"What a fiasco it was when I gave you that name."

I know the story even better than the song, but she's going to tell it anyway.

"The first time I heard it, just weeks before you were born, I *knew* that would be your name. Dad loved it, too, but your grandparents had a fit. You were supposed to have a family name. When we told them you'd be named Shilo, *mama mia*, they went crazy!" Right on cue, Mom rolls her eyes like she does every time. "My mother kept reminding me about Nonna Marie's role in my pregnancy, but I was tired of all the Italian traditions. And so you are Shilo *Marie*. And when you came into this world, your grandparents adored you. They weren't too happy with me and Dad, though."

"They seem to have gotten over it. And I'm glad my name's different."

Her smiling eyes linger on me. "It suits you. Now let's finish up and hit the toy store so I can get home and start the lasagna."

A sea of possibilities stretches before us at the giant toy store. In the end, we choose a stuffed dinosaur, a huge ball splashed with greens and blues, and a dump truck noisy enough to endear itself to any boy. I buy Julia a little mesh bag of bubble-gum that looks like real rocks. Back on the road again, we head for Sonrise House.

The two-story building looms larger than the surrounding houses. Other than that, there's nothing to show it's anything more than a family home. But inside these walls are girls like Misty, whose lives took an unexpected turn. My knock produces a friendly voice from an intercom mounted on the doorframe. Mom gives her name, and the door swings open.

"Hi. Welcome to Sonrise House. I'm Kelly." The girl in the doorway flashes a warm smile. "If you'll just follow me, I'll take you to meet Pat. She wasn't expecting you today, but I'm sure she can take a few minutes."

Walking down a short hallway, we pass a living room with a flat screen and two comfy-looking green couches. A rocking chair occupies one corner; bean bag chairs and stuffed animals fill another. Further down, girls talk and laugh as they microwave nachos in a country-blue kitchen. So not the sterile atmosphere I expected. Actually kind of homey.

"Here we go." Kelly gestures toward a room just past the kitchen. We follow her in and find the queen of travel on her hands and knees, scraping something off the floor. Again, not what I expected. Dressed in jeans and a powder blue sweatshirt, she digs in with determination.

"Pat, this is Annie Giannelli and her daughter. She talked to you about a girl named Misty."

Pat stands up, beams a smile, and wipes her hands before extending one to Mom. "Nice to meet you. Excuse my appearance. Cleaning day." Caramel-colored hair feathers about her face. So cool. My hair wouldn't do that even if I went to a Beverly Hills hair salon. She reaches for my hand. "Hi. Pleasure to meet you." Something about the way she says it makes me like her already.

"Hi, I'm Shilo." Palm meets palm, our fingers clasp, and there it is again. Warmth. It permeates my heart, then disappears when we break contact. I look closer at Pat, seeing beyond the smile. Pale skin, tired eyes. Sickness invading her body. I glance at the floor, afraid she'll see it in my face. How often is this going to happen? And the bigger question: What now?

"Have a seat." She gestures toward two chairs. "I'd love to hear more about the young lady you're trying to help."

Mom gives Pat the rundown on Misty, leaving out the healing part and downplaying Tyler's injuries. Pat's brows knit during the tales of Misty's trials and tribulations. She lets out a sigh when Mom recaps the part about Jake beating Tyler. When Mom finishes, Pat just shakes her head.

"We do have an opening coming up, and she sounds like an excellent candidate. I'll have to interview her though, just to make sure."

Mom's face lights up like Julia's when she's at the Museum of Science and Industry.

"Please keep in mind, we have rules." Pat pulls a paper from a file drawer. "Those who don't have a high school diploma are required to get their GED. Also, your Misty will have to find a part-time job. The daycare center and meals are free. Naturally, no drugs or booze. That'll get a girl kicked out." She hands Mom a brochure. "Any questions?" She radiates compassion. She obviously cares about the girls, and I'm glad. They set up Misty's interview for tomorrow.

"It may look ordinary on the outside, but let me tell you, I've seen miracles happen within these walls." Pat's smile seems to hold a million stories. "All these girls need is a feeling of security. Encouragement. Some of them have been squashed into the ground their whole lives. We try to help them rise up and discover who they really are. I hope we can do that for Misty."

As we follow her to the front door, my heart quickens in anticipation of another contact. She says goodbye and, looking all friendly and beautiful, reaches out her hand. I take a breath…and hold it. Our palms meet again. Soft heat envelopes my heart, fills my chest.

Confirms my fears.

"This is really a nice place." I hold on, fueled by curiosity. Will it continue and spread like it did with Tyler? Beams of warmth radiate into my shoulders before streaming into my upper arms. The Sonrise House entrance becomes hazy blue. My muscles relax. Peace floods my soul.

Pat lets go. The lovely blue mist disappears, taking the warmth with it, but it's momentary presence leaves no trace of doubt. I can no longer hope it was just my imagination.

On the ride home, Mom's excitement explodes

through the car, but I can't seem to share it. I stare out at the strip malls and restaurants, houses and schools, with my mind fixated on Pat. What could be wrong with her? Mom chatters on, recapping the meeting from beginning to end, talking about her hopes and dreams for Misty. Wasn't Pat great? Wouldn't it be wonderful if Misty got into Sonrise House? Took some classes? Got a job?

Silence. How long ago did she stop talking? Mom reaches over and lays her hand on mine. "Why so quiet, Honey? Didn't you like Sonrise?"

Her question jars me from thoughts of Pat. "Yeah, it was great."

"Well, something's bothering you. What am I saying? Of course something's bothering you. I'm sorry. I got so caught up in Misty's situation, I lost sight of yours. How are you holding up?"

"I'm fine."

She opens her mouth to say something, then lets it go. There's a shimmery look to her eyes. Maybe from the sunlight.

We ride in silence for the next few blocks, giving me a chance to focus on options. On one hand, I could just stay quiet about Pat. If I don't bring it up, we don't have to dive back into this morning's discussion. On the other hand, this happened for a reason, and I need help figuring out my next move. I have to heal Pat. The woman is amazing. A beam of light, brightening lives darkened by insecurity, fear, and oppression. She doesn't just offer compassion, she provides solutions that change lives.

The weight of such responsibility crushes me, pushing out a sigh, long and loud as I confront an endless future of making these decisions.

"What is it, Shilo? Tell me. It's better than letting something eat away at you."

I glance at Mom, who stayed up half the night sharing Nonna's story with me so I'd understand what I am, and what's at stake. She and Dad are the only ones I can talk to about this. At least, the only one's on this side of the Atlantic. I breathe deep and gather up my thoughts. "Pat's sick."

"What?" She glances at me, then back to the road.

"She's sick. Very sick."

"How can that be? She looked so healthy and vibrant. How do you...what am I saying. Of course, you would know."

Of course, I would. I am the blue-eyed great-granddaughter of Nonna Marie. I am Shilo, the healer.

And I just got my third assignment.

CHAPTER TEN

Misty

Jake's in jail, Tyler's all better, and we got invited for a free dinner. Man, it feels like Christmas. Not the kind with Jake, though. Feels like the kind I used to have with the Howells, when I'd look at the presents under the glowing tree and feel all toasty from the fireplace. I dig through my drawer and pull out my best t-shirt, then search in the bathroom for the sample of fancy shampoo that came in the mail. I'd put it away somewhere, savin' it for a special occasion. My fingers feel the edge of the foil packet under the bottle of vitamins I stole for Tyler. Guilt shudders through me. Never thought I'd turn to stealin', but I've got to take care of my boy, and those darn chewy vitamins are so expensive. I lay out my clothes on the bed, which Tyler's using for a trampoline. It's okay, long as I'm watching. There's not a whole lot to entertain him in this place.

"Look at me, Mommy! Look! I'm gonna touch the ceiling."

"All right, mister, settle down. You can watch TV while Mommy takes a quick shower. I think the Wiggles are on."

He wraps warm arms around my neck, and I scoop him off the bed. Two years, and it still melts my heart. If everybody had that kinda love, there sure wouldn't be so much ugly in the world.

Tyler curls up in the corner of the couch, singing with the Wiggles. I grab my special shampoo and shower fast, knowing I've got about ten minutes before he loses interest. The scent of lilacs and roses envelopes my senses. It's like I can't even sniff hard enough to get my fill. Mmm. To think some people get to use this stuff all the time. Lucky. I should write this down, so I can read it over and over and remember this really good day. The day everything went right, and I didn't feel scared or hungry or dirty.

"Tyler! Time to get dressed." He's still watching the Wiggles. I join him and find out why. They have animals on the show today. That boy sure loves critters.

"Look at the bunny, Mommy! Can we have a bunny? Please?"

I inhale, hanging on to the smell of lilacs. How can I tell him I can barely take care of *him*, much less a bunny? "We'll see, Sweetie. For now, let's get you dressed and go have a real nice dinner." No macaroni and cheese tonight. No Ramen. That Annie is a real chef; says so on the card she gave me. But she's not going to sucker me into spilling my guts again. Man, that woman must have put a spell on me that day in the hospital. Can't believe I opened up to her. I know better than to start gettin' close to someone. They all leave. First Dad, then Mom, then the Howells. Only one that ever stuck around was Jake. Lucky me.

Clean and dressed, we head for the door. I swoop up Ty and swing him in a circle, then set him down with a tickle. He tickles me back, and we giggle like big sillies. I glance again at the clock, satisfied I planned it just right. Mrs. Howell said you should never be late when someone invites you for dinner. We're still laughin' as I reach for the knob.

My cell vibrates, followed by music that cuts through the giddiness, chopping it into little pieces. I freeze.

"Phone, Mommy." Tyler's smile disappears.

We look at each other, somehow knowing it ain't goin' to be good. I reach into my pocket and grab it, but don't recognize the number. Deep breath. "Hello."

He curses at me, and I know for sure who's on the other end. "What do you want?"

"Payback, you little tramp!" The angry voice is not Jake's, but it's the next worst thing: His brother, Jeremy. "If you hadn't gone trottin' off to the stupid library, this never woulda happened, and Jake wouldn't be in jail."

"Tyler almost *died*. Did Jake mention *that* part?"

"You're the one who left him with the kid. Some mother you are!" He's shouting so loud now, Tyler's starin' at the phone, eyes wide, body trembling. "If you didn't call 911, he wouldn't be in this messed up situation."

If I didn't call 911, I would have spent today at my baby's funeral. "What do you want?"

"I want you to know one thing. He won't be in there forever. Just twenty more days. When he gets out, you'll get what's coming to you." The phone goes dead...and so does my soul. I don't want to look at Tyler. Don't want him to see the terror in me; the ocean of tears I'm holdin' back. But if I don't suck it up and be the Mom he needs, then who will? I glance at my boy, hugging his ragged teddy bear, and find the strength.

"Okay, you silly goose, it's time for us to go. You ready?"

"Uh huh." He squeezes my hand, and I walk out singin' "we're off to see the wizard," just like Dorothy. Even when she was scared, she sang that song like everything was fine. I'm doin' the same, hoping Tyler believes the lie.

Because this sure ain't Oz.

CHAPTER ELEVEN

Shilo

A green Kia sits in front of our house. As we pull onto the driveway, its driver gets out and walks toward us. He looks late twenties, short blond hair gelled for spiking, sunglasses veiling his eyes. As he gets closer, I see the cell phone in his hands, which shouldn't bother me. And yet…it does. Maybe it's the way he's holding it at chest level, like he's pointing it at us.

Mom's eyes ask the question before her words come out. "Do you know this guy?"

"Nope." What I don't say is I don't trust him either. Can't explain it. Just one of those things.

As he approaches, we step onto the porch and greet him with forced smiles. He does the same.

"Can we help you with something?" Mom uses her crispy, cordial tone, usually reserved for door-to-door solicitors.

"I'm hoping you can. Name's Paul Kaminski. I'm with the Weekly Star." The guy's eyes settle on me before turning back to Mom. His phony grin spreads wider. "I heard there was quite a miracle that took place at the hospital. Something about your daughter healing a little boy." He gestures toward me. "This the girl?"

I stand with my back against the door, holding my breath. It's only been twenty-four hours.

Mom's eyes narrow. "I'd like you to leave now."

Can he hear the low growl rumbling beneath her words? He'd be wise to heed her warning, but I'm guessing that won't happen.

"Sure, sure. I understand. I just want to ask a question or two. Won't take more than five minutes." Stepping closer, he keeps his cell raised high enough for me to see the recording app running, confirming my initial mistrust. "There's X-rays that show the boy's bones were broken one day and fine the next. And is that Shilo with an H at the end, or just an O?" He turns to me again. "Are you Shilo? Can you verify the healing took place?"

He takes a step back, then another, as Mom advances on him like a lioness stalking a rabbit. "My husband is Sgt. Nick Giannelli of the Cedarcrest Police Dept. Feel free to verify *that*. Unless you want to be arrested, you'll remove yourself from my property before your next blink." She moves in for the kill. "Am I clear?"

Man, I'm glad she's on *my* side.

"Mrs. Giannelli, please, I don't mean to invade your privacy. How about just confirming it happened? Yes? No?" He backs away as he speaks, words flying faster and faster. "Will the lack of evidence in the X-rays affect the brutality case? Was there some kind of ritual that took place?"

Seriously? Does he think I have a voodoo doll? My eyes focus on Mom, while her lioness eyes remain glued to the reporter. She whips out her cell, a motion heavily laced with Italian drama, and starts to scroll down to Dad's work number. The gesture works. Paul what's-his-name high tails it into his little green car and takes off.

Once inside, I collapse on the couch, afraid my legs won't hold me up much longer. Evidence. Just perfect. They have X-rays and obviously someone leaking info. Could it be that nurse with the beautiful accent? Adanna. Somehow I just can't picture it.

"Thanks, Mom. How did you know what to say?"

"Sometimes it's just a matter of living long enough." Mom hovers near the edge of the window, peeking out to make sure our visitor doesn't return. "He threw me with that zinger, though. Could Jake go free if the evidence doesn't support his crime? We'll have to ask Dad."

I search for words that will smooth the wrinkle forming on her forehead, but I know little about court cases, other than how they play out on TV. I doubt a producer would even consider this. Too unbelievable.

Mom eyes the clock and heads for the kitchen, her sanctuary. "It's getting late, and we've got a meal to cook. Let's focus." The wrinkle disappears, making me envy her ability to move on.

In minutes, the huge silver pasta pot sits on the stove. In her favorite yellow bowl, fresh ricotta joins eggs, salt, garlic, and grated Parmesan that will magically blend to create Mom's famous lasagna filling. As Chef Annie rules the kitchen, I head upstairs to wrap the clothes and toys, anxiously anticipating Misty and Tyler's reaction.

A quick scan of my room reminds me it's not exactly kid-proof. Visions of Tyler wreaking havoc with my stuff prompt me to move precious possessions to top shelves. Up goes the music box from Aunt Rita and Uncle Vince, my miniature crystal guitar, and the framed photo of me and Mel at the carnival when we were six.

We'd met a few weeks earlier on the swings at Veteran's Park.

"How come you don't match your parents?" It didn't make sense that her skin was dark, and her mom and dad were both fair-skinned redheads.

"Cuz I'm adopted. Bet I can swing higher than you."

"Betcha can't."

And the adoption conversation got lost in the wind as we raced to touch the summer sky.

I slide my real guitar under the bed, accompanied by my photo albums and iPod. Julia better hide her rock collection when she gets home, or it will be reduced to a pile of rubble. I wonder what she'll think about...

Julia! My nightstand clock says she'll be home any minute. I fly down the stairs, pulse racing, breaths coming in bursts. "Mom, what did you tell Julia? She doesn't know, does she? About me?"

"Calm down. It's not the kind of thing you explain to someone as they're rushing off to school. Now's not good, either. I'm a little nervous about telling her. She's young enough to think her friends will keep secrets."

"Well, it's not like she has that many. But still..."

"Dad and I will figure this out. This morning I told her you weren't feeling well."

"I would die if she told people. *Die*!"

"I guess there's no reason we couldn't keep it quiet for awhile."

As if on cue, the doorbell rings. Julia presses her pixie face against the window, nose squished like a snout, eyes crossed. Her silliness washes away my anxiety and makes me laugh. I make a face back at her and open the door.

"Faker." Julia's accusatory tone reveals her jealousy.

"Hi to you, too."

"You don't look very sick."

"I'm feeling much better." And it's true. At least, better than this morning.

"Well, I guess somebody got out of her genetics test." Julia plops down her backpack and pulls out color-coded folders, apparently anxious to begin her homework.

"Oh, no, the test! It's forty percent of my science grade!"

Mom assures me it will be waiting for me tomorrow. "You've got an excused absence." She mixes goopy white lasagna filling with a large wooden spoon. "Just make sure you're ready for it."

Genetics. Nothing in that textbook will explain what I got from Nonna Marie.

"So why did you stay home, anyway?" Julia's math book lays open in front of her, with familiar looking equations staring up at me. Equations I worked on just last year. Next to it, a pair of perfectly sharpened number two pencils await their demise.

"I told you; Shilo wasn't feeling well." Mom spreads the rich ricotta mixture between layers of noodles, tomato sauce, and slices of mozzarella.

"Like how?"

The repulsive memory of running to the bathroom during last night's conversation pops into my brain. "I threw up last night."

"Gross."

Mom smiles, then tells mini Einstein about the company we're having, without mentioning the healing fiasco. "Tyler's mother is going through some hard times," she says. "I thought it would be nice to invite her over."

Short and simple. Smart move.

"But, Mom, I'm supposed to go to Danielle's after dinner to work on our science project. I *have* to do this. There's only three more days until the science fair."

Perfect! Let her go, let her go, let her go. The last thing I want is Misty bringing up the healing thing with Jules around.

"It's fine. You don't have to stay. It will still be light out, so you can roller blade over there, and I'll pick you up later."

Julia digs into her math assignment with gusto, pencil moving madly across the page. Unbelievable.

"Stop looking so happy. It's geometry, Jules. It's *homework*." I tug on her ponytail. "You're not supposed to enjoy it."

"Genetics is calling, Shilo," Mom lays the last slice of fresh mozzarella on the top layer. "And Italian, plus whatever else you missed today. Go. They'll be here soon."

"*Non preoccuparti tanto, Mama.*" I walk away with another flick of my sister's pony.

"No fair talking Italian," Julia says. "What did you say?"

"It means Mom worries too much."

A couple of texts and emails later, I have today's assignments, but my enthusiasm for academics doesn't match Julia's. Not even close. Still, the books await. Sumptuous aromas drift up from the kitchen as I work on Italian. Mmm, *lasagna*. My favorite Italian word.

My iPod clock shows ten minutes to go before Misty arrives. Imagining a conversation with her constricts my insides, stealing away my desire for dinner. If Misty understood what happened, if she told people...

The doorbell interrupts my thoughts. She's early. Perfect. And here am I, still clueless as to what I'll say when she starts firing questions.

"Shilo." Mom calls from the living room. "It's Kenji."

My heart soars at his name, then tumbles. What if Misty shows up while he's here? I *do not* want to explain who she is, or have him telling Miya she was here. I can only imagine the interrogation tomorrow at school. He needs to leave. Fast.

Kenji stands in the doorway wearing jeans, a gray hoodie, and a smile that makes me forget I want him to leave. Strands of windblown hair hang over one eye.

"Hey, Blue."

"Hi. Surprised to see you."

"Yeah, well, I needed to stop by World Market, so I figured you might want to come. I mean, if you're done doing whatever you were doing."

So sweet. I love that store. He has no idea how much I want to jump in the car with him and go. "Yeah, I mean, no. I'm kinda done, but we're having company for dinner."

"Yeah? Who? Your aunt and uncle?"

"No, just a….a…friend of the family." I stand in the doorway, holding the storm door partway open as we talk.

"You're not going to invite me in?"

I scan the street behind him, fearing Misty will pull up any second. "Sorry, I can't. She'll be here soon, so I have to get ready."

Sounds like I'm dressing for the prom.

The smile vanishes, just like it disappeared from our conversation last night. "Well, maybe next time."

"Definitely. Thanks for coming. Wish I could go."

"Me, too." A quick kiss, then a "See ya," and he's gone.

I stare out at the empty street and imagine sitting in his car, kissing in the parking lot. Kissing on my porch. But there will be no warm Kenji kisses tonight.

Misty's arrival time comes and goes, with Mom firmly planted by the living room window. Come on Misty;, do this. All you have to do is show up. Don't bail on Mom after all she did for you today. Another five minutes go by. Mom stirs the sauce again, while I grate more Parmesan. She's not coming. I just know it.

"She's here!" Mom's voice warrants an appearance by the Queen of England.

I glance outside, where a rusted blue Ford rumbles in the driveway, duct tape securing the right front bumper. It seems to have collapsed there, with no intention of ever moving again. Our guest of honor unbuckles her son's car seat, holding his hand as they walk toward the house. I run upstairs and pound on Julia's door.

"Come on, Rockhound. She's here."

"Almost ready. Still putting stuff away so that boy doesn't get it."

Mom already has the door and her arms wide open. Misty smiles a cheery hello, but dull eyes tell another story. Beyond the sad eyes, however, a slightly improved version of Misty sports a less faded t-shirt, somewhat smaller than the tent she was wearing at the hospital. The faint smell of flowers hovers around her shoulder-length hair.

Tyler leans against her leg, clinging to the sorriest excuse for a teddy bear I've ever seen. Frayed stuffing hangs from the seam of it's back. A, an ear is dangling on it's last thread, and the thing has one eye. One. It's creepy. I scan my mental calendar and schedule another trip to the toy store while Annieconda hugs the life out of Misty.

Okay, Mom, let her up for air.

"Thanks for inviting us." She speaks softly, studying the carpet. "We don't get out much, so this is kinda like an adventure for me and Tyler."

She seriously needs a life.

"Mmm. Smells good, Mommy." Tyler's bright eyes sparkle with life and mischief, especially compared to how he looked the previous day. It's like watching Pinocchio come alive. Yesterday he was frail, pale, and limp as a rag doll. But today, his healthy glow is tangible proof The Gift is real. God used me and my ordinary hands to perform a miracle.

And I still have no idea why.

"I hope you like lasagna." Mom talks in a cheerful lilt, clearly seeing the misery on Misty's face. "If not, we've got chicken, meatballs, and green beans. Oh, and fruit salad."

"Thanks, Annie. You didn't have to do that for us." Misty shifts her feet, holding tight to Tyler's hand.

"Don't worry," Julia says. "Mom loves feeding people. It's her thing."

Mom ignores the comment and sends Julia upstairs to get our surprises. With Jules out of earshot, Mom turns back to Misty. "Julia doesn't know about what happened in the hospital," she whispers. "She's leaving after dinner. We'll talk then."

Misty nods.

Loud thumps announce Julia's return trip, though her face and half her body are hidden by packages and my bag of clothes. She reaches bottom and extends her load to a wide-eyed Misty.

"I don't understand. What's this for?"

"Just because." Mom grabs two of the packages, handing them to Tyler. "That's a good enough reason, isn't it? Now go ahead and open them."

"Presents, yippee!" Tyler jumps and claps, grinning wide enough to split his freckled face in two. He tears through the paper with dramatic gasps that cause all three of us to laugh.

"A truck! A truck! Can I keep it?" Triple assurances convince him the truck is all his. Shreds of paper fly as he rips open packages containing the ball, stuffed dinosaur, and two outfits, his enthusiasm extending even to the clothes.

"Mommy, look!" He boings up and down like a Tigger toy, trying to wrap scrawny arms around the entire booty. "Ohhh, nice! Open you presents, Mommy."

Trembling hands slowly tear through pastel tissue paper, revealing the new outfit. Misty holds the shirt against her body, then folds it and places it back in the box. "Thank you. They're real nice, but you don't need to be buyin' me stuff." Misty's eyes glisten. She turns away.

"If you don't like the clothes, it's perfectly okay." Mom's tone is gentle enough for a frightened child. "We have the receipts. We can exchange them for something more your style."

The comment elicits a sad smile from Misty. "My style? If I had one, these would probably be it. They're great, really." But her tone doesn't say "great" at all.

It's not the clothes, Mom. Get a clue. But I can't say what I want with Jules standing there. "Julia, why don't you take Tyler on the deck and show him how the truck works?" I scooch down to face Tyler. "You can put stuff in the back of it, Tyler. Then you press that black button and it dumps everything out."

Julia glares. "Why don't *you?*"

She doesn't want to miss a thing, but despite her crazy-high IQ, she's easy to manipulate if you know her weaknesses. And I do.

"Okay, I'll do it. Come on, Tyler." I reach for his hand. "Maybe there's some lava or cedar rocks out there."

"Lava? There's no lava in Illinois. And what the heck is a cedar rock? Are you crazy? You're going to mess him all up! Come on, Tyler." Julia pushes my hand away and replaces it with hers. "I'll find you some good rocks *and* teach you their real names."

"Tucking the truck under one arm, Tyler walks off with Julia like he's known her forever. "Let's go."

The screen door slams. Misty, still wrapping both arms around her gift box, turns to Mom. "I'm sorry." Fog hangs above us. Misty opens her mouth again, and we wait for an explanation for her tears. "I'm sorry."

"Sorry for what?" Mom loops an arm around Misty and her box. "You haven't done one thing to be sorry about."

"You made dinner, bought me this cool stuff. Then I'm all late and stressed. You must think I'm such an idiot."

"Not even close. I think you are someone with a broken heart and a broken spirit. I'd be stressed, too, if I'd been through half the things you've experienced."

"Really?"

"Really." She strokes Misty's hair, something that might seem weird if anyone else did it, but somehow Mom gets away with all that warm, fuzzy stuff. "Come, sit." Mom motions Misty onto the couch. "Why don't you tell us what's got you so upset today?"

Misty runs shaky fingers through her hair, then sits on the edge of the couch. She says she and Tyler had been excited all day about coming over. Then, the phone call. Anger flashes in Mom's eyes as Misty tells about the blaming, the threats.

How I wish she could get the monster and his brother out of her life.

Mom takes Misty's hand in both of hers. "Here's what I want you to do: Go up to the bathroom, wash away those tears with some nice cool water, and think about this. You are safe at this moment. Jake is in jail, and you're with people who care about you. We're going to have a lovely dinner, then talk about some ideas I have for you. Now go.

A hint of a smile graces Misty's face as she heads upstairs.

Dinner a la Chef Annie is worthy of a *Bon Appetit*

cover story. Her lasagna never tasted richer and cheesier. Tyler winds a strand of hot, gooey mozzarella around his fork and smacks his lips. The kid is hilarious, but it's Misty who seems most affected by the food. As we eat, talk, and laugh, her face softens. The pain in her eyes melts, replaced by a sparkle. Hope? The big mystery is how stick-figure Misty is packing away food like a sumo wrestler. I fight back a laugh as she reaches for yet another meatball.

"You're eating like a true Italian, Misty." Mom beams, surely considering Misty's hearty appetite a compliment.

Misty laughs. "Yeah, it's been awhile since I've had food like this. But I don't have any Italian in me. Just English and Irish. Last name's Morning."

Julia nearly chokes on her garlic bread. "Morning? Your name is *Misty Morning?*"

The only thing Jules likes better than rocks and planets is cool names. A sparkly notebook in her room is filled with the best ones she's heard over the years. Doesn't matter if you're alive or dead, a celebrity like Rip Torn or a homeless woman, like Beulah Bleu who hangs out by the bus stop and gets a sandwich from Jules every day. If you're name meets her criteria for coolness, it's in the notebook. Pretty sure Misty's just earned a spot.

"Yep."

"That is *so* cool! Oh my gosh, wait till I tell Emma. Awesome!"

Only a Harvard geology professor could have impressed her more.

"Who's Emma?" Misty asks.

I can't resist. "BFF and fellow rock nerd."

"*Geologist.*" Julia glares her disgust at me before turning back to our guest. "Misty Morning." Julia sighs the word with enough theatrics to make a pop star proud. "You are so lucky!"

Misty smiles. "I guess I am." She looks at Tyler and gives his arm a little squeeze.

The feast continues, with Julia complaining that Mom made meat sauce for the lasagna, Tyler spilling his chocolate milk, and Mom beaming at Misty's constant compliments. After we clean up, Julia grabs her backpack and heads to her science partner's house.

"What happened that day?" Misty lets loose the question before Jules reaches the backyard gate. "What did you do? I'm grateful and all, but you've gotta tell me. What *are* you? Why did Tyler get better? "

Misty glances from me to Mom. The only thing keeping me from falling off my chair is knowing Mom handled that reporter, so maybe she can handle this, too.

"You know what, Tyler?" Mom takes Tyler's hand and leads him down to the family room. "We have some great kids' movies. Would you like to watch one?"

She's leaving it to me. It's one of her famous "learning moments," but come on, this is not the kind of thing you mess with.

"Movies?" His excitement rises. Maybe he doesn't get to watch them. Maybe they don't even have a TV. Mom sets the DVDs on the floor, then Tyler lays them out in a row, pointing to each one as he strives to make the perfect choice.

My hands grip the edges of my chair. "I…I'm not sure. I prayed for him."

"My son was in bad shape, ya know? Broken bones, the spleen thing. Then you came along and boom, he's better. It's crazy."

My attempts at telepathy fail miserably. Mom doesn't hear my silent pleas for her to come upstairs and handle this. It's not that I don't want to;, it's just the giant risk is paralyzing my tongue. One wrong word, and the chaos could begin. Thanks to that reporter, it may have already started.

"Want some coffee?" It's pathetic, but it's all I've got.

Misty shakes her head. "No, thanks. I just want to know what happened at the hospital. I want the real story;, that's all."

That's all. That's *everything*.

Mom heads up the four stairs leading to the kitchen. "It's not that simple, Misty."

"Well, give it a shot. I'm not quite as dumb as I look."

I feel my eyebrows arch. Where did *that* come from? Probably got called dumb and a whole lot worse by the jailbird boyfriend. "We never thought you were dumb."

"I stayed with Jake, didn't I? Not exactly a rocket scientist."

Compassion radiates from Mom's eyes. "Lots of smart women make bad choices when it comes to men, for all kinds of reasons. I think you were just trying to protect Tyler and didn't realize you had options."

"Yeah, well, maybe. I don't know. Thanks, though. But anyway, what happened in the hospital? It just doesn't make sense."

Clearly, Misty was not to be swayed from the topic she came to discuss.

"Fair enough," Mom replies. "It was an answer to a prayer."

She didn't just say it. She *didn't*...and yet, she did. I suck in a breath, derailed by her honesty. Not that I expected Annieconda to lie, but I thought she'd at least dilute the truth.

"Prayer connects us with God. He always hears us, but sometimes it's a long wait and sometimes the answer's different than expected. But not this time, Misty. You got exactly what you hoped for. Even better. Be grateful, but not to Shilo. She was the vessel, not the potter. Know what I mean?"

She makes it seem so simple. Or I make it way too complicated. God gave me The Gift, so it stands to reason he'd give me the words. Maybe I just need to make the effort.

"I guess so. Mrs. Howell used to say stuff like that, too." Misty's tone softens. There's something about that woman's name that derails her.

"Your foster mom?" If I can get her on a new topic, we can leave the other one behind. "The one you ran away from?"

"Yeah, well, more like the other way around. They dumped me with her weirdo sister when they went to buy a house in North Carolina. *That's* who I ran away from. They said it was just for a few weeks, but no way they were comin' back for me." Pain shadows Misty's face.

"You miss them a lot, don't you?"

Misty looks down. "I don't want to talk about them. I want to know more about the healing."

Mom stands. "You two talk. I'm going to keep Tyler company." She heads to the family room, and Misty turns to me, her face a question mark. And for reasons I can't explain, I'm ready to handle this on my own.

"It's like she said. An answer. A miracle." My words flow without fear. I remember Mom's earlier conversation with the doctor and borrow her words. "Seriously, there's medical reports about prayer and healing. It happens."

Misty picks up the creepy teddy bear Tyler left on the table and stares at its Cyclops face. "I don't know. Seems like there's more to it." She sets it to the side and looks up. "I see this guy on TV sometimes. His name is Samuel something, and he says he's a faith healer."

This can't be good.

"He says he can heal anyone, no matter how sick. All you have to do is call the phone number, and they mail you a shower cap. You put it on, think hard about your sickness, then mail it back with fifty bucks, and he prays over it."

Pretty sure my eyes are popping out of my head. I thought those people disappeared in the 80s.

"He guarantees you'll be cured," she continues. "People on his show swear he cured them. I never believed it, though. His eyes look snaky to me."

That's it. We're kicking Samuel out of the Faith Healer's Union.

"You're smart not to believe him." I stand up to grab a refill. "He's a fraud."

She shakes her head. "I don't know anymore. Look what *you* did."

This just keeps getting better. "I'm nothing like him. Not even close." I explain there's a huge difference between a sincere prayer and the baloney Mr. Shower Cap is pulling. "A true healer wouldn't take money or need props. And how can a person promise a miracle? It's up to God."

Misty looks at me like I'm not of this world, and the question in her eyes is practically verbal. Here it comes. Don't ask me. Please.

"Are you a true faith healer then?"

And there it is. I squeeze my eyes shut, exploring the depths of my heart and mind for the right words. Deny it, and I'm lying. Admit it, and I'll be a one-girl freak show by tomorrow morning. No words come. I open my eyes, and she's still staring at me. "I never had this experience with any other people." It sounds clumsy, but it could work. She doesn't need to know about the dog.

"Really?"

"Yeah. And here's the thing. If you talk about this,

people will get all crazy about it. Reporters, scientists, social media." I pause for dramatic effect and gaze right into her eyes. "It would be a mess, Misty. Please don't ruin my life."

She stares back. Shakes her head. "Never. You saved my life when you saved Tyler's. I won't say a word."

The resolve in her eyes confirms her words. I exhale, inhale, slump in my chair. My secret's safe for now.

But what about next time?

CHAPTER TWELVE

Misty

They're hidin' something, these Gianellis, but it's okay for now. They're real good to me and Ty, and that matters more than the secret. But there's more to this healing thing. I just know it.

Annie's hot coffee warms me from the inside out. She put stuff in there to make it creamy and sweet. Even a little chocolaty. Breathing it in is almost as good as inhaling the scent of that fancy shampoo. I take little sips to make it last longer while she talks to me about Sonrise House. Maybe this could be a new start for us. Sounds pretty good. We'd have our own room, and they've got computers I can use, a kitchen, babysitting services, everything.

"There's a van that'll take you to the library," Shilo says. She musta remembered I love the library. "It'll take you to stores, too. And church, if you ever change your mind."

Truth is, I didn't mind church so much when I went

with the Howells. Kinda liked it, actually. It was all peaceful in there, and the pastor talked about Jesus like he was really with us, watchin' over us, wantin' the best for us. Jake got mad when I mentioned going, though. After awhile, I felt like God wasn't with me, anyway. Maybe I just couldn't see His light in the middle of all that darkness. Or maybe I just forgot to look.

"Guess I could talk to Pat tomorrow and see how it goes."

Annie looks like she just won the lottery. I don't know why she's doin' all this, but I'm glad she is. Even with that stupid call from Jake's brother, this day has been the best in ages.

"We're set then," she says. "I'll pick you up at three-thirty. But keep in mind they don't have an opening for four weeks."

All my insides slump. "We gotta be out in two. Rent's due, and I don't have it. And no way we can be there when Jake gets out." Images of Jake walkin' through that apartment door with his eyes blazing and his fist up make me shudder. Annie promises to help figure somethin' out. I sure hope so, cause I don't want to be hanging out in one of those homeless shelters with Tyler.

"Promise us you'll call if you hear from that Jeremy creep again," Shilo says. "He can't just threaten you. My Dad's going to have an attack when he hears about that."

Annie packs plastic containers into a bag, ; each one labeled with what's in it. "She's not kidding, Misty." In goes a container of lasagna and meatballs, followed by another with chicken, and a zip-lock bag nearly burstin' with chocolate chip cookies. "I want to know."

When it comes time to leave, she sends us home with enough food to last days, along with our gifts and a hug that nearly crushes me. No wonder Shilo calls her

Annieconda. Pretty funny. I like that Shilo, even if she is a princess with a fairytale life.

CHAPTER THIRTEEN

Shilo

My life is a nightmare. I just came within a hair of this whole healer thing blowing up and lighting the sky like the scoreboard at a night game. I can't even talk about it to Mel, not that we've talked in days, anyway. And for the second night in a row, I blew off Kenji. I grab my cell and start to text, then decide I need to hear his voice.

"Hey, Blue. Company gone?"

"Yeah. Sorry about before. I really wanted to go with you."

"It wasn't the same without you. I got lost in the Greek aisle. Wandered aimlessly for hours until some kind old lady helped me find the exit."

Grinning into the phone, I give him a "Yeah, right." I love his humor. His intelligence. His heart. We talk about the day, and he reminds me about Saturday's meeting to find out more about the mission trip to Kentucky.

"You're coming, right? You asked your parents?"

"Not yet, but I will. There's been a lot going on lately."

"Like what?"

My hand squeezes my cell a little tighter. It's great that he really wants to know; that he's such a good listener. I love how much he cares, but it doesn't change my situation. "Just stuff. Anyway, don't worry, I'll ask them before Saturday."

No response.

"Is that a problem?"

"I don't know. You've been kinda distant lately, and you practically pushed me off your porch when I came by. Want to talk about it?"

I do. I want to tell him everything about Tyler and the miracle. Everything my mom told me that night. Nonna's story, my mother's plea, feeling like I'm floating on air one minute and weighted by panic the next. My heart wants to pour out all the wonder and turbulence that has filled it since the unveiling of this incomprehensible gift. If only I could, without fear he'd think I was crazy and leave me forever. "No. I'm fine. Really."

"Okay, see you tomorrow. I'll catch you by Italian if Mrs. D'Andrea doesn't boot me out again. I still have no idea what she said. Probably better that way."

I laugh. It was true. Mrs. D'Andrea has a thing about couples hanging out by the classroom. Fortunately, she also has a funny streak, which makes Italian my favorite class.

I find Mom to make plans for visiting Aunt Rita tomorrow after soccer practice. So glad tomorrow's Friday, then the weekend and Saturday's game. My mind needs a break from the tornado winds spinning it in spirals of darkness and light. Focusing on soccer will ground me.

Friday morning moves at a normal pace, despite my

fear that "Healer" is tattooed on my forehead. With each passing hour, the ordinary rituals help me relax. Brittany stops at my locker to ask if I'm going on the mission trip. Lauren suffers like the drama queen she is over a D on an English quiz. Melody hands me a note in the hallway, her first communication in days. I like that it's a note, though, instead of a text. There's something more personal about unfolding the paper and seeing her familiar handwriting scrawled with her favorite purple pen. Maybe, just maybe, I can master the art of leading a normal life and keep this healing thing under wraps.

The genetics test strains my brain, but I'm feeling pretty solid about most of the answers. Others…not so much. On to Italian, where Mrs. D'Andrea guards the door like a sentry. Kenji comes along and flashes his celebrity smile.

"*Ciao*, Mrs. D'Andrea. You are looking *bello* today." I roll my eyes. Mrs. D'Andrea does the same.

"*Signor Romeo, vai via* . And by the way, if you want to say I'm looking beautiful, it's *bella*, not *bello*. I am not a man. You take my class, and I'll teach you how to speak Italian properly." She walks inside the classroom, beckoning me to follow her, but Kenji grabs my hand.

"I have to talk to you." His whisper quickens my pulse, but not in a good way. He's said those words many times, ; always at a normal volume. Always preceding something like "James and Becca want to hang out with us Friday night," or "My mom invited you over for dinner." But his tone was never this low, or his eyes this dark. Why now? Something tells me I don't want to know.

"Miya said rumors are going around at the hospital. About *you*, Blue."

I open my mouth, but nothing comes out. My knees threaten to wobble. Still struggling to respond, I jump at the bell, and Kenji takes off down the hall with a "We'll talk later."

The word is out, and Kenji will be one of the first to know his girlfriend is a freak. My pretty little delusion of leading a normal life just hit a very ugly brick wall. Will I lose him? Will I end up like Nonna Marie, in some middle-of-nowhere convent? Thoughts reverberate around my brain as I head for my desk. I can't...*won't*, let fear control me. God didn't give me The Gift just to let it destroy my life. I don't know why Nonna did what she did, but there's got to be a better way, and I have every intention of figuring it out.

Lunch finally arrives, but with no desire to eat, I veer away from the cafeteria and head for the Art & Pottery Room, which is thankfully empty. The scents of paint, clay, glue, and wood mingle and envelope my senses. I breathe deep. And again. There's something about this place. Maybe it's the endless possibilities or the sunlight beaming through smudged windows and illuminating the freshly glazed bowls. Or the silence. I find what I need, let my mind wrap around it, and sit down.

I smack down the clay to prevent air bubbles, and get it centered so it won't be lopsided like the bowl I made on the first day of class. Wet clay coats my fingers as the potter's wheel whirls a soon-to-be vase. The soft clay rises a short way from the pressure of my palms and finger tips. I dip my hands into murky water and thumb an indent, then gently squeeze until the height is right for daffodils and tulips. What was a formless, useless lump just moments ago transforms before my eyes. It rises, drops, and rises again at the slightest pressure from my hands. Another dip in the water before my thumbs and finger tips form a curled-out rim. The final creation is nothing like I'd imagined, but if the glazing turns out right, it will be filled with flowers and presented to Aunt Rita. Hopefully, it will sit on her kitchen table, not her hospital windowsill. My new creation joins others on the drying table awaiting the kiln's intense heat.

I head to my next class with a slower pulse and clearer head than when I walked in. When the final bell rings, I leave through a different door, avoiding Kenji and the conversation that might make everything spiral out of control. It is not the brave thing to do, or even the appropriate thing to do. And yet…it's what I do.

The call comes as I pass Melody's house. Knowing it's him, I ignore it, passing a cluster of blooming crabapple trees, gazing at fragrant pink blossoms and breathing in their delicious scent. Anything but answering my cell. My only hope is that coach will work us nearly to death today, so I'll be too wiped out to think about Kenji.

Massive lights illuminate the hospital parking lot. Dad walks next to me, his teasing and jokes lifting the anxiety that's entombed me since Kenji's comment in the hall. The levity is more appreciated than I let on. Tonight, I just want to focus on Aunt Rita.

"You and Jules remember the plan, right?" I grab his arm so he'll stop and assure me we're all on the same page.

"We keep a lookout for docs. You do your healing thing with auntie."

"And Julia thinks…"

"That we're sneaking in a cannoli for auntie." He holds up the bag from Franco's bakery, which hopefully still contains a cannoli. "And just for the record, Miss CIA, I coordinate drug busts, hunt down murderers, and have broken up several rings of car thieves, so I think I can handle *this*."

I nod. "Don't eat the cannoli."

"No promises. Don't go around fixing all the sick

people in there. Those docs won't know what hit 'em."

"You're hilarious." Healing the entire hospital is the least of my concerns. "But seriously, what if this doesn't work?"

Dad sighs. His smile fades. "I don't know. This whole thing's pretty much a mystery to me. It's not on you to make it happen, Shi girl. You have to accept that."

He's right, and yet, acceptance feels impossible. To possess The Gift without the ability to heal Aunt Rita would crush my soul beneath a mountain of failure. And it wouldn't matter that it was actually God's plan, *not* my failure, because either way auntie loses. I force the image from my mind, determined to walk into the hospital room with a smile.

"Let's just go have a nice visit," he says.

Like it's the easiest thing in the world.

Aunt Rita's ebony eyes are open this time. Hanging back, I let everyone else get their hugs and kisses in before wrapping my arms around her. How odd, not to smell her Forever Yours cologne or feel the stiff strands of over-sprayed hair against my cheek. The remainder of her hair lies sparsely against her scalp. I wait, willing the warmth to come.

Please, God. If I can only heal one more person in my life, let it be her.

Nothing. Maybe it's a hand thing. I break away from the hug and cup my hands around the frail, boney hand that has made countless raviolis, dried my tears, crocheted the afghan at the foot of my bed.

Still nothing.

My throat closes up. My eyes sting. This doesn't make sense. What good is this gift? What's the point?

She places her other hand over mine. "Honey, are you okay?"

"I'm fine. What about you? They treating you alright in here?" My smile is a sham, and her eyes tell me she knows it.

"Oh yes, those nurses are so sweet." She lets it go, class act that she is. "Of course, the tall one is a little abrupt, not really the friendly type, you know, but she does have lovely nails. Different shade every day."

Laughter warms the little hospital room. Cancer can't stop Aunt Rita from being Aunt Rita. Dad hands her the cannoli bag and says he and Jules will stand guard in the hall, but she thanks him and graciously refuses. The nausea has stolen her desire for food, even her favorite dessert. Dad looks to me for a Plan B, but all I can do is shrug.

There will be no miracles in this room tonight.

We all find spots to sit. I perch on the edge of her bed, while Mom and Dad get chairs and Julia scrunches down on the floor, back against the wall. Aunt Rita gives us the rundown of her treatment and says she's coming home in a couple of days. "They said the spreading has slowed—so I have a good chance of recovery. Forty percent, one doctor said!"

Which gives Team Death a sixty percent advantage. Mom and Dad exchange a tormented look. Out of the corner of my eye, I see Jule's face go pale as she raises her hand to bite her almost nonexistent finger nails. And me, all I can think is I felt the warmth with two strangers and a dog, but not someone I love.

Back home, I'm dying to talk to Mom and Dad about what I *didn't* feel when I touched Aunt Rita, but Julia keeps hanging around, making it impossible. Instead, I tell them about tomorrow's mission trip meeting with Pastor Frank. They ask all the usual questions and say they'll consider it.

"You don't have to worry. There will be church leaders there. It'll be safe."

Dad grabs a dishtowel, dries a pot, and tucks it into

a cabinet. "We *do* have to worry. It's our job."

Mom shakes her head, opens the same cabinet, and moves the pot to its proper location. "There's no doubt you can handle the work and the accommodations. It's you and Kenji that worry me."

Julia makes obnoxious kissing noises in the background, totally ignoring my best glare.

"Thanks for the trust." I fold my arms, lean against the kitchen counter, and dream of the day I can do what I want without needing anyone's permission.

"It's not about trust, Shilo. I know how you feel about this boy."

"*Kenji*, Mom. His name is Kenji. You know that."

"Apparently, he feels the same way," she continues. "Temptation is hard to resist, especially when you're far away."

My jaw tightens. "I can't believe this conversation. It's not like I'm heading for Florida to star in *Girls Gone Wild*. It's a mission trip. We'll be repairing a school and talking to kids about faith."

"And your boyfriend will be there."

"Alright, let's table this conversation for now." Dad finds the leftovers from Mom's Creative Candies class and munches the head off a chocolate macadamia bunny. "Go to the meeting and find out what you can. We'll talk when we have all the facts."

"Fine."

I retreat to the privacy of my room and call Melody. Any minute now, her voicemail will kick on, and I'll leave yet another message that she'll hear late tonight after rehearsal.

"I can't believe we're finally connecting."

"Me, either." We used to talk ten times a day. Now the sound of her voice is like winning a prize at the fair. "Are you in mid-leap, or can you actually talk?"

She laughs that bubbling brook laugh I miss more

than words can say, before reminding me the word is *jeté*. I hadn't forgotten. We catch up on the past few days of life, with me leaving out everything major. All the mind-blowing things I *really* want to tell her. But telling even one person could be disastrous. Even if it's Mel. Instead, I focus on the mission trip conversation, which elicits the desired sympathy and a similar story about her going away for a few days with her troupe.

"So…"

The pause that follows tells me we're changing topics.

"I saw Kenji in music hall. He asked if I thought you'd been acting weird lately. I told him no."

Her lack of perception pricks my heart. We used to practically read each other's minds. The slightest change of voice or body language would be like a foghorn blaring "something's wrong." Kenji knew something was up, but my best friend didn't have a clue. How would she? She's never around anymore. Dance class, dance rehearsal, dance shows. No time for me.

"Oh."

"So are you? Acting weird?"

"Aunt Rita's in the hospital. It's been hard, you know? Also I had a bunch of stuff to do before we went to see her."

I wait for an inquisition about the "bunch of stuff," but none comes. Maybe I expect too much. Maybe Mom is right about Mel just needing to focus on her goals. But the river between us grows wider as the conversation progresses. Something *has* to be done before the murky water becomes too wide to cross. An idea illuminates my brain.

"Hey, why don't you come on the mission trip?" This is it—the answer. Ten days together, away from the dance studio, and we'd be Shi-and-Mel again. I feel myself grinning, imagining us talking for hours on the bus.

Doing this trip with Mel and Kenji would be too awesome for words. "It will be a blast, and you're great with kids. You could dance for them. And we would really have time together. It would be so much fun!"

I hold my breath, waiting for my excitement to echo back from Melody. Instead, a deafening silence tells me her answer.

"Shi, you know I can't just disappear for that long, especially not then. My coach would kill me. We've got a show at the end of June. I'll be rehearsing every night 'till ten."

Thoughts pound my head. Selfish. Shallow. Forget ballet! It's stupid! You're ruining your life! You're ruining *my* life. Why can't you just play soccer like a normal person? The silent reaming screams through my brain. I tell my emotions to *shut up*, but they do their own thing.

"Yeah, well. I guess it was a dumb idea. I just thought it would be fun." My finger itches to press the "end" button.

"It *would* be fun. It's just not possible. Thanks for asking, though." Melody *jetés* over my disappointment. "You're coming to the show, right? It's going to be fantastic! We've got these great costumes, and the scenery is so cool. In this one part, I'm dancing toward a cliff, well, it's not a *real* cliff of course, but the scenery guys are making it look real." The more excited she gets, the tighter my hand grips the phone. "Then I run and leap to another fake cliff with my costume billowing out like wings. It feels like I'm flying! You've *got* to come!"

"Yeah. Of course." As I search for a valid reason to end the call, another one comes in. Thank you, Brittany, queen of perfect timing. I say goodbye to Mel and hello to Brit, who informs me there's a pizza plan for after tomorrow's meeting. Yes, something normal. Hanging with friends. Talking about boys and clothes and what we're going to do on the trip.

"Sound's good. I'm in."

"Okay. See ya at ten-thirty. Gotta go."

Pastor Frank's blond hair shows signs of thinning, but his easygoing smile takes about ten years off his age. He welcomes each person and talks with parents about the mission trip while waiting for the remainder of the group. As the parents leave, Pastor Frank heads to the front of the room. "Alright, everyone, have a seat."

Amidst voices and scraping chairs, I hear my name. Kenji waves from across the room, tempting me to leap over chairs and into his arms. Instead, I point to my friends. It would be rude not to sit with them. Plus, sitting with Kenji will mean continuing the conversation he started in the hall. Do I even want to know what he heard from Miya? He tosses his hair out of his eyes and flashes the okay sign as I sit between Brittany and Lauren.

Pastor Frank clears his throat. "They say pictures speak louder than words."

Down comes the screen. Good, a PowerPoint. I can just veg and not think for awhile.

"I have to warn you, though; you're going to see a part of our world quite different than our own. The Appalachians run through twelve states. When God's hands created these mountains, they sculpted a place of incredible beauty. Deep green forests, winding rivers, waterfalls, flowers, wildlife." Gorgeous scenery fills the screen. I sit up straighter, anxious to be in the midst of it. "Unfortunately, it's also a place of staggering poverty. At least, parts of it, which brings us to the Kentucky-Virginia border."

The screen shot switches to a U.S. map, and Pastor Frank beams his laser on the mission trip area. "Many of the people there lack basic needs. Food, shelter, medical care, education. These photos were taken on last year's trip."

"He sounds intense." I whisper to Lauren, who nods in agreement.

Three children and a naked baby, sitting on the floor of a dilapidated wooden shack, gaze at us from the screen. Solemn little faces framed by dirty, tangled hair. Scrawny bodies clothed in ragged t-shirts, like the ones Mom uses for dusting. Smudged cheeks. Hungry eyes. One child has a dirty wound.

Ragamuffins. I can't remember where I'd heard that word, but it comes to mind as I look into those haunted faces. *Ragamuffins.*

Next slide. A woman kneels in a weedy garden and holds tomatoes, smiling at the camera with yellowed teeth. In another, the pregnant belly of a girl no more than fourteen protrudes from shorts that are way too small.

And so it goes, slide after slide. A school room that looks like something from a third world country, a church where people sit on grocery store crates, a toddler crying on a dirt road. Rusted cars, garbage, old tires, and beer cans fill in the background.

The slides end, and we sit in silence. Staying with the girls had been a good idea. I swipe a tear from my cheek, glad Kenji can't see it.

"I know." Pastor Frank's voice sounds more gravelly than usual. "This is not a trip for the faint of heart, or for anyone thinking *vacation*. These people need help, and we're going to work from dawn 'till dusk to make sure they get it." He flips on the light. "Some of you will do school and home repairs. Others will build cribs. By the time you finish dinner, all you'll want is sleep. It will be one of the toughest experiences of your life, and one of the most rewarding. You won't come away unaffected."

More silence. I believe him...and I'm ready to be

affected.

"Who's with me on this? Hands up."

Every hand in the room shoots into the air.

Pastor Frank smiles. "Let's do it. Operation Green-wood Kentucky is underway. Have your parents sign those papers by May twenty-ninth. We head out at five a.m. sharp on June twelfth. Prior to that, you will be required to attend two carpentry workshops. Keyword – *required*. Details are in the papers. Questions?"

Kenji's hand is the first in the air. "What about rafting?"

I roll my eyes, and my friends stifle laughs.

Pastor Frank smiles as though he'd anticipated that particular question from that particular boy. "Almost forgot. We'll finish up on Friday, then hit the Tanger River for some white water rafting the next day. Saturday night is party time, but don't stay up late because we leave for home at the crack of dawn. Sunday service will be on the bus."

While we're sleeping?

He ends with a prayer, and we head out into a spring-scented windy afternoon. I figured Kenji would find me, and he doesn't disappoint.

Brittany sees him, too. "We'll meet you over in the courtyard."

I don't argue, fearing Kenji might say something I don't want them to hear. I shift my purse strap higher onto my shoulder and force a smile. "Hi."

Kenji's melt-my-heart grin is noticeably absent. "Hi, yourself. What's goin' on, Shi? You didn't return my call, didn't meet me after school." The wind blows a strand of hair into my face, and he brushes it away. "You trying to tell me something?"

The simple gesture makes me want to wrap my arms around his neck, but I hold back. I need to get away before he brings up a topic I'm not ready to discuss. "No. It's just...I've been really busy and yesterday I had to visit my aunt."

"But I needed to talk to you. Just five minutes. A text. Something."

"I know. I'm sorry. Thing is, I can't talk to you now, either. My friends are waiting."

"You can't just give me a couple of minutes?"

"Not really. Lauren and Brittany are..."

"Whatever." A chill ices his words. "Go have fun with your friends. I wouldn't want to *inconvenience* you."

Wow. Where did that come from? He turns away, but I can't let him go. Not like this. "Kenji, wait. Kenji!"

But he keeps walking without looking back.

CHAPTER FOURTEEN

Misty

I sink into the faded green couch, scrunching against the corner where the spring won't poke me. So glad Tyler finally fell asleep. I love that boy to death, but man, oh, man, he sure can wear me out. Time to chill. I grab the remote, hopin' to watch Part Two of that show—the one I can't stop thinkin' about. People rescuing girls stuck in brothels over in foreign countries. Some as young as six! And the rescuers, so brave, are just regular people tryin' to make the world better. I don't know which part touched me more; that these little girls are sold like meat, or that strangers were willing to risk everything to free them. I was just goin' to watch for a minute, but the weirdest thing happened. The minute turned into ten, then fifteen, then thirty. And I thought, maybe I could be a hero for somebody someday. It's been forever since I thought about "someday."

Where is that show? I shoulda wrote down the stupid channel. I click from one dumb reality show to the next, then cooking, then oh, cool, somethin' about Hawaii. But I don't stop, because I want to learn more about those girls. Some are stolen by strangers. Others betrayed by people they trusted and loved. Kinda like me in some ways, only way worse. I imagine getting my life together enough to be one of the rescuers. Goin' over to India or Thailand and helping those girls, like the Giannellis are helping me. When I asked Shilo why she was givin' me those clothes, she said people should take care of each other. Jake always says we all gotta take care of ourselves. So far, his way hasn't worked out so good.

Click. Disney teenagers singin' and dancin'. Click. Chefs tryin' to outcook each other. Click. There it is! And now a commercial, with probably twenty more to follow. Figures. I turn down the sound and close my eyes, trying to picture me on one of those rescue missions, bringing those girls to a safe place. Do I have that kind of strength? Mrs. Howell always said God gives us strength to do good things, if we ask Him. Guess I stopped askin' after she left me.

My cell music tears me from my thoughts. I grab it fast, not wantin' anything to wake Tyler.

"Hello?"

"Yeah, it's Jake."

My hand clenches, along with the muscles in my stomach. "Oh."

"Listen, uhhh, sorry about that call from my brother. He's just upset, you know?"

How dumb does he think I am? He wants somethin', I know it. "Okay."

"Listen, I pulled some strings to make this call, but I only got a minute. You gotta do somethin' for me, baby, understand? It's really important. You can't mess this up."

My pulse throbs in my wrist, keeping time with my

pounding heart. He ruins everything. Even this tiny little peaceful moment. "What?"

"First off, get money outta the closet for rent. Otherwise, we'll get kicked out. There's an envelope in my old Nikes." My mouth drops open. There's money in the closet? "Take *only* enough for rent. Put the rest back. *All* the rest, Misty. Get it? Don't be messin' with that money."

"Okay, Jake. I get it."

"Now, listen good. There's three packages you gotta deliver. They're under the bed, way in back. The people waitin' for them are pissed, so get this right. Meet them at four-o'clock tomorrow. Duke's Arcade. Tyler can play some games or whatever over there." I shake my head. He must be insane to think I'd put Tyler in danger. "You'll see two guys in green and gold jackets," he continues, racing his words. Must be runnin' out of time. "One has a swastika tattoo on his hand. Tell them they'll get the fourth package when I get out. I didn't have time to get it. Make sure they know that, Misty. Don't mess this up."

That's when I'm interviewing at Sonrise House. No, he is not going to ruin this, too. I have friends now. Me and Tyler have a chance now.

But even from jail, he still scares me.

"Okay, Jake." I play along. Nothing more.

"You do it, Misty, and maybe I won't be so pissed when I get outta here."

How considerate.

"You got it?"

I squeeze the phone tighter. "Yeah, I got it."

"Gotta go!" Click.

"Whatever." I say the word to no one and head to the closet, stepping lightly past the bed where Ty lays sleeping. The closet door creaks, and I freeze, but he just breathes softly, like a slumbering angel, so I scoot down to search. What I find inside the shoe sucks the air from my lungs. Seriously. More than a thousand dollars in fifty and hundred-dollar bills. Maybe I fell asleep on the couch, and now I'm dreamin'. This can't be real. We never have money, just enough for rent and cheap food. And meth, of course. There was always money for Jake's drugs.

Where did he get this? Images flash across my brain. Jake robbin' a bank. Jake sellin' drugs. Stealin' from a jewelry store.

Hands trembling, I take enough for rent and put the rest back, just like he said. Under the bed, three packages lay stacked on the floor, each about the size of a hardcover book and wrapped in brown paper. No names or addresses. Prickles crawl across the back of my neck. All I want to do is go back to my little spot on the couch and watch those brave souls do somethin' big and meaningful. Somethin' that changes people's lives. But first, I have to make a call.

CHAPTER FIFTEEN

Shilo

Kenji hadn't called all weekend. Every time I thought about calling or texting, I chickened out. It didn't take a brain surgeon to figure out Miya heard about the "strange occurrence" at the hospital and told him. I long to divulge everything to him, but he'd think I was crazy, or get caught in the chaos that could erupt any moment. And that can't happen, so I just do nothing, waiting for time to magically fix everything.

How dumb is that?

Heading into Monday morning, I fear what he'll say when we meet by Italian. Fearing even more that he won't be there. A variety of awkward scenarios fuel my imagination, but not the one facing me now. The dark Asian eyes watching me from Mrs. D'Andrea's doorway do not belong to my boyfriend. I'm still halfway down the hall when Miya motions for me to hurry. Picking up speed, I anticipate the inevitable questions with no clue how to respond.

I barely get out a "hi" when she cuts me off with a whisper. "They're talking about you at the hospital."

Here we go. I need a strategy. Maybe a fake seizure. No, too complicated and I can't risk someone calling an ambulance. I'll just stall while I think of something brilliant. "Who?"

"Everyone. What happened?" Miya raises one eyebrow, a cool expression I've never been able to master. "Tyler was way better when I saw him that night, then he left the next morning. They're all saying *you* did something."

I search my mind, now a black hole sucking up anything remotely resembling intelligence. "Really? They're saying it was me?" Awesome response. Downright dazzling.

"Well?" The whispered word hangs over me like a thundercloud. "Did you?"

"I just prayed for him. His mom asked me to."

"His *mom*? They shouldn't even let her near him! She ought to be locked up, along with her idiot boyfriend."

I picture Misty and wince, knowing the harsh comment would hurt her feelings. Miya's words mirror my judgmental thoughts before I saw the heart beneath the ragged t-shirt. "Misty's not so bad. She's trying to be a good mom. Just had lots of problems."

"Misty?"

"Tyler's mom."

"You're *friends* with her?" Miya's eyes narrow to slits.

Mrs. D'Andrea appears at the door, hair pulled back with a barrette the size of a Hershey bar.

"Shilo, *vieni in classe. Fai presto!*"

"Sorry, Miya. She's telling me to come to class."

"Call me."

"Okay."

"Promise"

There's no way I'm calling her. "I will. I promise." What's wrong with me? The worst part is, I won't break that promise. And I have no idea what I'm going to say.

Halfway through the morning, Kenji appears down the hall in a sea of students. He walks into U.S. History as the bell rings, never glancing my way during class. Not once. Mr. Myners' lecture drags on for days. When class finally ends, Kenji bolts before I even leave my seat. I pick up my book bag and scrape my heart off the floor before heading to lunch. As the final bell blares, the tidal wave of students pushes me toward the outside world. Our meeting spot under the old willow is conspicuously void of life.

If only I could talk to Melody—the pre-ballet Melody, who used to hang on every word, knowing all the right things to say. But even if I could, I'd have to leave out the one thing at the root of it all: healing hands. I stare at them for the millionth time. And still, they look deceptively normal. But they healed Tyler and felt the sickness in Pat. How can such a miracle be hovering inside these hands? I'm the queen of average. There's got to be hordes of people who are smarter, holier. People who would know what to do, how to handle it. Priests and pastors. Theologians. Missionaries. But *me*? It doesn't make sense. I sigh and trudge home, wishing these hands could fix whatever's broken between me and Kenji.

The clock strikes eight-thirty before I finally keep my promise to Miya. Nausea oozes through my stomach as I wait for her to answer. Using some of Mom's words and phrases, I downplay the miracle and move on to Misty and Tyler's visit. Miya listens, sometimes interrupting with a "really?" and ending with a "well that gives it a whole new twist."

"So, let's think. What does she need right now?"

Miya seems to be talking more to herself than me, so I wait. "Not food. She'll be eating at your place. Babysitting? Me and the squad could help. Money's always good. Yeah, a fundraiser." She can't see my grin, but suddenly I'm very glad I made this call. "Alright," she continues, "let me run this past the girls. Keep me posted, okay?"

"Yeah. Definitely." Good, no mention of Kenji. Even though I'm dying to talk about him, doing it with his sister would be weird. Plus he'd find out.

I escape into a book, hoping it will help me sleep, but thoughts of Kenji create a fortress between me and dreamland. I miss him so much it aches. Literally aches. How is that possible? The bigger question: how is it fixable? How is any of this fixable? Me and Mel. Misty and the mess she's in? Pat and her sickness? Aunt Rita would whisk my worries away with "oh, Honey, God is bigger than our problems. Everything will be all right." But right now I don't even know if Aunt Rita's going to be "all right."

My body sinks deeper into the mattress as muscles relax and nonsensical thoughts float through my brain. The outside world slips into a land of clear blue skies and lush mountains surrounded by azure water. Warm, wet sand oozes between my toes as a tropical sun melts into my skin. I walk along the water's edge, gazing at the sparkling ripples and waves dancing on the shore. Could this be Heaven? Gulls and pelicans soar above me, sandpipers scamper along a beach laden with the prettiest shells I've ever seen. A warm breeze kisses my face.

Ahead of me, a small white something lies on the sand. As I get closer, I see the sweet, innocent face of a baby harp seal staring up at me.

"You're a long way from home, little one." I squat down for a better look. "You don't belong here."

The seal moves, revealing a bloody, half tail. Bite

marks paint a picture of the horrific encounter that must have taken place. Out on the water, a shark fin slices back and forth. I run my hand along the seal's furry white back. Warmth surrounds my heart, filling my chest and spreading through my arms. I jerk away as I consider the shark.

"If I heal you, you'll go back in the water and get eaten. If I don't, you'll bleed to death."

The seal gazes at me with saucer eyes the color of bittersweet chocolate, then licks my hand like a puppy.

I nod, knowing what he wants me to do, and lay my hands on the crimson tail. Sticky red blood stains the white fur and sand. I lose myself in the healing warmth, letting it fill my body, my soul. I call out to the Great Healer, asking Him to use me, to heal this beautiful creature and protect it from harm. His answer comes as the heat intensifies inside me, shooting through my wrists and into my hands, bursting through my fingertips in brilliant rays of light.

When the power fades and disappears, I lift my hand. The white, fluffy seal bears no signs of the horrid shark attack. Not even a smudge of blood. Hopping into my lap, the seal snuggles against me, tickling my face with wet seal kisses that make my heart smile. But the moment ends too soon. The seal bounds out of my lap and into the crystal blue sea.

I look out at the water, glued to the sand by pure terror. "NO!"

My scream shatters the tranquility, startling the gulls, whose screeches send the sandpipers skyward. The shark slices through the water like a jet boat, heading straight for the seal pup. Other fins follow close behind, closing in on the leader. I stand on the shore, powerless to prevent the inevitable feeding frenzy. The menacing gang of fins nears its prey, overtaking the first shark. One leaps into the air... then another, and another.

Dolphins! Not sharks, *dolphins!* They ram the shark until it races into the open sea, then form a protective ring around the seal as it, too, heads out of sight. I smile, knowing my furry friend is safe.

Brushing sand off my legs, I continue along the shore toward something else in the distance. Something larger. As I move toward it, I see another form, and another. I stop, wanting to turn around because it would be safer, easier, than whatever lies ahead. But my heart pulls me forward more powerfully than fear holds me back.

The lullaby of gulls and waves is suddenly overtaken by the harsher sound of guitars and drums. Music radiates from everywhere—the sky, the ocean, the sand beneath my feet.

I open my eyes. The beautiful seashore is gone. No more sun-kissed waves or soaring gulls. No more mysterious figures on the beach. The lavender walls of my room have replaced the island sky, and next to my bed, my cell phone alarm announces the beginning of a new day.

CHAPTER SIXTEEN

Misty

Annie and Nick sit on my lumpy old couch, listen-in' to my story about Jake's call. We all talk quietly so Ty doesn't wake up. The boxes and money are on the wooden crate we use for a coffee table. Nick just shook his head when I showed him.

"Drugs and drug money," he said. "No doubt about it. That boyfriend of yours is a mule, Misty. A courier."

"*Ex* boyfriend." I want them to know that idiot is behind me forever.

"What else did he tell you about the drop?"

I tell him about what they'll be wearin', and the one guy's tattoo.

"Green and gold jackets, huh? Great. Just great." Nick shakes his head again, then runs his hand through his hair like he's real tired. "The Warren Street Warriors. What a fine group of young men. We like to bring them into the station for little visits."

"The Warriors? Oh, Nick!" Annie's eyebrows crinkle. "You're not going to let Misty near them, are you?"

Her question makes a little lump in my throat. Guess it's been awhile since anybody cared if I got hurt. "Who are they?"

"Gang bangers. That pretty much says it all. And Jake's their delivery boy."

Pretty sure I saw them in the newspapers I read at the library. That real nice librarian, Allison, always grabs the newspaper for me when she sees me comin' so I can read while Tyler plays with the trains. Those guys are bad news, that's for sure.

Annie puts her hand on my arm. "Well, Misty's not going anywhere near them and that's all there is to it."

The lump gets bigger.

"I'm not so sure, Annie. Let me think about this." Nick picks up one of the boxes, shifting it from hand to hand as his eyebrows knit together. "Misty, would you be willing to help nail these guys?"

Hard to believe he would trust me with somethin' so important. "Seriously?"

"Seriously." He turns to Annie. "Make sure Shilo and Julia are nowhere near that arcade tomorrow. Same for Tyler." Nick shakes his head. "What kind of a father puts his son in a situation like that?"

"The same one who put him in the hospital." Annie moves her hand from my arm to Nick's, giving him a little squeeze. If only my sweet boy could have gotten a daddy like her Nick.

"Yeah, that guy's a real prize," Nick says. "All right, ladies, I've got calls to make, then we'll talk about how we're going to handle this. Misty, we'll need to meet with you first thing tomorrow after the girls go to school."

Fear and excitement swirl inside me. To be part of somethin' important—somethin' that makes a difference! "I'll be there."

Annie asks if she can say a prayer for me and Tyler. Mrs. Howell used to pray for me, but that's in the past and there's no use thinking about it. Annie's prayer is real nice. She asks God to protect us and improve our situation. Still not sure if it's God or coincidence, but I gotta admit, that seems to be happening. After all, the Giannellis came into my life, and me and Shilo are kinda becoming friends. Been a long time since I had a girl-friend, other than the library ladies. They both hug me before leaving the apartment. It's weird to be gettin' hugged again by someone besides Tyler.

I head up to bed, with all the good and bad stuff making my head spin, wonderin' what tomorrow will bring.

CHAPTER SEVENTEEN

Shilo

The hall by Italian was void of a certain dark-eyed "Romeo" all week, much to Mrs. D'Andrea's joy. No Kenji there for a quick kiss before class. No Kenji sitting with me at lunch or texting me during study hall. I sweep the crowd of kids as they break up and head in different directions.

No Kenji.

It's like he fell off the planet. He keeps using that same move in history. Coming in at the last second, bolting out before I can reach him. I might as well be poison personified. I start to head home, but a vaguely familiar girl blocks my path, walking toward me. Long legs strut beneath a swishy skirt that barely covers the butt of her supermodel body. The whole package is topped with a billboard-perfect face. Generous doses of eyeliner and shiny pink lipstick finish the picture. She looks straight at me, eyes unblinking, and I remember where I've seen her before. Soccer. One of the other club teams.

She stops, planting herself in my path. "Are you Shilo?"

"Yeah."

"I know Kenji."

He must have sent her to give me a message. Weird, but I'll take it. My heart races with a little shot of adrenaline. "Oh."

"Did you guys break up?" Sunlight glints off super glossed lips.

"What?"

"I'm in Kenji's Language Arts class. I always see you guys together, except for lately. Just wondering if you broke up."

This isn't making sense. Where's my message? My holy healing hand wants to strike out and slap her. Probably not the best use for it. I stand up straighter. "Why do you want to know?"

"Why do you *think*?" A thick layer of smug coats her many layers of makeup.

Okay, it took a house to fall on my head, but I get it. Stay away from my boyfriend, Miniskirt, or I'll...

"So, what is it, yes or no?" A light breeze blows her hair like she's posing for a Victoria Secret photo shoot, which makes me want to throw up on her pink leather heels.

"Why don't you ask Kenji?" I walk away, my heart beating loud enough for the marching band to use at half time. She tosses a "whatever" at the back of my head, but it's so not worth a response.

I fly home, wanting to distance myself from school and all the horrid people who go there. Okay, only one. But that's enough. My house is in sight, and in it is my room, where I will scream into my pillow until my voice runs out. But when I walk through the door, Tyler's little freckled face looks up at me and grins.

"Hi, Sheebo." He holds up a plastic dinosaur. "Look!"

Just shoot me.

Misty sits next to him on the floor, turning the pages of a dinosaur picture book. "Hi." Tyler picks up the book for a closer look and she points to a pterodactyl. "Surprised to see us?"

"Uh, kinda."

In the kitchen, Mom's on the phone saying something about changing an appointment.

"I have to go somewhere with your mom. Any chance you could watch Ty for a little bit? Sorry it's last minute."

I don't even have time to process this before Mom walks in with a strained smile. "How was school?"

Just wonderful, especially the last part. "Fine."

"Listen, Honey, we need you to watch Tyler."

Something's up and they're not going to tell me. Seems like something's *always* up these days.

"Misty and I have to go somewhere," she continues.

"I heard."

"It's just for an hour or so. Julia will be home soon, then she can help you."

"Pretty sure I can handle a toddler, Mom. You guys going to Sonrise House?" I already know the answer, but maybe she'll tell me what's *really* going on.

"That got changed to tomorrow."

"Because?" I glance from Mom to Misty, but Misty only laughs nervously.

"Tell you later. Promise. Right now we have to go to that arcade. The one your Kenji likes."

I try to envision Mom at Duke's, but it's just not working. She must be referring to someplace else. "Duke's?"

"Yes. Dad's meeting us there."

"What? Why?" Has the whole world gone crazy? "I thought Dad was working."

"He is. I'll explain later. We've got to go. Make sure you and your sister stay away from there. Hopefully your friends will do the same." She grabs her keys off the counter. "Come on, Misty."

With a hug and kiss, Misty says goodbye to Tyler and brings him to me with apologetic eyes. "I really appreciate this. You already worked a miracle for me, and here I am asking for another favor. There's a sippy cup and toys in my tote bag. He'll tell you if he has to go potty. Bye."

And they're gone. I try to sum up the past minute in hopes of finding a shred of sanity. My mother and a soon-to-be homeless teenager are meeting my police sergeant father for a secret mission at a video arcade. Nope. Nothing there even remotely resembles normalcy. My life has officially become a cheesy reality show.

Two seconds after the car disappears, Tyler's scream shatters my eardrums.

"Mommy! Mommy! Mommy!"

The little face that happily flipped pages of the dinosaur book seconds ago is now contorted into something from a "Saw" movie. Teardrops rain down his cheeks, melting my heart into a giant red blob of compassion.

"Hey kiddo." I kneel down and wipe soggy cheeks with my palm. To my amazement, he wraps his arms around me, sobbing into my shirt. Good start, I guess, at least he trusts me. Now what would Annieconda do? I rub his back and search for a children's song to sing. Julia's favorite was always "Mockingbird," so I go with that. The hysterics subside. Now for a good distraction.

"Hey, let's go see the toys in your bag!"

"No! No toys."

"Well then, let's go in the back yard and dig for

worms."

He shakes his head. "No! No worms."

"Maybe we'll find some good rocks."

Another theatrical head shake. "No. *Julia* find good rocks."

As always, he pronounces Julia's name perfectly. "I have a great idea. We can kick around my soccer ball."

"No, Sheebo! No balls. No kicks."

Oh, this is fun. I smile through gritted teeth. "What would *you* like to do, Tyler?"

"Play with Julia and truck."

Great. Perfect. I check the clock, which betrays me by announcing there's ten minutes before my little sister walks through the door. I finally convince Tyler we can sit on the front porch with a Popsicle and wait for her.

"Blue Popsicle. I like blue."

I open the freezer and, thank you, Mom, find a blue raspberry Popsicle. Tyler slurps away as we sit outside. His concentration on the icy treat gives me time to think again about the Duke's mystery, and unfortunately, the scenario with Miniskirt. By the time Julia shows up, I've decided to call Kenji...without a clue what I'll say.

"Hello, Shilo." Kenji's mom? I glance at the number and see that I dialed the house, instead of his cell.

"Hi, Mrs. Hiyama. Sorry to bother you. I meant to call Kenji's cell."

"No bother at all. Kenji wouldn't hear it anyway, with all the noise at that game place. He's there now with his friends."

"Dukes?" My fingers tighten around my phone.

"That's the one. "

He's at Dukes. How could this happen? "Okay. Thanks. Bye."

"Don't be a stranger, now."

I'm trying not to be, but failing miserably. I freeze, picturing Kenji, *my* Kenji, at Dukes, where something's happening. Something bad. I call his cell, mentally commanding him to pick up, but apparently telepathy is not my strong suit. Of course, you can't hear anything in that place. Sprinting outside, I tell Julia to watch Tyler until I return, then grab my bike from the garage.

Why don't I have a car? Everyone else has a car. Except Melody. And Lauren. Actually, most of my friends don't have cars. Still...this is ridiculous.

I race past two blocks of houses, the park, school, more houses, then finally reach the busy intersection of Tenth and Warren, where that gang hangs out. It looks so normal. Seems like there should be barred windows and armed guards.

More traffic now, which forces me to slow down and pay attention. In seconds, I pass the Jewish temple and Market Square strip mall. The sign at the bank blinks 3:55 p.m., and I still have two blocks to go. A couple of girls my age walk out of Claire's Clothing, swinging bags and laughing as they talk. When's the last time me and Melody did that...or *anything*? When did we get buried under a mountain of responsibilities with no time for each other?

I put that mental conversation on hold and keep pedaling toward the red and blue Duke's sign looming half a block away. Nearly crashing into the bike rack, I jump off and run inside. Beeps, buzzes, and voices besiege me as players compete in pinball and video games.

Just find Kenji and get out.

Flashing lights and a few familiar faces, but no Kenji. I head for the second room, home of the air hockey and foosball tables. Chances are, that's where he'll be. I squeeze past game tables and bodies until my theory proves correct. Air hockey puck in hand, Kenji throws his hands up in victory and laughs after scoring the winning point against Nico. As if sensing my presence, his eyes meet mine and his beautiful smile fades.

Eyes widen as I walk toward him. Can he hear my heart pounding above the din of noise? We stand face to face, his friends exchanging glances. No one speaks.

I stop a couple of feet away. "I have to talk to you. It's important."

"What's up?" He says it calmly and without expression. Those dark eyes used to light up whenever I was near. Used to. "Kinda busy right now. I'm with my friends. You know what that's like, remember?"

Great time to play games. I walk closer, leaning in to whisper. "This can't wait. Something is happening. Right now. Please, Kenji, I know you're mad, but trust me on this." His eyes soften.

Kenji turns toward the guys. "Back in a minute."

They snicker a "yeah, right."

He leads the way back to the first room, where we pass two skinhead types in green and gold jackets. I ignore them and grab Kenji's arm. "Stop. Just stop. I came here to tell you to leave."

"What? Shilo, what's gotten into you? I thought you wanted to talk about *us*. Maybe even apologize for blowing me off. No way I'm leaving."

How can I make him understand? "Listen. My dad'll be here any minute. Something's going down. I don't know what, but it's bad. Dangerous. They told me to stay away, but your mom said you were here, so I came to get you out."

"My mom? When did you talk to her?"

Heat rises to my cheeks. "A little while ago. I called you and dialed the house by accident."

"Called for what?"

He steps closer. I smell his soapy scent, feel his warmth. "I don't know. Kenji, please, we can talk about other stuff later. We have to get out of here!"

He rolls his eyes. "Look around you, Shi. Everything's fine. Same old Duke's. Kids playing video games, little squirts with their moms, gang bangers trying to make time with some skinny girl."

I close my eyes, goose bumps icing my spine. Noooo! Don't let it be her. I whip around in the direction of the "skinny girl," only to have my fears confirmed. There stands Misty, jaw set, fear etched across her face, talking to the Warriors. Her quivering hand reaches out to them with a plastic shopping bag. The two gang bangers peer inside, then back at Misty, fire shooting from their eyes, mouths twisted in rabid dog snarls. Mechanical noises and crowd voices mask their words, but not their tone. One points at the bag and then to Misty. I turn to Kenji.

"What is it?" Concern shadows Kenji's eyes.

"She's my friend. Something's wrong. We have to help her."

The conversation between Misty and the Warriors tanks fast. One grabs her arm, his tattooed hand squeezing hard enough to make her wince. It's the kind of thing you can get away with in a crowded arcade where nobody's watching.

But we are watching.

Kenji stares at the ugly scene unfolding before us. "I'm going. Stay here."

We are so not doing the protective thing right now. "No way."

He grabs my arm, pulls me toward him. "Shilo!" Ebony eyes pierce mine. "Don't take another step."

I jerk my arm away and rush forward. "No time to argue."

As we close in on Misty, the Warriors words become clear. "Three ain't gonna cut it. We came for four and we ain't leavin' without four. Where's the rest? "

In some sort of ninja move, Kenji disappears from my side and is in the guy's face. "You got a problem?" If he's scared, which he should be, he masks it well. "Or you just like picking on people who can't fight back?"

"Stay out of it, punk. You do not want to mess with us. Move it."

"Shilo!" Misty uses her free hand to motion me away. "Get out! You're not supposed to be here." She messages me with her eyes, but the message eludes me.

"Yeah, Shilo," the tattooed guy mimics, "get out, and take your little boyfriend, too."

"Get your hand off the girl." Kenji's voice is deeper, stronger than I've ever heard it before. His eyes could incinerate rock.

"You lookin' to get cut, boy?" The Warrior sneers, getting up in Kenji's face.

But my boyfriend doesn't back down. "Get your hand off her." He jerks the guy's hand off Misty's arm.

"I tried to warn you." Tattoo guy swings at Kenji, who blocks the move and pushes him back. He doesn't have time to block the punch from the other guy, though. With blood oozing from his upper lip, Kenji thuds to the floor. Red-hot anger flashes through me, driving rational thoughts from my head. I lunge at the Warrior, but I'm no match for his street fighting experience. He grabs both my arms.

"I got no problem hittin' girls."

And I got no problem hurting bad guys. This idiot doesn't know I'm a cop's daughter. Dad taught me a thing or two about self-defence. My knee flies up hard and fast, catching the targeted tender part. He doubles over with an "aghhh!" and a string of curse words. Pain scrunches up his face as he cups his crotch with both hands. Mission accomplished. My victory lasts less than half a heartbeat before his partner draws back his arm for a retaliation punch.

Oh, God.

Every muscle tightens for the inevitable burst of pain. But Skinhead stands frozen, looking behind me. I dare not turn around.

"Police!"

I turn around. The gun in Dad's hand isn't nearly as scary as the cold, hard steel in his eyes. His men have the Warriors on the ground and handcuffed in seconds. Near silence has replaced the chaotic noise of the arcade. Kenji and I watch the cops lead the gang guys out the door, afraid to say a word. Dad turns to Misty. "You okay?"

She nods.

"All right, then go to the parking lot. Annie is waiting for you."

Misty doesn't need to hear it twice. She's gone like a comet, but not without whispering a "Thanks, Shi." Her absence leaves me and Kenji to face a version of Dad I've never seen. Nor do I ever want to again. The message in his eyes is clear.

My life is over.

"You two, come with me. Now!"

It is not a request.

In the craziness of the scuffle, I hadn't noticed the crowd staring at us. Silence hovers like storm clouds. No one speaks. No one plays. But everyone raises their cells for photos. This will be headline news at school for weeks to come. Dad's going to kill me, and Kenji's going to hate me. If banishment to a deserted island were an option right now, I'd happily go.

Dad strides to the door, with Kenji and I close behind, trying to avoid eye contact with the onlookers. A bright flash on my left nearly blinds me, followed by another on my right. Newspaper reporters? Seriously? A television crew's truck is parked at the curb. Our local parades don't even get this much attention. We head for Dad's squad, where surely a slow, painful death awaits us both. Dad opens the car door.

"Inside!"

Still silent, we get in. The car shakes like an after-shock as Dad slams the door. I look at Kenji, hoping to read something in his face, hoping we'll exchange a ro-mantic mental message, like "as long as we're together, we can handle anything." But he just stares ahead, saying nothing. Another slam trembles the car as Dad gets in.

"Dad, I was trying to…"

"Don't even speak. Do not say one word. Not one!"

I stop breathing. Nails dig into palms.

"We're getting out of this parking lot and the three of us are going to have a little talk," he continues. "Meaning I will talk, you two will listen. Is that clear?"

"Yes sir," we say in unison, which might have been followed by a laugh…under normal circumstances.

Dad tosses a napkin on the back seat. "Wipe your lip, Kenji. Don't bleed on my squad."

Kenji winces as he dabs the blood from his swollen lip. We drive a short distance to a forest preserve, the kind of place where families picnic, kids fish, and cou-ples walk hand in hand. But none of those people are there. Dad parks in an empty corner of the lot, steps from the woods. The place where, someday, someone will find our bodies rotting beneath a tree.

Everything in me desperately aches to open a win-dow, but I don't dare ask. Dad turns, face crimson, thick vein throbbing in his neck. "Do you have any idea what the two of you just did? Any clue at all? Do you?"

"Dad, I just wanted to…"

"Be quiet! I'll tell you when to speak! You almost ruined an investigation, embarrassed me in front of my own men. Worst of all, you could have gotten your-selves killed. What were you thinking?" The vein throbs faster. "Don't you know those guys carry weapons?"

I force myself to breath and remember this can't last forever. My mind tries to escape to my room, where

I could sit alone, wrapped in my afghan from Aunt Rita.

"Didn't Mom specifically tell you to stay away from Duke's?" Dad's shouts shatter the vision before it can form. "And yet, there you were, deliberately disobeying. And what about Tyler? Hmm? Don't tell me he's with Julia. He was *your* responsibility, Shilo, not hers." He runs his fingers through his hair, which seems to be sporting more strands of gray today. "You are in more trouble than you can possibly imagine." He says this last part calmly, almost monotone, which is far scarier than all the yelling.

I stare at my lap as Dad turns to Kenji. "As for you, Rocky, what was your role in this, other than getting your face punched?"

"Sorry, sir." Kenji dabs his lip again, probably terrified of one drop hitting the car seat. "I saw them harassing the girl. Just wanted to help."

"Do you know the girl?"

"No."

"Do you know why they were harassing her?"

"No."

"Did either one of you hotshots consider calling the police? Telling the arcade manager?"

"No, sir."

"Did my wayward daughter tell you anything about what was going on?"

I cringe, waiting for Kenji's next words.

"She just told me to leave Duke's. Wouldn't tell me why. Then we saw the guys hassling the girl and went over."

"So you don't know anything?"

Give it a rest, Dad. He doesn't know. I don't even know. No one tells me anything. I say all these things to him inside my head.

"No sir."

"Good. Stay away from the Warriors, and Duke's,

and anywhere else they hang out. You crossed them. Both of you." I look up, assuming that means I'm back in the conversation. "Do you know what that means?" He continues. We both shake our heads. "Revenge. They'll be looking for you two. *Capish?*"

"I didn't think of that."

"No, you were too busy trying to be a hero. That's all for now. What's your address?"

We pull up to the familiar two-story house, where Dad walks Kenji to the door. Apparently we haven't suffered enough humiliation already. Kenji's mom appears on the porch, forehead furrowed at the sight of her son's bloody lip and Dad at his side. If only I could hear their conversation, but I don't roll down the window or move. Or breathe.

When Dad returns, he slams the door, rumbling the car yet again. "Well, I didn't plan on meeting your boyfriend's mother under these circumstances."

My boyfriend? Not after today.

The ten-minute ride home drags on for hours. Days. Eons. But the silence is better than the yelling. We finally pull into the driveway.

"Alright Shilo Marie Giannelli." He turns to face the back seat.

Oh please, not the whole name. It's all downhill from here, and I didn't think it could go any lower.

"We'll discuss this tonight. Remember you are not safe. Do not leave the house. It's not a request." He faces front again, starts to open the door, then stops. "And know this: I've never been as disappointed in anyone as I am in you at this moment."

Gutting me with his fishing knife would have been less painful. Hardly able to stand, I force myself out of the car and into the house, where Annieconda's arms open to embrace me in a fortress of love. Her tenderness dissolves me, but I walk past her with an "I'm fine" and try to ignore the dull pain pulsing in my throat.

"It's okay," she says. "Everyone's home safe. Everything's okay."

"Everything is *not* okay, Annie." Dad tosses his keys onto the table and stands next to us.

Oh, to have the power to make myself disappear. Right now I'd take that over healing.

"She nearly ruined the whole damn thing." Anger still smolders in his voice.

In the arched opening between the living room and kitchen, Julia and Misty watch and listen, propelling my humiliation to a higher level. It's not their intent. They ooze compassion, which I neither want nor need in this miserable moment. Without a word, I retreat to the beautiful silence of my room, thankful it's only occupant is me, and turn off my cell. But from behind the closed door, the words "she almost messed up everything" punch me in the gut. He doesn't get it. I was trying to protect the people I care about, same as him. We just had different methods, that's all. And maybe if someone had clued me in on what was going on...

"Misty, you need to come with me to the station to give a statement." Dad's words are muffled, but clear enough through my closed door.

Good. Go away. Both of you.

"Misty did great, Annie." No more anger, now. Just overflowing pride for the girl who is not his daughter. "Especially considering the circumstances. She was very brave."

I flop onto my bed, listening to Tyler wail in protest over Misty leaving. Wondering how, in less than a week, my life went from soccer and school and Kenji to pure insanity.

CHAPTER EIGHTEEN

Misty

The pain in Shilo's eyes made my whole insides hurt. She was tryin' to protect me, willing to get beat up just to save me from those jerks. To me, she and her cute boyfriend were heroes…big time. I mean, doin' that for me? And then to get yelled at, well, it was just wrong. And I was wrong, too, when we first met. I judged Shilo just like Elizabeth judged Mr. Darcy in that *Pride and Prejudice* book. Seemed to me she was just a spoiled kid who probably didn't care about anybody else, but she's been proving me wrong from the start. Maybe it ain't my place to question Nick, him bein' a sergeant and always bein' so nice to me, but I have to stand up for Shilo. As we leave the station to head back, I gather up my guts to do it.

"Hey, Nick?"

"Yes?"

"I know you're really mad at Shilo."

"You bet I am."

"But, um, well, I was thinkin' she was trying to do a good thing, you know? Tryin' to get me away from those guys. And I know it's none of my business, but…"

"But you think I was too hard on her, right?"

"Kinda. Well, yeah."

"Here's the deal, Misty. I love Shilo the way you love Tyler. That's more than anyone can measure, right?"

I nod. That's a pretty good way to put it. I loved the Howells for awhile, but it was nothin' like what I felt when Tyler was born. Holdin' that sweet baby in my arms melted everything inside me, but terrified me, too, because I was too young and so unprepared. Still, from Day One, I knew I'd do anything for him.

"So I don't want anyone hurting her. Those two morons could have done serious harm if me and my guys hadn't been right there."

"No kiddin'."

"Shilo was specifically told not to go there. She was supposed to watch Tyler and stay home. That's all. By disobeying me, she put her life, Kenji's, and yours in danger. That's why I got so angry. I don't tell her to do this or don't do that just to be controlling. It's because I want the best for her. I want her to be safe. I do it because I love her."

His words make sense. It's like me telling Tyler not to touch the electric outlets or pet stray dogs. "I get it, but she really had good intentions. I was thinkin' maybe that could count for somethin'."

Nick stops for a red light and turns to look at me. "If one of you had gotten stabbed, would it count for something? What if Tyler had to go through the rest of his life without you?"

A shudder runs up my backbone. I may not be Mom of the Year, but I don't want him growin' up without me. "Guess I didn't think of it that way."

"I'm not perfect, Misty. I don't always get it right, but in this case, my anger is justified." He turns to me with a half smile. "But," he says with a deep, official tone, "I will reflect on the testimony of the key witness and consider leniency when sentencing." He slams an invisible gavel and ends with "court adjourned."

Shilo's so lucky to have a dad like Nick.

CHAPTER NINETEEN

Shilo

I hate him. What kind of a father gets red-faced furious when his daughter tries to do the right thing? It's like he didn't even consider I was trying to help Misty. Didn't even care.

Footsteps on the stairs announce Mom's arrival.

"Sweetheart?"

"Yeah?"

"Dad called."

Oh, joy.

"He says he'll be home late tonight, and you two can talk about this tomorrow."

Maybe the guilt is getting to him. Maybe he's realizing he reacted like a crazy maniac. "Fine."

"Just thought you'd want to know."

Twenty minutes later she calls "dinner ready," but I'm so not interested, even though something smells pretty good. I don't want to sit there with the Giannelli women and Misty trying to make small talk like nothing happened. Or worse, talking about what happened. No, these four purple walls, my guitar, and books are all I need.

"Not hungry, Mom." That works for awhile, until Julia runs up's feet run up the stairs, and she taps the door like there might be a fire-breathing dragon on the other side.

"Hey, Shi?"

"What?"

"Can I come in?" She forces a little happy into her voice, ; her attempt at making this afternoon's disaster go away. If it were only that easy.

"No."

Oh, okay. Well, Kenji called."

I open the door. "What? Why didn't you tell me?"

"I *am* telling you." Julia's voice morphs from perky to wounded.

"I mean when he was on the phone."

"Oh." She pauses. "He said he tried your cell, and it was off. I figured you didn't want to talk to anyone."

"Alright," I say softer. No point taking out my misery on Julia. "Thanks for telling me."

"Shi?"

"Yeah?"

"I don't think you did anything bad. I think you were very brave."

"Thanks, Rockhound. I wish Dad saw it that way." I reward her with a smile, nothing huge, but it's the best I can do. "You're not so bad, you know?"

She grins, reminding me I need to say nice things to her more often.

"We can look at my new specimens later, if you want to." The hope in her voice could light our whole basement at midnight. "One is kind of sparkly. Possibly from northern Peru. Maybe we can research it, and it'll take your mind off all this stuff."

Will the torture never end? "Sounds great."

"And I have a new book that shows which gems, rocks, and minerals come from which countries." Apparently my "sounds great" was all she needed. "If it's not in there, we can try the Internet."

I silently wish I could offer up a less painful activity in return. Maybe a root canal, minus the Novocain. "Sure, Jules."

"Tomorrow? You can't go anywhere anyway. Dad's worried about the gang guys wanting revenge."

"Tomorrow it is."

Jules heads to her room, and I return to my solitude, instantly turning on my phone to call Kenji, but as I scroll to his name, my finger stops. Why did he call? He was so angry in the car he wouldn't even look at me. In fact, if I hadn't pleaded with him at Duke's, he wouldn't have talked to me, either. Whatever he's got to say can't be good, and I'm just not ready to face another punch right now. Especially if it comes in the form of a breakup. Tossing my phone on the bed, I pick up West With the Night, an old book Misty recommended, and try to lose myself in the pages. Any other day, the story would have drawn me in, but too much has gone down, and anxious thoughts keep me from the African adventures in my book.

Marking my page, I gaze out past the swooshing limbs of the ancient willow into the manicured backyards of all the normal people. What would they think if they knew about my healing power? Would they come bearing gifts, begging for a miracle, or march with pitchforks and baseball bats, demanding I leave town?

Morning filters through my curtains on beams of sunlight, but it's the aroma from downstairs that awakens me.

"Shilooo!"

Dad's voice is not the first one I want to hear this morning. Or even the second. Or third.

"Time for breakfast."

It's not a question. I throw a hoodie over my t-shirt and trudge downstairs. The scent of orange spice tea draws my eyes to the steamy cup waiting on the table. Mom gives my arm a squeeze as I pass, while Julia fixes doe eyes on me, then turns her focus back to spreading homemade strawberry jam on a crusty croissant.

"Sit down." Dad's calm words flow like tranquil water veiling the rip tide below. "We're going to get this over before breakfast."

I sit. He launches into the story about Misty and the phone call from Jake, without even stopping to sip his coffee. He tells me about the boxes filled with cocaine, explaining Jake was a drug courier and the Warriors paid him to do his job perfectly. No mistakes.

"The night Jake beat Tyler, he was supposed to pick up a fourth box, then deliver all four together." He continues in that painfully calm tone. "But getting arrested prevented that. The Warriors were furious, so Jake arranged for Misty to make the drop. She never knew he was a drug courier." He rips open a blue packet of sweetener and dumps it in his coffee.

"Dad, I'm sor…"

He holds up his hand. "Jake sent a lamb to the slaughter, and his little son too. These punks resolve everything with violence. When they're angry, they want revenge."

I swallow hard, knowing exactly where this is going.

"And now they're angry, Shilo. Do you understand?"

"Yes."

"Do you?" Dad's voice rises in the otherwise silent room. "They blame you and Kenji for their buddies getting arrested. They will seek you out. This is why the police, not teen vigilantes, enforce the law." The story continues with undercover officers inside the arcade, uniforms standing by, and Misty wearing a wire. "We were just about to grab them when you two entered the picture."

"Nick." Mom's voice fills the room like a favorite song. "I think you should consider the fact that Shilo had good intentions."

"I've heard all about her good intentions from Misty."

I feel my eyebrows arch. Way to go, Misty.

He turns back to me. "This won't happen ever again, *capish*?"

"Got it."

Yes, we're done. That wasn't bad. I celebrate the moment with a sip of tea and reach for a croissant, knowing I can finally move forward with my day.

"You'll need to stay put the rest of the weekend."

I drop the croissant. "What?"

"And come home immediately after school. No stopping to talk to friends. Stay off social media. All of it. I don't want these guys knowing anything about you."

"But I'm not friends with them on social media. I don't even know them."

"Doesn't matter."

He doesn't get the damage this will cause. A week might as well be a month…or a year. By next week, I'll be little more than a hazy memory floating aimlessly through the halls. Friends will make references to private jokes I won't get. Couples will break up or get together without my knowledge. A thousand tweets, posts, and snaps will come and go. In one week, I will cease to exist.

"That's not going to work."

"No choice. We're not just talking about you being in danger. Do you want to risk Kenji's life? Misty's?"

He's killing me.

"You may have had good intentions, but the result is bad guys with bad tempers and dangerous weapons who want you and your friends dead. You better think hard before you act, especially considering your special circumstances."

"What special circumstances?" Julia pounces as the last word leaves Dad's mouth.

"Never mind." Mom and Dad answer in unison, and Julia lets it go.

Before noon, I'm already so sick of the house I could throw up. Out on the deck, I play guitar, losing myself in the music, taking comfort in the cool, smooth wood against my body, the metal strings beneath my fingers. All the pressures in my head begin to fade, until Julia strolls outside with her *Gems, Rocks, and Minerals of the World* book. I squeeze my eyes shut and take a deep breath. Time to keep a promise.

"Hey, I got it. You ready?"

I shove enthusiasm into my voice and paste on a smile. "You bet."

Jules sits next to me, her pixie body making me feel colossal in my size five jeans. She opens a book that is roughly the width of a coffee table. It extends past her lap and probably outweighs her. The photos are cool though, making it easier to feign interest. I particularly like the crystals with their otherworldly shapes and iridescent hues. "Wow, this stuff is pretty."

She beams. "That's fluorite. It's found all over the world. Of course, you probably know it's the Illinois state mineral."

"Naturally. Who doesn't?"

Julia squints her eyes at me. "Sarcasm?"

I give her a thumbs-up. In response, she closes the book and stands.

"Jules, sit down." I grab her sleeve and tug. She sits,

but stares straight ahead.

"I was being funny, Rockhound. Come on, don't abandon me when everything else in my life is falling apart. The book is cool."

"Really? Or more sarcasm?" She looks at me with eyes narrowed to slits.

"Definitely not sarcasm. I want to see more. Tell me about the fluorite. Is it in the same rock family as quartz?" It is the most intelligent rock question I can conjure.

Julia opens the book again and scooches over so we're knee to knee. "It's not a rock;, it's a mineral. Illinois used to be the largest producer of fluorite in the country, but they closed the last mine in 1995."

Someday that girl's brain is going to explode. Still, it's kind of interesting, in a depressing sort of way. "All that gorgeous crystal…gone. That's sad."

She squints at me again.

"Seriously. It is sad. It's so beautiful. Seems like we humans either consume or destroy God's best stuff, you know?"

"I know." She nods, emphasizing those two words like we've just agreed on the solution to world hunger. Her eyes twinkle at me. Guess I redeemed myself for the whole sarcasm thing, at least until next time. I listen to Julia's mini lectures and somewhat enjoy the rock and mineral pictures for the next ten minutes. Another ten go by, and I'm getting edgy. Ten more, and I'm about to rip out my hair.

"Hey, how about a little soccer, Jules? We haven't done that together in ages." How desperate am I? There are people in nursing homes with more athletic ability than Julia. Dad pushed her into soccer one year, and it was downright painful to watch. I hold my breath, hoping I didn't just trigger another emotional scene.

"Okay." Her voice echoes the same fake eagerness I

used for her book.

We set up imaginary goals and kick the ball around. Well, I kick. Julia mostly chases. Twice she trips over nothing. But it feels good to be moving, inhaling the earthy smell of our neighbor's fresh-cut grass, feeling my heart pumping. Julia lasts twenty minutes—ten less than me and the rock book.

"Hey Jules, isn't it about time to visit Aunt Rita?"

"No. We've still got an hour."

Ugh. How am I going to fill an hour? "How about we play a little more? Come on, it'll be fun." I've hit a record low on the desperation scale.

Julia grimaces. "I was just going to make a card for Aunt Rita."

My conscience prevents me from talking her out of it. Auntie comes first. "That's nice. She'll love it."

"Then if there's time, I'm doing extra credit in math."

"Um…okay." She's getting an "A" in sophomore level math, and doing extra credit. The girl seriously needs therapy. She disappears through the door, leaving me to practice alone, but all I can think about is Aunt Rita. What will happen an hour from now? I have to feel the warmth when I touch her. I have to. I close my eyes, and her loving smile fills my mind. I can almost smell her perfume. Feel myself wrapped tight in her signature bear hug, though she hasn't had the strength for it lately. That chemo better be doing something besides making her weak and nauseous.

Please, God, bring healing today. End Aunt Rita's suffering.

Poor Uncle Vince. Seeing her this way, so fragile, so limp, has got to be killing him. Just a few months ago she was talking about their Hawaiian cruise, then broke into a hula that had us rolling on the floor. Now this. I smack the ball into the goal. Not much of a triumph with no goalie. I , and head over to pick it up. But in my head, I'm in that hospital room, holding her hand, feeling the healing power flowing into her body, incinerating those cancer cells.

The back door slams, an unexpected sound that jars me back to the present. Mom walks toward me, her face pale as flour, eyes glazed, mouth drawn into a thin, quivering line. Julia follows, palms out to indicate she doesn't have a clue.

"Come sit, girls." Her voice is thick. Slurry. The words land on my shoulders, pressing down, down, down. She sits on the deck bench, and we sandwich her, awaiting her next utterance. Words that I fear will change my world…again. She stares at the vegetable garden, where young tomato and pepper plants bask in the sun. We wait and watch as a fluffy orange cat strolls across our lawn, then climbs the fence and leaps into our neighbor's yard. And still, Mom is silent. Finally, she sighs, clasps her hands, looks at me.

And something inside me dies.

Oh, God. No. Not this. Please let it be anything else.

A tear slides down her pallid cheek.

"Mom?" Julia's voice shakes. "Mom? What's going on?"

"Aunt Rita." She whispers the name. "A stroke. It happened so fast."

No, please. Don't take my auntie. Undo it. Give her back.

My hand flies to my mouth, holding in screams that would shatter windows. White hot pain sears my heart. I want to run inside and cry 'till I pass out. But my mom…she is bent over, her whole body trembling with sobs that glue me to her side. Jules wraps both arms around Mom's waist, and I do the same. We sit there, three broken spirits mired in darkness, clinging to each other because at this moment, none of us can stand alone.

And the healing power in my hands feels like nothing more than a cruel, sadistic joke.

CHAPTER TWENTY

Misty

The funeral is the worst. I've never seen so many tears my whole life. People everywhere. I tried takin' Ty to the room with the little cakes and cookies, but people were cryin' in there, too. I never knew Aunt Rita, but she musta been something.

Shilo looks like she stepped right out of The Walking Dead. So pale. So agonized. Vacant eyes, like she can't figure out what happened. I want to help, but my experience with this stuff is pretty much zero. Mrs. Howell's cousin from Boston died a few years back, but she was super old, and Mrs. Howell hadn't seen her in ages.

"Come on, Mommy." Tyler tugs my hand. "Let's go by Sheebo."

I grab his hand before he interrupts her huggin' her friend, Melody. Pretty name for a pretty girl. Probably has a perfect life, just like Shilo, with a mom and dad and all the fancy trimmings. She must be a good friend, because Annie seemed really glad to see her, too. Another hug and Melody heads out the door—our cue to fill the spot so Shilo's not alone in her misery.

"Okay, Tiger. Now we can see Shilo." Tyler doesn't need to hear it twice. He's at Shilo's side in two blinks. She ruffles his hair and stares at a photo collage of Aunt Rita.

"Hey, Shi. You okay?" It's lame, but I don't know what else to say.

She nods, but doesn't look at me.

"I saw you talkin' to Kenji. That was nice, you know, that he came by." He didn't talk more than a few seconds to Shilo. In fact, from where I stood it pretty much looked like a sentence or two and a quick hug. I hope he doesn't blame her for that big mess at Duke's.

"Yeah. Yeah, that was nice."

"You're auntie musta been pretty great." I hope that sounds okay. Just looking at her makes my eyes feel glassy. "I'm real sorry she died."

Another nod. "Thanks."

Tyler let's go of my hand and takes Shilo's. "Why you sad?"

"Shhh, Tyler! We talked about this. Remember?"

"Oh, yeah, cuz of that lady." Tyler fully extends his scrawny arm and points up front to where Aunt Rita's laid out. I gently push it down, feelin' the blood rise to my cheeks.

"Don't be sad, Sheebo." He takes her hand. "We love you, kay?" His words speak to my heart. They musta spoke to Shilo's, too, because she scoots down and hugs him.

"Thanks, kiddo. Love you, too."

Her words shine inside me like a thousand fireflies twinkling on a summer night. No one except me ever said that to him before.

"Julia!" Tyler's arm flies up again as he points to

Jules sitting by herself on a couch. And again, I push down gently and remind him not to point. Julia folds her hands in her lap and looks around like she's wishin' somebody would sit with her.

"I go by Julia." Ty looks up at me with those big puppy eyes. "Kay?"

That child can make me smile even in the saddest situations. "Okay, Tiger. You be good." Little legs get ready to bolt. "And no running."

A hint of a smile forms on Shilo's ghost face. "He's pretty amazing."

"Thanks." Silence follows, with nothing comin' to my head until I realize there's all these pictures in front of us. I point to one of Aunt Rita dressed real fancy, dancing with her husband. "She had a real nice face. She looks so happy there."

"My cousin's wedding. Joey." She nods to a nice looking guy talking with a couple of elderly women. "His brother is Charlie. O, over there." This time she nods to a guy handing tissues to her uncle. They both look so handsome in their suits.

We stand real quiet together, looking at the photos, 'till it starts to feel awkward. "I'm sorry you couldn't of healed her, you know, like you did with Ty."

A light flickers in Shilo's eyes. Not the good kind. I want to take back the words, but they're out there, hanging over us like a black cloud. I clench my hands, remembering all the times Jake glared at me like Shilo's doin' right now. I hold my breath, knowin' her next words won't be anything I want to hear.

"Yeah, thanks. I really needed that." She strides away so fast, she nearly collides with a little girl. In a heartbeat she's gone, and I stand frozen, wondering how I could have said somethin' so stupid. But why was it stupid? I replay my last words, searching for the part that drove her from sad to angry, but come up empty.

Mrs. Howell used to say when you make a mistake, turn it around fast as you can. I glance at Jules and Tyler to make sure they're doin' fine, then walk into the lobby, the cake room, the bathroom. Nothin'. It's like she just evaporated.

My heart starts racing as memories attack me. M: my daddy leavin' before I was born, then mom dyin', then the Howells movin' out of state, leaving me behind. Is Shilo going to leave me now, too? Is this going to keep happening over and over? What is it about me that drives people away?

Please, God. Help me fix this. I'm not real sure yet where You and I stand, but I sure would appreciate it.

I find her outside in the little courtyard, sitting on a bench under a flowery tree. Nobody else is out there. She glances at me and stares at the street, but doesn't leave. I sit down at the opposite end and grip the arm rest. Fine. She can leave me if she wants to. I've handled it just fine all the other times. But I'm not goin' down without a fight. "Can we talk?"

"No."

"Just wanted to say sorry."

"It's fine. Whatever."

Her voice sounds like a dead person's, if dead people could talk. I hate the silence. It feels like a wall of fire between us, burning up the friendship that was just startin' to blossom like those crabapple branches hanging over us. Everything in me wants to run back into that funeral home, because even the sadness is better than this firewall. But I won't. I never really had a best friend, but I've read about a lot of them. Sherlock and Watson used to argue, and those Harry Potter kids, but in the end, they were always there for each other. Protecting, encouraging. Maybe Shilo needs somethin' like that right now.

"I know you're really upset about your aunt. She

sure was lucky, though."

Shilo looks at me like I just said Martians landed in the courtyard. "She just died, Misty. She had *cancer*."

"Yeah, well, that part wasn't so lucky. But man-oh-man, she sure had a lot of people who loved her. All those folks so sad about her passin'. Being loved like that…" I shake my head in awe of Shilo's Aunt Rita. "Must have been a great life. And then she died real quick, you know, instead of sufferin' with the cancer."

She turns her gaze to me and stares like she's never seen me before. Her eyes soften from ice blue back to sky blue. I sigh. Maybe I should have said that part first.

"Hmm." She picks up a white blossom from the bench and holds it in her palm until a breeze plucks it off, carrying it to some unknown destination. "I guess you're right."

"Anyway, about before, I didn't realize I said somethin' that would make you mad. Guess I'm good at that. I used to make Jake mad all the time."

"Please don't compare me to Jake."

"I wasn't. Not at all. I just meant my words don't always come out right."

She sighs. "That's not why Jake always got mad, Misty. He's just an idiot."

Her answer makes me laugh, even though it's not really a laughin' sort of situation. But her lips turn up a little like there's a laugh inside her, too. My hand releases the arm rest, and I lean back. "Anyway, I'm real sorry. Forgive me?"

"Yeah. I do." Her words come out softer than before and I can tell she means it this time. We stay quiet, watchin' the cars go by. It feels like she wants to say something more, so I wait, figuring she'll get to it sooner or later.

"I prayed like crazy for Aunt Rita. Not just once, like I did for Tyler, but lots of times. But she died,

Misty. She died, and I couldn't prevent it."

She looks at her hands, then back to me. I remember her hands that day, how they moved from Tyler's arm to his scarred cheek and the tender part over his spleen. All the places that were broken. All the places that weren't by that night.

"But Shilo, you're not God. You can't just fix whoever needs fixin'. You told me what happened with Tyler was a miracle. I may not share your faith, but aren't miracles up to God?"

She nods, flashin' me a little smile to let me know we're okay. "You sure don't sound like somebody without faith to me."

It was in me once, burning bright, until the people who helped me find that light threw me back into the darkness. Then Jake came along and pulled me down deeper. It was a painful descent – one I don't ever want to repeat. I don't tell her any of that, though, because I feel that light flickering inside me, and can't help thinkin' it might be worth another try.

CHAPTER TWENTY-ONE

Shilo

Misty's right. About miracles. About Aunt Rita. She's smarter than she realizes, but she's got to stop blaming herself for Jake being a violent jerk. At least she's safe now, and, unlike me, not under house arrest.

By Monday morning I'm more excited about school than I've been since Kindergarten. Five days of living in isolation still lies ahead, but here in these halls I can see my friends and feel like a real person again. More importantly, I can talk to Kenji in person and apologize for getting him involved in that stupid mess at Duke's. Maybe if we talk face-to-face, he won't want to break up with me. Maybe we can just make things right again.

Classroom doors open and shut, teachers rustle papers, and students slam lockers, laugh, and call out to friends. The music of my world. I breathe in the scent of chlorine from the pool and glance at the smiling, framed faces of award-winning athletes. My comfort zone. Here I can blend in with the crowd and feel normal again. Hope fuels my heartbeat with each footstep. Maybe he'll be at my locker.

I freeze, staring at the small crowd gathered at my locker. Eight? Ten? Some I know;, others look vaguely familiar. The rest, no clue. They huddle together like paparazzi waiting for

Kim Kardashian. Confusion glues my feet to the floor. I stare at the dreamlike scene ahead of me. Am I in the wrong hallway?

"There she is!" The girl who shouts is in my gym class, but we've never even talked. "Shilo, hurry up!" She knows my name? "Bell's gonna ring soon, and we want to hear all about it."

Which *it*? My brain struggles to figure out how much they know and what I should say. A whirlwind of voices and questions whips around me as I stand in the center, trying to make sense of the craziness.

"What happened at Duke's?"

"Did you really punch a Warrior?"

"What happened to Kenji? Someone said he got stabbed."

"Is Kenji dead?"

Kenji. My stomach drops to the floor. Don't let him be dealing with this, too, or our on-the-edge relationship will crash for sure.

"Come on, you guys;, let her talk before the bell rings." Brittany grabs my arm. "Fess up, Shi. What happened Friday night?"

"It was no big deal, really." Warmth rushes to my face, making my head feel detached from my body.

"Oh pleeeeeeze." The gym girl seems to be auditioning for a part in the school play. "It was a very big deal. Everyone knows about it. I heard your father arrested you and made you spend the weekend in jail."

I roll my eyes. "Uh, no, not exactly something my Dad would do." Though it did feel like jail, minus the steel bars and group showers.

"So what happened?"

Man, this chick doesn't give up. Nearly a dozen pairs of eyes stare me down, waiting for my answer. I need to say just enough to make them go away.

"Me and Kenji saw Warriors harassing a girl at Duke's. She looked scared, so we went to see if she was okay. That's when we got into the fight, but it only lasted a couple of seconds and then the police arrived. And my Dad, of course. The gang guys got arrested, and my Dad took me and Kenji home, alive and well."

"What about ...."

Brriing, brriing!

Saved by the bell.

Relief washes over me as everyone scatters. But thanks to my new groupies, there's no time to drop stuff off at my locker. On the bright side, U.S. History is close, and Kenji will be there. I fly down the hall, hoodie flapping and book bag bouncing. In the final second of the bell, I fall into my seat, panting and blushing like a freshman. Kenji stares at his open book, apparently captivated by the timeline of events leading up to the first moon landing.

Mr. Myners, in the midst of grading papers, looks up. "Cutting it a bit close there, aren't we, Miss Giannelli?"

"Sorry."

Sorry, Mr. Myners. Sorry, Kenji. Sorry, Aunt Rita, and Dad, and the rest of humanity. Is this my destiny? To spend the rest of my life apologizing? If I can just get through history and biology, maybe Kenji will be waiting for me by Italian and one more painfully genuine "sorry" will make the world a slightly better place. Maybe.

The dream comes true. Carrying one book by its spine, with the other hand shoved in his pocket, Kenji stares solemnly as I draw near. Somehow, some way, he'd gotten hotter over the weekend. We only have two minutes. M; might as well dive in. "Kenji, I'm sorry. I had no idea it was going to turn out that way."

"I'm not here for an apology." Monotone words. Unreadable face. "Just wanted to see if you were okay. You and your aunt were pretty close."

The thought of her gone from my life thickens my throat, but I can't cry. Not again. Not here. "I'm okay. Thanks for coming to the funeral."

"No problem. Take care." He touches my arm, a polite gesture that would make anyone think we're little more than acquaintances, then takes a step back. "Well, I gotta go. See ya around."

"But…"

Too late. He's disappears into the crowd and leaves the word hanging in the hallway's atmosphere. I strain to see him through the flow of bodies, but he's gone. And he stays that way until re-emerging in the same spot three days later. I smile at him, hoping it will create a mirror response, but he is once again expressionless as he waves me over.

"Look, I know you're going through a tough time, and I don't want to make it worse, but there's something I just have to know."

"Okay." But it's not okay, because that "something" could be anything, and what if it's a ("something" I can't answer?

"Why did you call me Friday after school? Before you came to Duke's. "And why *didn't* you call me back *after* Dukes?"

The reasons that totally made sense at the time sound incredibly lame now. Way too lame to say out loud. "I don't remember."

"Yes, you do."

He's killin' me. How are we supposed to have this

conversation with the clock ticking away our seconds? "Okay, okay. I just wanted to talk. You know, about us."

"So you thought not calling me back after Dukes was the best way to do that?"

"Yes. No. I wanted to wait so we could talk in person. You seemed pretty angry in the squad."

Anger sparks in his eyes, but he strains to hide it, probably because he knows I'm grieving. "Of course I was. First you blow me off a bunch of times when I want to talk to you, then you show up at Dukes, out of the blue, and tell me to leave. Next thing I know, I'm face-to-face with some gang moron." His voice rises enough to solicit glances by two guys walking past us. "And then the best part, an entertaining ride in your dad's squad."

"I know. You had every right to be mad."

"And I still am. There, I said it. And now I feel like a jerk because of what you're going through. But, man, Shi, after everything that happened, you still couldn't make time to talk to me."

This isn't going at all the way I envisioned it. And the worst part is, I get it. Everything he's saying, everything he's feeling, makes more sense than my weak explanations. But he doesn't know the reasons behind my actions. The residue shock-and-awe I'm still dealing with after finding out about The Gift. My fears that he'll find out I'm a little different than…well, most of the world. And once again, there's no way to share these thoughts and feelings with him without revealing my secret. Nor do I want to tell him I didn't call because I was afraid he'd break up with me.

The sparks become a fiery glare as he waits for my response, but my blank mind is not producing anything worth saying.

"That's it, then?" He gestures with palms up, as though expecting me to hand him something. But I've got nothing to give.

The click-clack of heels sounds behind me, and I know exactly what's coming next.

"*Signorita Giannelli, vieni in classe.* Ciao, Romeo."

My stomach cringes at the familiar voice of Signora D'Andrea telling me to come to class. I can't decide if I want to hug her or strangle her for interrupting. It wasn't exactly going well, but then again, there's no chance now to turn that around.

"I know that much Italian," Kenji says. "Guess I'm outta here."

His words sink my heart, so I throw out a lifeline. "Wait." He turns away, but I've got to give it another try. "Kenji, wait."

"Why?"

"Meet me by the tree." Maybe that's what we need, a moment by the willow, so sturdy and familiar, where I can tell him we need to take a break for awhile so I can straighten out some things going on in my life. He'll agree to that, because it will be easier for both of us than him telling me he wants to break up. Then we can just drift apart, without him ever finding out my secret.

"What's the point?"

"We'll talk, okay? I promise."

He sighs. His eyes lose their hardness, and I know he'll come. "Fine. The tree." And with that he races toward the technology hall, with no chance of reaching his class on time.

Anticipating the loss of Kenji weights me down through Italian and presses harder with each passing hour. By the time the final bell rings, I trudge toward those doors with Nikes of lead. He can't be part of my life if I'm going to supernaturally save other lives. There's too many complications that come with The Gift. Too many risks he didn't sign up for. Too many misconceptions that could soar through the world in a flash and torpedo my life and all those connected to me. But Kenji is entwined around my heart. He is my friend, my confidant, my morning sun. He is all that is right with the world. He is love.

And now, he is my sacrifice.

As always, Kenji keeps his promise; one of his most lovable traits. He calls when he says he will, shows up on time, does whatever he promises. Not like some other guys I've dated. He squints in my direction, shielding his eyes from the afternoon sun as a small breeze ripples his t-shirt. Prince Charming in blue jeans.

And twenty feet away sits the evil king, parked in a familiar black and white police car.

This is so not happening. I must be dreaming, because Dad wouldn't do this. He trusts me. Loves me. I look at Dad, back to Kenji, back to Dad. Nope, not a dream. A nightmare. One step in Kenji's direction, and I'll be dealing with more lectures and who knows what else. Kenji maintains his salute pose, obviously confused about why I'm not heading his way. He waves. Yes, I see you. Dad glares at me from behind his bullet-proof windshield. Yes, I see you, too, watching to make sure I go straight home. And guess what, you win. The last thing I want is him not trusting me and getting Kenji involved in another lecture. After getting Kenji's attention with a wave, I extend my arm and point to the police car. He sees Dad, then takes a step toward me. My insides crumble. I want to run into his arms in slow motion, like in sappy movies where the crowd disappears and the couple can see only each other. Instead, I shake my head and put up my palm. He gets it. With a final wave, he turns toward home, and I do the same.

I walk past Melody's house, and my heart drops from heavy to dead weight. She's on her way to the studio now. Probably won't get home until ten. Maybe I'll text her later and tell her about how much this day sucks, how much I wish the two of us could just go to Florida and hang out on the beach for a few days. Maybe Pat Nicholls, the travel queen, would give us a discount now that we've met her. It's so cool that she's helping all those young moms get a fresh start. I wonder how she's doing, what sort of sickness she has. It just isn't right that I felt The Gift with her, but not Aunt Rita. Why? The question has battered my brain for the past two weeks.

Why, why, why?

Because God wants me to heal her. The revelation hits me like a goal kick to the face. What's wrong with me? He practically shouted it from the stadium microphone, and I let it go.

"Stupid." I shake my head. The One who placed the sun and stars in the sky gave me the power to do something phenomenal. Life giving. And all I've done is complain that He isn't listening to me. That He didn't choose Aunt Rita. Shame rises in me, filling my heart until it spills out in a tear I quickly swipe away before anyone sees. How did I get so caught up in who I couldn't heal, that I forgot about someone I *could*?

Please, Lord, don't let it be too late.

I am the God of second chances.

My feet sprout wings. I fly down the next few blocks and burst through the door—a woman on a mission. "Mom? Where are you? Mom?"

The dryer door slams from the basement. "Down here, Honey. Are you all right?"

Heavy footsteps clomp up the stairs. The basket emerges first, followed by a weary-looking Annieconda.

"We have to do something about Pat Nicholls. I mean, *I* do. Well, *we* do. I've been thinking and…"

"Slow down before you break yourself." Mom laughs at her little joke as she sets the laundry basket on the living room floor. "Here, grab the other end of this sheet and talk to me while we fold."

"I need to do something about Pat. When I feel that warmth, it's a sign, right? I was walking home, thinking about things, and it just came into my head. I'm supposed to heal her."

Her smile fades. Worry lines etch her forehead. "Stop right there. We talked about this. I like Pat. A lot. She's a wonderful person, and hopefully she's getting the medical attention she needs." She brings up the end of the sheet to meet mine, and I see a complexity of emotions battling in her eyes. "But you need to let it go, Shilo, or it will ruin your life. All our lives."

She cares about Pat;, yet her priority is protecting me. I get it. But this is bigger than her fears, and I'll do whatever necessary to make it happen. "What about *her* life? I have to get to her. We need to figure out a way." My pulse is racing as I pick up a pillow case and fold it in quarters.

"Did you hear what I just said?" Volume and pitch tangle and rise. "Let it go. She can afford the best doctors. You're not to get involved."

She doesn't understand. I already am. I didn't choose this gift, but I'm definitely choosing to honor the Giver. I want to scream that it's not her decision to make, that she's contradicting everything she's taught me, but that won't get me to Pat. I take a breath and will myself to be calm and rational. If there is any hope of getting her to help me, I need to present an argument she can understand. "Mom, this is Pat we're talking about. Think of the girls she's helping. Girls like Misty. Think of the lives she's changing. What becomes of them if she's too sick to run Sonrise. Or if she dies?"

She collapses onto the couch, her face a reflection of the forces clashing inside her. Fists clench and unclench. "No, no, no! Just forget about it."

As if.

"It's in me, Mom. In my heart and flowing through my veins. Etched in my soul." Determination grants me clarity and drives my words. Fire burns inside me, ; not the healing warmth, but a fire born of conviction. "I couldn't forget about it any more than I could forget I'm a girl, or a Giannelli." I take her hand, like she always does to me when she's saying something really important. "Please. Help me help Pat. I want you to be part of this." I keep my voice low so she understands I'm not being confrontational when I say my next words. "But you have to realize I'm doing it either way."

Mom and I lock eyes, and the pain in hers breaks my heart. Part of me wants to tell her I won't do it, but a bigger part knows that's not an option.

"*Mama mia*, Shilo. Do you realize the risk?"

"Yes."

She shakes her head. "Oh, Lord. I can't believe this is part of my life again."

My heart soars. She is not happy, but she's caving. "So you'll help me?"

"Better that, than for you to get discovered or pass out with no one to get you home. Let's think about it tonight and…"

"No." The word practically leaps out of my mouth, making Mom's eyebrows arch. "Now, Mom. It needs to be now." The thought grows in me like a living thing. "I know it sounds crazy. I know you've got stuff to do, and we didn't plan it, but this feeling in me, it's…it's…real. Powerful. It has to be now. Please."

Mom opens her mouth to speak, then closes it again. Seconds tick by. Precious seconds. Does she understand? Do I? Not really.

The front door opens, and we jump, gazing at Julia like she just beamed down from Mars, which I often suspect she did.

Mom gives her a hug and kisses her head. "Keep

your jacket on, Sweetie. We have to take a little ride." She turns to me. "Let's go." She grabs her purse and keys. Before Julia can ask the first of her usual two hundred questions, we are on the way to Sonrise House.

"So let me get this straight." Mini drama queen injects a truckload of disgust into her voice. "I'm supposed to sit in the waiting room, reading stupid magazines about celebrities and fashion trends, while you guys have a meeting with Mrs. Nicholls."

"Yes." Mom and I answer in unison.

"I still don't see why I can't be in the meeting."

She's making my head pound. Judging from my mother's expression, the Julia drum is beating against her brain as well.

Mom sighs. "Julia Theresa Giannelli."

The dreaded full name. She's in trouble now.

"I have already explained it to you six different ways." Mom's words squeeze through clenched teeth.

"No, you didn't. Just twice, and it was the same both times."

I'm pretty sure lava is about to shoot out of Mom's eyeballs.

"You are not joining us because you are too young." Mom slowly emphasizes each word. "You are not joining us because we have things to discuss that do not concern you. You are not joining us because I said so!" The last three words explode from her mouth and reverberate through the car. "Is that clear enough?"

"Yes." Julia's voice downgrades from tiger to kitten.

"Thank you."

We arrive at Sonrise where a girl about my age opens the door. She's holding a squirming baby with a pink bow stuck to her nearly bald head. Cute kid, but the pouty lips tell me she's not having a happy moment. Mom introduces us and explains we need to speak with

Pat.

"Sure. I'll take you to her office, but I gotta warn you, she's not feelin' so great. She seemed pretty wiped out this morning."

Her wiggling bundle scrunches up her face, opens pink petal lips, and lets out a scream that shreds my ear-drums. How can so much volume come from some-thing so little? The struggling young mother bounces in place, but nothing calms the wild child in her arms. "It's this way, just follow me."

Mom gives Julia the look and points to a couch in the waiting room. Julia rolls her eyes and trudges toward it, making sure we hear her exasperated sigh. I can re-late, though. It's not so different than Aunt Rita asking me to leave the hospital room so she could talk to Mom. No one likes feeling left out.

Another scream rises from tiny lungs and sets off a series of sobs. The girl turns to face us. "Sorry. I was just warming her bottle when you guys rang the bell. I really need to feed her."

"By all means," Mom says. "We've been to Pat's of-fice before. Go take care of your baby. We'll be fine."

Relief floods her face. "Thanks. Sorry." She sprints toward the kitchen as we turn down the hallway leading to Pat's office. At the end of the hall, Pat's door is cracked open. Mom knocks softly, which widens the crack. She opens her mouth for her usual perky "hello," but stops as Pat comes into full view. The travel queen is slumped over her desk, head resting on her arms, eyes shut, breathing deep and steady.

Mom turns to me, resolve darkening her eyes. "This is it."

I turn my palms up in a silent "what?" But the an-swer smacks me in the head before she has a chance to respond. Oh, God. Oh, no. This fast? A soft snore from Pat answers my question. The opportunity has been handed to me on a silver platter. Failure to grab it could change the course of many lives, and possibly bring an end to one.

Easing my way toward Pat, I cringe at every squeak in the floor until I reach her and look back at Mom. She holds out her hand and places it on her opposite shoulder. I nod, mimicking her move, but placing my hand on Pat's shoulder instead. This has to be the most awkward situation I've ever been in, and for me, that's saying a lot. Hopefully, Pat hears the mental message I'm straining to send her. : Please don't wake up. Not until I'm done and out of here.

Unlike the failed attempts with Aunt Rita, this one works immediately. As my palm rests softly on Pat's shoulder, warmth floods my heart. Mmm, so comforting, so sweet. It ripples outward, filling my body, washing away worries and fears. Gravity disappears. I am floating on waves of peace, joy, love so pure it's crazy. Unconditional. My knees feel the soft padding of carpet. My other hand reaches for Pat, guided by an unseen force.

I feel His presence.

Lord, please use Your incredible power to heal Pat. You created all things. You command the wind and waves, placed the sun in the sky, taught the birds to sing. You can do anything.

Mom moves closer, but like my surroundings, she is fading away as The Gift grows stronger in me. Heat pulsates from my arms and into my body, flowing through my veins, radiating through my arms. Intensifying in my hands. They glide over Pat, touching skin, then cloth, as the warmth fills me and envelopes me like loving arms.

Please take away her illness and let her continue to care for these teen moms and their babies. I ask this of You, the Great Physician, the Savior of the world.

I drift on a sunlit cloud, enshrouded by soft, white mist. With a final word of prayer, the heat shoots through my fingers, draining the warmth and energy from my body. I fall in slow motion, feeling the carpet beneath me. Soft fibers brush my cheek. Arms hook under mine, lifting me. Mom. She stumbles.

"Try, Shilo." She whispers. "Try to walk, just a little. You can do it."

No energy. No desire to do anything but sleep.

Her arm wraps around my waist, guiding me. As the mist clears away, my eyes take in the dreamy room, where Pat still sleeps with her head on her desk. She stirs. Mom freezes, then nudges me forward again.

"Take a step."

I struggle to comply with whispered words, but manage to force a step.

"Keep going."

Step, step. A carpeted hallway stretches before me like an endless bed. Oh, that soft, wonderful carpet. How I'd love to collapse and tune out the world. My legs wobble, threatening to grant my wish. If I could just rest. Five minutes. Step, step. A couch, a table with magazines. A bouncing foot. I raise my eyes to see a hazy version of Julia.

"Mom, what happ…?"

"Shhh." Mom cuts off Julia's question. "Don't speak;, just get on her other side."

Julia's skinny arm encircles my waist. If I fall, she's going down with me. But there is love in her touch. Love from both sides, giving me strength to move forward. Step, step. Out the door, down the stairs, into the car, where I flop onto the back seat and fall into darkness, knowing something wonderful and amazing just happened.

But I can't remember what.

CHAPTER TWENTY-TWO

Misty

A knock at the door stiffens my spine, but I don't panic. Since Nick promised Jake can't leave jail 'til his trial, I don't worry anymore about him bursting through the door. Still, I'm not touchin' that doorknob without knowin' who's on the other side.

"Who is it?"

"Kyle. Got your mail again. Looks like a card."

I let out my breath. Guess there's still little bits of worry left inside, after all. I open the door to Kyle's smiling face.

"Thanks." I want to say more, like askin' him all about college and what he's learning and what books he's readin', but I just take the envelope and start to close the door.

"Birthday card?"

"Don't think so. My birthday's not 'til September." What I don't say is there's nobody who would send me a card, anyway.

"You doing okay, Misty?"

He knows my name? Probably heard Jake screamin'
it enough times. I just nod. My eyes flick to the pink
envelope. Not a bill, not junk mail. A real card with my
name on it. That's a first. I pretty much became invisible
when I ran away and met Jake.

Kyle shifts his backpack, which looks like it's
burstin' with books and papers that help him learn all
sorts of cool things. "I saw them carrying your little boy
out on the stretcher last week. He okay?"

"Yeah. He's much better. Thanks for askin'."

"Good." He smiles at me, and somethin' about his
smile makes me feel different. Pretty. He takes a step
back. "Well, take care. I better get to class."

"You, too." I hold up the envelope. "Thanks for
this."

Huh. That was so nice, him askin' about Tyler and
everything. Like he actually cared, even though he
doesn't know us. I walk toward the couch with a little
spring in my step.

This past week without Jake made me realize I've
been livin' under a big, dark storm cloud. Tyler, too.
Now, even with all the stressful stuff goin' on, it's like
there's this beam of sunlight in our lives. I just hope it
don't disappear. We laugh more. We play more. And
we're eating great, thanks to the Giannellis. It felt so
good to spend time at the park, then go to the library
without checkin' in with Jake. Without bein' scared he'd
be mad when we got home. Nope, none of that anymore. We came home, scooped out some of Annie's
homemade peach ice cream, and read two library books
before Tyler's nap. Now if it all works out for us to live
at Sonrise House, maybe, just maybe, we can get a do-
over. Tyler deserves a way better life than this, that's for
sure.

The envelope tingles in my hand. What could it be?
I rip it open. Inside, there's a fancy card with bright col-

ors and sparkles. When I open it, a hundred dollar Target gift card falls out. Unbelievable! Who would send this? I read the swirly handwriting.

Dear Misty,

We give you this gift in the spirit of love and friendship.

Sincerely,

The Cheerleaders of Cedarcrest High

P.S. I was volunteering at the hospital the night Tyler arrived. I am a friend of Shilo Giannelli. Hope you don't mind that she told me a little bit about your circumstances. Been praying for you—Miya Hiyama

I plunk down on the couch, fearing my legs won't hold me up much longer. Weird enough that Kyle asked how we were doin', now this? Total strangers sending me a pretty card and money? I read it again and again. My heart floods with love and appreciation for people I've never even met.

So here's what I need to figure out: Is it luck that Tyler got healed? Is it coincidence that good things have been happening ever since Shilo prayed that day? Was meetin' the Giannellis just my fate?

Or is it somethin' much, much bigger than that?

CHAPTER TWENTY-THREE

Shilo

Julia knows. Mom told her everything while I slept like the dead for five hours after praying for Pat. This is not good. Julia may be a genius and all, but she's only twelve, and not the best at keeping secrets. Mom says Julia "comprehends the severity of the situation and the need for complete secrecy," but I still have my doubts. To make matters worse, Jules has asked me about three hundred questions since that day, and wants to conduct experiments on me using electricity and radio waves. One of these mornings I'm going to wake up to jumper cables clamped to my toes. But Rockhound isn't my biggest problem. No, that would be Kenji. Or rather, the lack of Kenji.

Not his fault, of course, but that doesn't make it any less painful. It was me who wrote the note. Me who turned my back on the best relationship I've ever had. What else was there to do? I never thought anything could be worse than losing Kenji, but if he finds out I'm a freak…that's just more than I can handle. I tucked the note in his locker yesterday.

Dear Kenji,

I know I've been unavailable lately, and I'm sorry. You have questions about things I can't answer right now. There's a lot going on in my life -- some personal stuff I can't really talk about. Maybe it would be better for us to take a break. Just for awhile, OK?

Shilo

I head down the hall toward Italian, staring at the spot where Kenji won't be waiting anymore. With each step, my heart sinks deeper into a cold, dark gulch. Until a firm hands grabs mine and pulls me toward the wall. He stares without saying a word. I search his eyes, trying in vain to figure out what he's thinking.

"What are you doing?" His words hold a quiet anger. His hand holds tight to mine.

My mouth opens, but nothing emerges. I keep thinking if he stares at me long enough, he'll see I'm not normal. The thought swirls through my brain, blocking any attempt at a reasonable response. But, oh….the fire in his eyes, the heat from his hand gripping mine, makes me love him more than ever.

"What are you doing, Shilo? We had something good, you know? I didn't figure you for a game player. I thought you were different."

I am different. Too different. That's the problem. But I can't say it. So I go with the two words I've become an expert at saying lately. "I'm sorry." My throat thickens, preventing any other words from emerging.

"That's all you've got?"

I nod, because it really is all I've got.

"What am I missing here? I thought we had this awesome connection, then suddenly, bam, it's gone, like a meteor hit and I didn't even see it." He shakes his head; let's go of my hand. "You want to break up? Fine.

But tell me what happened. I deserve that much."

This can only get worse, because nothing I say will justify us splitting up, unless I tell him the truth. And that's not going to happen. "I've got some personal stuff going on. This is something I need to do right now. Just for awhile."

"Awhile? It doesn't work that way. I'm not going through this again, not unless I know what's going on."

"I can't, Kenji. I'm sorry. I can't give you the explanation you want."

"Whatever."

No, no, no. Not "whatever." I hate "whatever," because that's not what it really means. It's always way worse.

He walks away, taking his floppy black hair, silly jokes and sweet warm kisses...and the shattered pieces of my heart. From across the hall, Miniskirt smirks at me with her shiny pink lips.

The only thing giving me a pulse is knowing there's only seven days left until school ends, but even that morsel of joy is ruined by the image of a Kenji-less summer. Now, instead of bursting with brilliant color, the months ahead blend into blacks and grays, sucking the happiness from all my awesome plans—: time with Kenji and Melody, working at Frosty Freeze, and hanging out at the beach with oiled-up friends playing volleyball. Even the main event, soccer camp at Notre Dame University, doesn't fire me up like it did a few weeks ago.

Saturday floats in on a blanket of clouds determined to block the sun for eternity. The monotony of the endless drizzle makes me crazy. It never lets up, never breaks into a full-fledged storm. No lightning, though, which means soccer won't be cancelled.

The game begins with mud on the grass, mud on

the bleachers, and mud coating every player walking off the field. Only one thing can make this day worse...and there they are——: The Redbirds. The pushiest, most aggressive team in the league. Both our teams are nine and two, so playing to win takes on a whole new meaning. I long to skip the pre-game warm-up and jump right in, but no chance of that. Bad idea, anyway. But it will be a great escape once the whistle blows and I can forget about Kenji, Misty, and even Aunt Rita for the next ninety minutes. Finally, the stretches, jumping jacks, and sprints are over. Determined to make this loss number three for the Redbirds, we hit the field in our black and purple jerseys.

Coach Dave whips out a clipboard from his soccer bag. "All right, Panthers, make me proud out there. Giannelli, you're left defense. Watch number twelve."

Even in spikes, the slippery surface of the rain-soaked field tells me we'll be hitting the mud a lot today. As I run toward number twelve, she turns to face me. Bleached hair, pouty lips, full-scale eye makeup. Mini-skirt. This is going to be a messy game. On many levels.

"Well, look who's here." She grasps the practice ball, her shimmering nails sporting a French manicure. For a soccer game.

"Hi." No need for conversation. This little soccer model isn't going to get under my skin. There's no room there for anything else.

"So where's your boyfriend? Doesn't he watch your games?" Her snarky tone accomplishes its task. My Panther claws unsheathe as muscles tense for the pounce. One lunge would do it. Just one. But instead, I give in to another temptation and glance over to the bleachers, where Kenji normally sits during games. This is a stupid move on two counts. One: I broke up with him, so why would he be there? Two: It gives Miniskirt way too much satisfaction.

"Obviously not here." I clench and unclench my fists, envisioning her Lush-n-Long eyelashes face down in the mud.

"Isn't he? Maybe you're just looking in the wrong direction."

The whistle blows. Somewhere in the back of my head I know the game has begun, but I'm hypnotized by the scene at the Redbird's wet metal bleachers. Kenji is sitting with the friends and families of my opponents. He's here to watch that painted, plastic Barbie doll! Our eyes lock, and the rest of the world disappears.

"Shilo!" He screams my name, pointing, arm fully extended. "The ball!"

Whack! It slams into my stomach, knocking me to the soft, mucky ground. Shocked and breathless, I lay in the grass, trying to suck in some air. Cold, sticky mud coats the back of my arms, my ponytail, and the entire backside of my uniform. Pain radiates through every square inch of my body. But none of that comes close to the pure humiliation of this moment, which will be tattooed on my brain for eternity.

Slate gray clouds flood my vision. A whistle silences the players, and seconds later, my coaches' faces replace my view of the sky. They squat down next to me.

"You all right?" Coach Cathy wipes mud off my cheek with her hand. Worry shadows her deep green eyes.

I squint up at her. "Pretty sure I left my guts somewhere on the field."

"Can you walk?"

"Maybe."

"Try sitting up." Cathy and Dave each grab an elbow and lift me to a sitting position. I glance toward the Panther bleachers, where Mom is staring at me as she heads down the stairs.

Go back, go back, go back.

"Hold onto our arms." Coach Dave hooks my arm around his. "Let's get you off the field."

A sub runs in, and the game continues. Emerging from the daze, I see Mom closing in. My battered stomach crunches in on itself. Heat rises, filling my mud-streaked face. An Annieconda hug in front of my team, the Redbirds, and a million onlookers will surely be the death of me right now. No, don't come over here! Why can't I have telepathy? Now that would be a useful gift. Through gritted teeth, I flash her my brightest smile and a thumbs up sign, but she takes another step forward. My eyes squeeze shut.

Somebody, pleeeze just shoot me.

"Annie!"

At the sound of Dad's voice, my eyes fly open and Mom - thank you, God - stops and turns. He waves her up, but she points to me. He motions again, shakes his head, and she returns to her seat at the top of the bleachers.

My sigh holds enough air to fill a beach floatie, but I can tell by Coach Dave's expression there's more pain to come.

"For Pete's sake, Giannelli, what were you looking at? Certainly not the ball. Where was your head?"

"Sorry."

"Sorry doesn't answer the question." Now that serious injury isn't an issue, the compassion from three minutes ago is dissolving like Kool-Aid. "You weren't paying attention, plain and simple. Did you come here to play or what?"

"Yes, Coach."

"Then get in the game. Have some water. Wipe off that mud. You're going in for Walters as soon as we call for subs."

"She's a forward, Coach. I'm defense."

"I'm aware of your position, but she's holding her

side, and we're short today. You'll just have to switch gears."

The sub call is made, and action begins on the sloppy field. I hit the grass with one purpose—: get that ball into their goal. I will not be distracted by the cleated beauty queen, or let traitor Kenji muddle my thoughts.

Girls run, mud flies, parents cheer, and coaches yell as the Redbirds send the ball flying over our keeper's head, smack into the corner. A collective groan rises from my teammates. We can not lose to this team. We run faster, pass more accurately, and up the aggressiveness. As the game intensifies, so does the weather. Rain pelts my face, soaking my jersey through to my skin. Dave and Cathy scream futilely into the wind.

"Washington, cover fifteen! I said fifteen!"

"Dribble, people, dribble. This isn't kickball."

"Here it comes, Giannelli, back up!"

"Giannelli, it's yours, it's yours, go to the goal. That's it, all the way. Shoot!"

My heart races as I head toward the goal. Despite the slick grass and annoying wind, I keep the ball under control and send it flying toward the net. A good shot, but no match for the Redbird goalie. With a dive worthy of Hope Solo, she grabs the ball just before slamming into the mud. Redbird fans go wild. They stand, scream, clap. Thunder erupts from the bleachers as feet pound metal.

Stupid! Why didn't I go for the corner?

Teammates trot over with back pats and encouraging words.

"Good shot, Giannelli. She got lucky."

"Nice kick, Shi. You shoulda had it."

"Man, you suck." The voice comes from behind, but I know exactly whose glimmerstick lips formed the words.

I whirl around. "Eat dirt, blondie."

And this is one of the many reasons I should not have The Gift. A better Christian than I would have handled that much more…saintly. It should go to someone with virtuous thoughts. Not the kind I'm having right now.

"Giannelli, keep it up." Coach Dave megaphones his words with hands cupped around his mouth. "You'll get it next time. Let's go, girls. We're O and two. Shoot hard;, shoot often!"

Five minutes later we score, thanks to Ellie The Boot, a credit to her name. The goal sends an electric charge through us like we're one unit. Pumped and fighting to win, we kick it up, playing for the pure satisfaction of shooting these Redbirds right out of the sky. But when the first half ends, the score remains one to two. Muddy, wet and tired, we trudge back to the bleachers for water and a pep talk. My eyes wander to the Redbird side, but there's no sign of Kenji.

Dave and Cathy try to overcome the eternal grayness of the day with forced enthusiasm. They tell us we're doing great, then tell us everything we did wrong.

"That should have been a corner kick, Giannelli."

Yeah, yeah, yeah. I know.

We get five minutes worth of strategies before the whistle blows and we're back in action.

"Walters and Patel, mark up!"

"Chaberski, attack that ball. Get in there!"

"Washington, get in position."

"Giannelli's open! Pass it, pass it now! You've got it, Shilo. Control it. All the way. Corner shot this time!"

My resolve to make the goal is even more powerful than the kick that sends it in. The Redbird keeper pounces, but this time the cheering and stomping come from our side of the bleachers.

Yes! I love this game!

Two to two, with five minutes to go. We spend the

first four on our side. Sweat slides down the sides of my face alongside raindrops. Finally Brittany sends it sailing, and I fly to intercept from Miniskirt. I beat her by half a stride and pass to The Boot, who scores a heartbeat before the whistle blows. For the third time today, hoots and hollers erupt from happy Panther fans. Umbrellas bob crazily as they cheer us with a standing ovation. Me and my teammates converge on each other, screaming, high-fiving, and hugging before forming a line to shake hands with our opponents. The humiliating fall is now a distant memory. I would have taken ten of them to make this moment happen.

A ray of sun bursts through pewter clouds, glistening the wet field. As I handshake my way down the row of Redbirds, there's no avoiding Miniskirt.

She smiles oh-so-sweetly as she reaches out her hand. "You won the game, but I won the guy."

Stopping to respond is not an option. I move to the next player in line, and the next. By the time I shake hands with the Redbird coach, the clouds have swallowed up that solitary sunbeam.

CHAPTER TWENTY-FOUR

Misty

Plastic boats, rubber duckies, and a bright blue sponge float through Tyler's sea of bubbles, as giggles from both of us bounce off the walls of our tiny bathroom. He's never had a bath like this before. Seems like there's been a lot of firsts since the Giannelli's came into our lives. Annie gave us the Mickey-shaped bottle of bubbles with the sponge, and I used that gift card from the cheerleaders for the rest. There's still plenty more money on there for the stuff we need. No more stealin' vitamins for Ty.

My cell phone buzzes in my purse. I tense, then remember Jake doesn't have this number. He doesn't even know I got this phone. The caller ID shows it's from the library. I gave my librarian friends the new number soon as I got it.

"Hey, Misty, it's Allison."

Allison's real nice, just like all those ladies. Nancy

always knows the perfect books for Tyler, and Yolanda greets me like seein' me just made her day. John's real nice, too. He helps me find science books, and he's got a boy right around Ty's age. But Allison's the one I talk to most.

"Hi, Allison. I'm not overdue on anything, am I?"

"You?" She laughs. "No, of course not. I'm calling partly because we got in a new book specifically for parents of toddlers. Thought you might like it."

"Thanks. Yeah, I would."

"But the other reason is that Lucy gave her two week's notice this morning. I don't know if you're interested, but I was just wondering if…"

"Lucy the shelver? You need a shelver? Seriously?"

"Interested?"

The water pooling in my eyes catches me by surprise. I'm no stranger to tears; there's been way too many, but happy tears? Now that's somethin' new. "Yeah. I am. Real interested."

"You okay, Misty?"

"Yeah. Just got a little somethin' in my throat." I clear my throat, hopin' I sound normal when I talk again. She don't need to know I'm all sappy about this. "So, like, what do I do?"

Allison explains I have to come in and fill out an application. Then if they call me, I come back for an interview. I never done any of this stuff before, but she said she'll get me a book about how to interview. She says it's got tips for what to say and how to act, and it even tells some of the questions that might be asked. I tell her we'll be there tomorrow, first thing. Then she says I'll need "references."

"What are those?"

"People who can vouch for you. The person who does the hiring might want to call some people you know and ask what your character is like, if you'd be a good worker, if you're honest, that kind of thing."

"Oh."

"You can list me as a reference, Misty. I'll vouch for you. I bet Yolanda and the others would, too."

Where is this coming from? All this good stuff keeps happening. People bein' so nice and everything. It's like my heart is near bursting with all the good things that have happened since that terrible night with Jake. "Thanks, Allison. That would be great. Thanks so much. I think there's somebody else I can use, too."

We say our goodbyes just as Tyler grabs my arm for attention. My mind is soarin' on wings of possibilities, images of workin' at the library, making my own money, learnin' new skills. But Tyler needs me to come back to earth. I squeeze the ducky, and a stream of water shoots from its beak. He squeals and slaps the water, splashin' me, which makes him laugh harder. It's the sweetest music ever. But the melody is silenced by three knocks at the front door. We both jump. Somethin' about the sound—more like poundin' than just a friendly rap. I force a smile for my son. "Be right back, Tiger."

Hands clenching, muscles tight, I head for the door, tryin' to convince myself its just Kyle with more of my mail. But forcing those thoughts don't make me believe 'em. Through the peephole I see three guys in green and gold jackets. I don't say nothin'. Pure terror swallows my words. Let them think I'm not here.

"Open up, or lose the door!"

Oh, God, protect my son. Help us!

"Open up now, or we break it down! You got two seconds." He pounds again, shaking the flimsy door and everything inside me.

"Mommy!"

Tyler's frightened call from the bathroom unglues my feet. I run to him and lock the door, but if they can break through the front door, this one won't take nothin'. I grab him outta the bubbles and wrap the towel around him.

"Mommy, I scared."

"Shhh, baby." I press finger to lips. "We're gonna use our new phone to call Sgt. Nick." They'd given it to me the day after the Duke's incident. Must have known trouble follows me like a shadow. I hit "contacts" and "send," and suddenly Shilo's on the other end.

"Get your dad!"

"Misty? What's…"

"Get your dad!"

I hear her call for him. Please be nearby, Nick. I need you.

Boom! The front door crashes in. Tyler screams. Fear rips through me, thundering in my head. I force it back. Gotta think.

"Misty?" Nick's voice gives me hope.

"They're here, in my apartment! Three of them. Help us, Nick. Please."

"Who? Where are you?"

"Warriors. We're in the bathroom." Crashes come from the living room as they trash the apartment looking for the missing package. Swearing and yelling take my terror to a higher level. Tyler squeezes his eyes shut, frozen in his fear.

"I'm sending units. Gotta hang up. Do whatever you have to, but do not let them in. " Click.

Loud stomps come our way. They can't hurt my boy. I won't let them. My eyes race to the medicine cabinet.

Please, God, a weapon.

Somehow, that don't sound right.

Keep my baby safe.

Inside the cabinet, there's just some baby aspirin, Jake's lighter, and my free samples. I grab the lighter, and a thought flickers in my memory. The chemistry

book I checked out a few months ago. The fiery photo.
I reach for the mini hairspray, hopin' I don't have to use
it.

CHAPTER TWENTY-FIVE

Shilo

Dad grabs his gun and races out the door yelling "Misty's in trouble. The Warriors broke in. She's moving in tonight."

He tears out of the driveway, phone to his ear. Unlike my gentle, warm healing power, the terror that fills me now is harsh and cold. Like an evil, living thing, it seizes me with images of Misty and little Tyler at the hands of the Warriors. I don't dare dwell on the possibilities.

Mom stands by the window, hands to her face. "Oh, no, not this, not this. I couldn't bear it."

Julia sets down the book Misty got her from the library. "What's going on? Can somebody please clue me in?"

I relay the few facts I know.

Wrinkles appear on Julia's brow. Her eyes glisten. "Do you think they'll kill her?"

Great. Just what Mom needs to hear. I shoot her "the look" and discreetly nod in Mom's direction.

"I just hope your father calls as soon as he knows something." Mom's eyes are as shiny as my sister's.

We each suffer through the waiting period in our own way. Mom makes coffee, pours a cup, and lets it sit untouched. I go for my guitar, mindlessly strumming songs I've known forever. Jules opens up her new bag of rocks and starts cataloging them on her laptop. Repeated glances at the clock show nothing more than hands frozen in time. I decide to join Mom in the kitchen before insanity permeates my brain. She's at the table, staring outside at the slow dancing willow leaves. An inch from her hand, the stubbornly silent telephone rests on top of her souvenir oven mitt from Wisconsin.

"It's been forty-three minutes." I don't know what else to say.

"I know." Her words are barely out when the phone rings. She strikes it like a cobra. "Nick, are they okay? What's going on?"

Jules races downstairs, and we both strain to hear Dad's words from the phone.

"Oh, thank God, thank God." Mom leans her forehead on her hand. Matching sighs emit from me and Jules.

"That was too close, Nicky. We could have lost them both."

Muffled words came from the receiver. Mom nods. "Okay, Honey, we'll be here. Just be careful. I love you. Bye." She clicks off the phone, leans back, and deflates like a soufflé gone awry. "Dad said his guys got there just as one of the Warriors was kicking in the bathroom door. Misty had Tyler on her back. He said she had hairspray and a lighter in her hand."

I get that she was desperate, but a lighter isn't much of a weapon, any way you look at it. "What?"

"Brilliant!" Julia beams as though Misty were her protégé. "A flame thrower."

"Again, *what?*"

Jules shakes her head, appalled that I don't get the connection. "The propellants in hair spray are flammable, Shi. Get it? She was going to spray the hairspray through the flame, which would cause it to shoot out like a flame-thrower. You know, to protect herself."

I really hate it that she knew and I didn't. Worse...Misty knew it, too.

"Oh, my, I don't even want to picture it." Mom's face is several shades lighter than pastry dough. "Talk about using your brains, though. That was pretty impressive. Dangerous, but impressive."

Mom says Dad arrived just as his men were cuffing the Warriors. He stuck around to help Misty get packed and out of there.

"All right, Giannelli ladies. We've got some work to do."

Julia and I harmonize a groan.

"Grab some cleaning supplies and hit the basement. You two are going to fix it up real nice down there. Clean sheets on the bed, fresh towels in the bathroom, everything spotless. And don't forget to vacuum. I'll be cooking. They're going to need a nice big dinner after all they've been through. How about chicken pasta alfredo? That's good comfort food. Shilo, you can make a batch of brownies for dessert."

And there goes my new diet plan. Maybe we could have giant slabs of whale blubber on the side.

"Mom, here's a crazy idea. Why don't we just have chicken, *minus* the alfredo, and save ourselves about ten-thousand calories?"

She laughs as if I were joking. "Oh, don't be silly. The alfredo is the best part. And you could use a few more calories anyway. You're always eating like a bird."

The creamy, Parmesan aroma of alfredo fills the house by the time Dad's key turns in the front door. Misty enters first, with Tyler clinging to her leg. She is instantly enveloped in Annieconda's arms.

"You're safe here," Mom says. "Don't worry about anything."

A sad smile crosses Misty's face. Does she even remember what "safe" feels like?

"Mmm, smells yummy!" Tyler tugs on Mom's arm. "Are we gonna have good food again?"

We laugh in unison, dissipating the tension that's thickened the air for the past two hours. Mom and Julia take our guests downstairs to unpack. I follow.

"Shilo," Dad calls from the kitchen. "Stay up here for a minute."

I couldn't possibly have done something wrong this time. I wasn't even there.

When they're out of earshot, Dad plunks down on a kitchen chair and pushes another one out for me. I join him at the table. "What?"

"Do you get it now? Why I was so mad at you after Duke's?"

This again? "I guess."

"Those guys had knives, brass knuckles, and a Beretta. They would have killed Misty and Tyler without blinking an eye. *That's* who wants revenge on you. And Kenji, too. You've put yourself and him in danger—so much, I can't even protect you without keeping you locked up day and night."

Pretty sure a person could die from that much protection. "But you won't, right?"

Weary eyes fix on mine, but there is something more in those eyes. Something I've rarely seen before. "I love you. I have to figure this out."

And it hits me. The "something" is fear.

"I get it, Dad." Sorrow seizes me without warning,

inviting Guilt to wrap its spiny arms around me as well. What's it like for him, the leader of our little pack, our protector, to worry about keeping me safe? It's like I've opened up the door to Hell and let demons into our lives. "I'm really sorry." Those words have never sounded so lame.

Dad tugs my hair, smiles. "I know. We'll get past this, Shi girl. We always do."

Not soon enough. But maybe for now, we can take a sidestep. "So, you going to give me the scoop? Let's have it. Every detail from the moment you left the house."

He grins. "Why do you love this stuff so much?"

"I don't know. It's just interesting. Other people just get it from the crime shows. I've got the real thing. Come on. I want to know everything."

"Okay, okay." The anxiety fades from his eyes, re-placed by the gleam that makes him…Dad. "First I put my key in the ignition and turned it carefully backward to start the engine."

"Dad!"

He laughs, thinking his little joke is hilarious. "You know I can't resist torturing you. When I got to Misty's, there were two squads there and another pulling up. I walked in just as they were frisking and cuffing."

"Then what?"

The rest of his story matches what Mom told us, except the part where the guys said they wanted their merchandise. They were there to "convince Misty to hand it over."

I don't even want to imagine what methods they'd have used.

"The Warriors are at the station getting charged with anything we can legally throw their way. I have to get over there, too."

My heart sinks. I was really looking forward to him

being home tonight. "Come on, Dad. You're supposed to be off today."

"Gotta be there, Honey. It shouldn't be more than a couple of hours, though. Don't eat all the chicken alfredo."

After Dad leaves, I head for the basement, but just as I reach the stairs, Miya's name appears on my vibrating cell.

"Hey, Shilo, do you know if Misty got the gift card?"

"The one from you and the cheerleaders? Yeah, she was pretty excited. Wrote you a thank you note and everything."

"Aw, that was sweet. She didn't have to. I just wanted to make sure she got it."

"That was pretty cool, Miya." I was surprised enough when she thought of it, but almost fainted when I found out she actually pulled it off. Who'd of thought all those hair-flipping, rah-rahs would be so thoughtful?

"Not bad for a bunch of shallow, superficial bimbos, huh?"

My face heats instantly. Did she read my thoughts? "I never thought that!"

Liar, liar, pants on fire. Shilo Marie Giannelli fails the judgmental and honesty test today.

"Some people do. I don't know why. Oh, well, that's all I called for."

My heart picks up speed, anticipating my next words, the ones I have to say quickly before I blow my chance.

"Um, so, how's Kenji?" Simple question, yet it sucks the air right out of my lungs.

"Oh, he's fine. You want me to give him a message?"

Yes! Tell him I'm sorry, so sorry, for everything.

Tell him we shouldn't be apart ever, and Miniskirt is all wrong for him. Tell him I love him so much it hurts.

But those are not words I can say. "No, no message. Thanks anyway, though."

"You know, Shilo, I think…oh, never mind. I probably shouldn't say anything."

"No, say it!" The words fly out with way more enthusiasm than I intend.

"Well, I think he misses you, but you didn't hear it from me."

"Oh." Okay, what do I do with that?

"Anyway, I'm glad the gift card made Misty happy. Gotta get going. See you at school. Just one week left!"

Downstairs, a better mood settles over the room. Me and Jules had pulled out the sleeper sofa earlier and covered it with sheets, pillows, and a quilt. Misty lays on her back, staring at the ceiling, looking like she could melt right into it. Tyler rolls around giggling next to her.

"Look, Sheebo, I sleep in big bed with Mommy!"

Miya's call and Tyler's laughter sweeps away the day's earlier torment. We sit around rehashing the break-in, applauding Misty for her bravery, then move on to a happier topic—Misty's future. Discussing Sonrise House and school bring Misty back to life. She sits up, eyes bright, talking about getting a college degree like it's a trip to Paris. Compared to what she's been dealing with, I guess it is. We head to the kitchen for tonight's feast, topped off with warm brownies and ice cream. The no-sugar plan starts tomorrow.

"Excuse me a minute." Misty slides her cell out of her jeans pocket. "Just want to see if Sonrise called. They said they might need more information from me."

Phone to her ear, Misty grabs a pen and notepad off the counter, writing frantically while listening. Her face pales. Fear glazes her eyes.

I lean toward Mom. "Maybe someone died," I

whisper.

Misty clicks off her cell, but continues to hold it in a white-knuckled grip. Lips drawn tight, she looks at us, shakes her head.

"What is it, Misty?" Mom breaks the silence. "Who called?"

"Jake. Always Jake. Ruining my life. Ruining every tiny grain of happiness that comes my way."

"He can't threaten you from jail, those lines are tapped. They'd be all over him."

"It wasn't him directly. It was Jeremy, his brother." Misty explains that Jeremy said Jake's hearing is in three days, and there's new charges against him now stemming from the incident at Duke's. He threatened her on the phone, saying she'd messed it all up, just like Jake knew she would.

"He said there's a good chance Jakes stayin' in jail cause of me." Misty's eyes pool. "Then he said, 'If you take away my brother's freedom, I'll take away the only thing you love. You know I can do it, Misty. I know people.'" She grabs a tissue from the counter to blot her eyes. "And he's right. He does know people. What am I gonna to do? I can't let anyone take my Tyler. I won't."

Mom wraps her arm around Misty, who stands rigid as an ice sculpture.

"I don't care who he knows, he's not going to get near Tyler. He doesn't even know where you are. Remember, you've got your very own cop now. And pretty soon, you'll be at Sonrise House and on your way to a better life—a life without Jake or his brother."

Silence pervades the room. Misty purses her lips, then nods. "I guess you're right. It's still scary, though. You don't know him. When Jake or Jeremy get mad, they make sure someone pays the price. I won't be able to stop worryin' about this."

I really hate those guys. Another reason I shouldn't

have been given The Gift. You're not supposed to hate people, but sometimes...

"Misty, lean on Jesus in times like this. He's more powerful than your fears, and way more powerful than Jake. Talk to him."

"Talk to him?'"

"Pray. Anywhere, anytime. He'll listen. I can't promise a lot of things, but I can promise that."

Misty opens her mouth to respond, then stops as Tyler bursts into the room.

"Mommy, play catch with Julia?"

"Sure, Tiger. You go ahead." She sends him off with a hug and kiss, but reaching the door, he turns around and grabs her hand.

"You come."

"I have to put some things away downstairs. I'll come out in a little bit."

"Kay." He let's go and runs to Julia.

"Julia, please don't let him leave the backyard." Misty's words tremble from her lips. "And promise you'll watch him real good? He can't be alone. Not even for a second."

Poor Misty. It just never ends.

"Don't worry, I'll be super careful." Julia takes Tyler's hand, tossing me a questioning glance before walking out.

Questions flash in Misty's haunted eyes as she turns toward me. "Can you help me put away some stuff downstairs? I can't reach the top shelf in that closet."

"Sure."

Now what? This definitely isn't about the closet.

Once downstairs, Misty continues the charade by handing me a small mirror and old, yellowing box of stationary from her suitcase. I play the game, setting them on the top shelf, until Misty sits on the edge of the sofa bed and hugs her knees.

"Uh, this is a little weird, but I have to tell you somethin'."

Great. There just isn't enough weirdness in my life at the moment. "Okay." I take the spot next to her and wait.

"Strange things have been happening to me since I met you."

No kidding. Strange things have been happening since I met her, too. But I don't say it. "You mean like all the trouble with the Warrior guys?" If it's that simple, I just may break into a dance of joy. But even before the question leaves my lips, I know the answer.

"No. I mean, that's been strange, too. But I'm talking about somethin' way different. I think it started that night you prayed for Tyler in the hospital."

Please don't talk about The Gift. Let's talk about anything else on the planet. Clothes, Tyler, Julia's rock collection. Literally anything. Seconds tick away and I realize she's waiting for a response. There's no avoiding it. "Really? Like what?"

"I never told you or your mom this, but I felt somethin' when you were praying. I was holding Tyler's hand, and it got really warm. Then the warmth was like…you're gonna think I'm so weird …it was flowin' from his hand into me. At first just my hand was warm, but then I felt warm all around my heart. It's hard to explain. Did you ever feel anything like that?"

Other people can feel it, too? I grab a pillow 'til my knuckles whiten, searching my mind for a way to explain it.

I try to imagine what Mom would say. Her voice drifts into my head. "Keep it honest and simple." My fingers release their death grip on the pillow. "Sometimes when I pray I feel warmth. It's a nice feeling, though, like God is there listening."

"That's the other thing."

I'm still dealing with the last thing.

"This is going to sound crazy, too, but I kinda felt like something powerful was in the room. Not creepy or anything, just....I don't know. Powerful. Ever since then I've been kinda thinking about Jesus and the stuff I learned when I lived with the Howells." That flicker of hurt shadows her face. I see it each time she mentions her foster parents. "Part of me wants to believe and trust Him the way you guys do, but part of me is afraid. There's just been a lot of let downs, you know?"

Everything about Misty's life—all the hardship, the hurt, the disappointments, and fear—wraps around my heart and squeezes tight. "No kidding. You've been through some heavy stuff."

"Yeah, so there's that, and then all my mess ups over the past few years. Let's face it, I'm kind of a loser. I mean, livin' with Jake and getting pregnant and, well, there's somethin' else. Somethin' bad I haven't told your mom or anybody."

"What?"

Misty covers her face with her hands. "I hate saying it."

I wait without saying a word, giving her the space and time she needs. Whatever it is must be horrible. I tense, fearing she might have killed somebody, implausible as it seems.

"I stole groceries and medicine. I had to. The parenting books all said kids need vitamins from fruits and vegetables. Jake, he never gave me enough. I always had to spend most of it on his beer and cigarettes. So I slipped apples and oranges in my pockets, sometimes a banana because they have potassium." Misty picks up Julia's old Barbie and braids her hair, fixating on the shimmery blond tresses as she talks. "A couple of times I shoved a handful of green beans or a potato in my pockets. The books said he should be havin' spinach and stuff like that, but it was too bulky, so I had to steal vitamins. Do you know how much those cost?"

I flop back onto the mattress and shove a pillow behind my head. With all my heart, I believe what Misty did was okay. Yeah, it's illegal. And then there's the whole "thou shalt not steal" to be considered. Aunt Rita's words echo in my head, "There's nothing that Jesus won't forgive, if you just ask." We sit in silence; me staring at the ceiling, Misty braiding and unbraiding the Barbie. She hates that she stole things;, that much is clear. Half of me is glad she hates it, but the other half doesn't want her beating herself up over it. She's done that too much already, for so many different reasons.

"You did what you had to do, Misty. You were just trying to keep Tyler healthy. Maybe someday, when things are different, you can pay it back."

"Oh, I will." She sets Barbie on the bed and faces me. "I owe $86.50 to Shop-n-Save; and $52.85 to Walgreens. Oh, and $32.00 even at Walmart. I took diapers and wipes from there a couple of times. Had to push them under my shirt and pretend I was pregnant. Thought for sure I'd get caught."

Misty leans back against the headboard as I digest the fact she actually memorized how much she owes each store. We stare at the fancy doll together, both lost in thought until I remember this conversation started with her talking about wanting to believe. "So what does this have to do with having faith?"

"I feel like if I walk into a church, a booming voice will say 'What are you doing here?'" Misty keeps her gaze locked on Barbie. "But when I listen to your mom and remember what the Howells used to say, it seems like trusting God would be pretty cool. It's just confusing."

Something creeps forward from the corners of my mind. Foggy bits and pieces of the prayer I prayed in the hospital.

Please help his mother, too. Help her find You. Give her friends who will care about her.

He answered. Why didn't I see it before? The friends are *us.*

"I'm no theologian, but there's one thing I know. The booming voice would say 'Welcome to my house.' Nothing less."

"I'm not so sure."

"I am. I'm sure." Insecurities about what to say or how to say it dissipate in the wake of my conviction. She needs to know it's not about judging. "No matter who you are or what you've done, He forgives you. It's a gift. You don't have to earn it; you just have to *want* it."

She turns to face me, eyes wide. Hopeful. "I think maybe I do."

"Yeah? Good, 'cause living with faith is like going into battle with armor, instead of naked. This world is kind of a mess, but with faith, you can ask for guidance and protection. I mean, you'll still have problems, because there's plenty of evil forces at work, but God will give you what you need, even if it's something totally unexpected."

And I should know.

Misty sighs and returns to braiding. We listen to Mom's padded footsteps crossing the kitchen above, and the trill of a cardinal outside.

"You know, Shi, I was onboard with having faith for awhile, so I get what you're sayin'. I just have some things to work out." Misty looks down, then straight into my eyes. The intensity of her gaze reflects a battle waging inside. "I'm just not good with getting close to people, and that includes God. But I'm workin' on it. You did good with your little sermon, though."

It is meant as a compliment, and given with complete sincerity. Still, the phrase "little sermon" strikes me as funny. "When you're ready, you'll know."

Seconds later, the basement door opens, and Mom call us to come up, saying Dad's home and wants to hear about the message from Jake's brother. We head up to the kitchen, where Misty recounts the Jeremy story, threats and all.

"Let me get this straight." He opens a soda can as his chicken alfredo spins in the microwave. "He actually left this message on your cell? He threatened you, and we've got a *recording*?" He grins like he just watched the Bears win the Superbowl.

Misty's brow crinkles with confusion. "Yeah."

"Man, this guy's dumb as his brother."

I've watched enough crime shows and heard a lifetime of Dad's true crime stories to know what's up. "This is perfect. It's evidence, right, Dad?"

"You bet." The microwave beeps, and Dad grabs the steamy plate. "I don't mean to sound flippant, Misty. I'm sure that message upset you. But this is the perfect example of a blessing in disguise. With Jeremy's comments on your cell, and all the other baloney Jake's put you through, you won't have to deal with him for a very long time. He's going to jail. In the meantime, we'll get Orders of Protection to prevent either of them from coming near you or Tyler. They won't know you're at Sonrise House anyway."

"Really?" Misty's hopeful eyes glimmer at Dad.

"Really."

"Huh. Kinda weird, you know?" She stares out the window, eyes focused on the sky. "Some very cool things have come outta somethin' pretty terrible."

CHAPTER TWENTY-SIX

Shilo

Dad walks from the driveway to the front door with a smile that says it all.

"Tell us, tell us!" Mom shouts through the screen door, swinging it open before he reaches the front step. "Is it good news, Nick? It is, isn't it?"

Feet pound up the basement stairs and run down from the second floor as Jules and Misty join us in the living room. Four sets of eyes zero in on Dad, who will no doubt take full advantage of his moment in the spotlight.

"Well now, I don't know if I can talk with this dry throat. A nice glass of ice water might help me get the words out."

Jules runs to the sink and back faster than she ever moved on a soccer field. Dad chugs the water for a lifetime until only ice remains.

"Ahhh. Thanks, Sweetie." He tussles Julia's hair. "Now what's everybody doing in the living room? Is something going on?"

"Stop playing games, Nick." Mom puts hands on hip. "We want the verdict, and we want it *now*."

"Okay, okay. You win…but Jake didn't." Dad stops to laugh at his little joke. "The hearing went even better than I expected. Dr. Shurden showed up with the medical report and Tyler's X-rays. "Fortunately, Jake's public defender either didn't know, or didn't care, that Tyler was released the next day. The doctor's testimony put Jake away for one year on child abuse charges."

"What about the drugs?" I can't help breaking in. "Didn't he get time for possession?"

"Yes, two years for possession with intent to sell."

Joy illuminates Misty's face. "That means he can't come near us for a long time!"

Dad chomps on a piece of ice. "Don't get too excited. He could get off early for good behavior."

"Who, Jake?" Misty laughs. "You're kiddin', right? He'll punch somebody before the week is out."

"You won't be hearing from his brother, either. The judge signed an Order of Protection against Jeremy after hearing his threatening message."

Seems like a perfect time to share the other good news. "Well that's the second victory today." I flash a smile at Misty. "Tell them."

Misty's normally pallid face flushes rose pink as all eyes turn toward her. "I got a job at the library. I'm gonna be a shelver part-time while I'm living at Sonrise House."

"That's wonderful, Misty." Dad beams at her. "I'm proud of you."

"Me, too." Matching beams emanate from Mom. "Today marks a new chapter for you."

Waves of joy wash over me, catching me by surprise. It's a good feeling. A powerful reminder that not all of life's surprises turn your world upside down and inside out. When I think of how I judged Misty...saw her as a tramp and a horrible mother. A total loser. Definitely not someone I'd want in my life. But now I'm nothing less than inspired by her survival skills in a world that knocked her around since she was a kid. If she can persevere through that, I can be strong in the face of whatever challenges The Gift may bring. "Perfect fit, too. Nobody knows the library like you."

"Ahem." Julia glares at me.

"Except maybe Jules, who thinks it's better than Disney World."

My little sister honors me with a combo eye roll/head shake, but Misty is too lost in her excitement to notice.

"Allison in the children's area called me soon as it was posted. Then she and Yolanda put in a good word for me with *the director*! Do you believe it?"

I open my mouth to answer, but the new, animated version of Misty keeps on going like the Energizer Bunny.

"The library is just three blocks from Sonrise, so I can walk to work, which is really good cuz I can't keep Jake's car. Isn't it perfect?"

"So, so, cool!" Julia grins like someone just handed her a moon rock. "I go there a lot, so I'll see you. They have an excellent geology collection."

Dad ambles over and pats Misty's arm. "I bet it won't be long at all before you get promoted, and who knows what might happen from there?"

We celebrate Jake's conviction and Misty's job with dinner at El Meson, where Tyler decides he wants to eat Mexican food "every day forever." How can that scrawny little body devour a cheese enchilada bigger than his head? Afterward, we drop off our live-in guests and head to Uncle Vince's house—a visit I both crave and dread. What does it feel like to lose the person who's been at your side for forty years? They'd met in high school, just like me and Kenji. I wonder where we'll be in forty years.

I wonder if we'll ever find our way back to each other.

A ragged Uncle Vince hugs me at the door and invites us into the kitchen for coffee.

"How are you doing, Uncle?" My question sounds lame, but I can't think of anything better to say.

"Fine, Shilo. It's hard. But she's with God. At peace." My uncle, my big, strong uncle who spent thirty years building Chicago skyscrapers, walking fearlessly on beams twenty stories high, looks at us with shimmering eyes that rip my heart in two. Aunt Rita may be at peace, but Uncle Vince sure isn't. Misty's words come back to me, and I remember finding comfort in the thought that my Auntie spent her life wrapped in love. Maybe Uncle Vince would, too.

"Aunt Rita was really blessed. She had you and Charlie and Joey, us, and all the relatives. Plus she had church friends and book club friends—more love than that funeral home could hold. All in all, a pretty great life."

The silence that follows sucks the air from the room...until my uncle smiles. "She was crazy and funny, my Rita." He shakes his head. "You're right, Shilo. Everyone loved her. I'm going to replay your words every time I feel sad. Of course, that might be nonstop for awhile."

Dad de-sombers the room with a story about a guy who robbed a 7-11 yesterday after he'd just paid for something with a credit card. The bad guy's stupidity provides the comic relief we need to get past the moment. By the time we stand to leave, Uncle Vince is dry-eyed and complaining about the doctor bills.

Back home, Tyler hugs each of us before he and

Misty traipse down to their new safe haven. His hug is particularly enthusiastic tonight, with plenty of squeeze action. Clearly he's been spending too much time with Annieconda.

"Night, night, Tyler. Sweet dreams."

"Happy sleeps, Sheebo."

"It's Shilo, you crazy boy. Shilo. If you can say Julia, you can say Shilo."

"Sheebo, Sheebo, Sheebo."

"Alrighty then. Good talk."

His soft little lips kiss my cheek, and suddenly it doesn't matter if I'm Sheebo for the rest of my life.

Long day, with too many highs and lows and terrors. My limp mind and body escape to my room, where my bed begs me to flop and stay there for days. But no, there's one more thing to do before I slip between those lavender sheets. My heart fears this next move could end in disaster, but I'll never get to sleep unless I try. I grab my cell off the dresser and call Kenji, just needing to hear his voice. Maybe we could find a way to be friends. It would be better than this bleak void that's shriveling everything inside me.

"Hey, guys, sorry I missed you. Do the message thing."

"Hi, Kenji, it's me." What do I say? I hadn't thought this out. Wasn't expecting his voicemail. "Give me a call, okay? Bye."

Twenty minutes goes by, then thirty. I know his schedule, and I know he's home. Of course, his cell might be dead, or maybe he's in another room and didn't hear it. Wishful thoughts, nothing more. Might as well go to bed, where sleep will spare me the torture of waiting for a reply.

It doesn't. Sleep finally finds me around 2 a.m., and four hours later, that hateful alarm jars me awake. It must be the middle of the night. *Has* to be. The sun disagrees, so I drag myself out of bed and dress for school.

One breakfast and one bus ride later puts me at my locker, where a note falls out of the little air slits in the top. Please let it be from him! Please, please, *please*!

The basic square fold, unlike the neatly tucked triangles my friends make, tell me it's from Kenji. I nearly drop it as my hands race faster than my speeding heart.

Shilo,

I got your message last night but decided not to call. This is all I want to say. I loved being with you. You were easygoing and fun, and I could talk to you about anything. You made me laugh, and you laughed at my dumb jokes. Being with you always felt better than anything else. You were honest and open, and I really liked that. But things changed. You got all moody and mysterious. Sometimes when you were with me, you seemed to be somewhere else. You stopped having time for me. Stopped telling me things. I don't know what's going on. You say you want to break up, but you can't tell me why, then you call me. Sorry, but I'm just not into playing games.

Kenji

I stop breathing and read it again. Still says the same words. And I'm still not breathing.

It's okay. It's what I wanted. My choice. Better this way.

My flimsy words are incapable of blocking the wave of pain that crashes into me, sucking me into a whirlpool. I lean against my locker, begging my legs not to give way. I squeeze my eyes shut and picture our first date at the carnival, when he spent nearly twenty dollars to win me a ridiculous stuffed rhinoceros. The student-filled hallway blurs. No. Not here. Not in plain sight of everyone.

I open my mouth for a deep, overdue breath, then another. I can do this. There's a bigger picture here that needs my focus. I can heal people. He chose *me* to perform miracles. How amazing is that? But Kenji…the thought rips my heart again. No. I need to focus on the good stuff. The miracle. I tuck the note into my purse and shuffle off to History, vaguely aware of my surroundings.

Each class drags on for days. Are the clocks even working in this school? The lunch bell finally frees me from the endless drones of teacher voices. I meet up with Brittany and Lauren in the lunch line and head for our table. They talk about anything but Kenji, and say nothing about my silence. My buds. We look out for each other. I join in here and there, eventually feeling the trauma subside into tolerable misery. But when Brittany's eyes dart to the aisle, mine instinctively follow…right to where Kenji is standing. Those almond eyes lock with mine, then break away as he continues toward his friends.

My heart hits the floor for the second time today. And for the second time, I scoop it back up, because the image of everyone seeing my pain is far worse than holding it inside. I toss the remnants of my lunch into the garbage. "I'm going to work on pottery."

Brittany grabs my arm. "Come on, give it a rest. There's only three days left."

"I know. I just want to finish a project."

Brittany reads between the lines and lets go. "It'll be okay, Shi. Really. You just need time."

The hall leading to the pottery room is nearly empty, and I'm hoping the room is even emptier. Just me and the clay and a million possibilities. Silence fills the paint-stained room as I move past art tables, the imposing kiln, rows of unglazed pottery, and into a hidden corner. Scrunching down on the clay-dusted floor, I rest my forehead on my knees and allow a waterfall to rain down my cheeks as images of Kenji waltz through my head. My self-absorption in misery prevents me from hearing the footsteps of Mrs. Dell, my art teacher.

"Shilo?"

I gasp, jump, and bump a shelf, sending a clay pot crashing to its doom.

She looks at my soggy face, no doubt accented with mascara streaks by now. "Goodness, what happened?" She pulls two chairs to the corner and sits in one, patting the other. I sit, heat flooding my cheeks, and try to find my voice, but only a sob emerges.

Mrs. Dell shakes her head, stands up again. "You just stay there and try to calm down while I find something to wipe those eyes."

I don't believe this. Why can't I just suffer in peace?

Mrs. Dell returns, tissue box in hand. I blow my nose, wipe my cheeks, then crumple the black-streaked tissue. No doubt I resemble a reject from the Rocky Horror Picture Show. The evil clock shows I have exactly twelve minutes to get my act together before Science.

Mrs. Dell sits back down. "There, now. Do you want to talk about it?"

"No, not really."

"Mmm. Well, I'm guessing it's about a boy."

I nod.

"Wondering how I knew?"

Another nod.

"After raising two daughters and teaching for seventeen years, I know the signs. Anyway, I'm not going to pry, but I just want you to know something. You are a beautiful, intelligent girl."

Yeah, right, okay. I focus on a broken shard of the clay pot.

"You have more strength in you than you can even imagine. And there's something else...I can't quite put my finger on it. It's almost like you have a quiet power about you. Shilo, look at me." She places two fingers beneath my chin and gently lifts until our eyes meet.

"You will get through this just fine, even if it doesn't seem that way right now."

I nod. Partly because she's waiting for a response, but also because hearing her say it makes me think it's possible. I *will* get through this. It's just hard, especially with my heart still grieving for Aunt Rita, who stayed strong in the face of cancer. She wouldn't want me losing it over a guy. But I love that guy. I do. And I don't want him mixed up in this Healer stuff. At least not until I get it figured out.

"Okay, young lady." Mrs. Dell stands up, crunching a small chunk of dried clay. "You've got exactly four minutes to get those eyes looking normal again before the bell rings. "Go work some magic."

I run to the girl's room in the hallway, racing the clock to clean off the smudges. The bell rings just as I'm sweeping on some lip gloss. With no hall monitor in sight, I run through the art hall to the main hall, slow to a fast walk, and enter Science a minute after the bell rings.

Mrs. Shah raises perfectly tapered eyebrows at me as I settle into a desk. "Shilo, it's not like you to be late."

"Sorry."

She marks me tardy and turns back to the class. "Today we will finish up our discussion on genetics. I'd like to hear about some trait, feature, or ability each of you received from a relative."

And so it begins, with Brian saying he's got a crooked toe, like his mother, and Carlos saying everyone in his family has straight black hair, and on and on. Guess I won't be giving voice to the thought streaming through my head. *I got my blue eyes and my miraculous ability to heal people from my Father…in Heaven.* No, definitely not saying that out loud.

But I will say it to myself from now on, to remind myself it's something wonderful and miraculous.

Stronger than my fears. And amazingly, even bigger than my broken heart.

CHAPTER TWENTY-SEVEN

Misty

I breathe in the scent of Annie's lemon cleaner as I hang clothes in my closet at Sonrise House. She's been wipin' down everything with that stuff while I unpack. Smells good, though, and it's real sweet of her to help me like this. I finish the closet and lay my three pairs of pants in a dresser drawer. It's so weird to have all these clothes, to have choices of what to wear. Gotta admit, I'm lovin' it. Taking a little break from Tyler is kinda nice, too. I hope he's havin' fun.

"It's sweet of Julia to watch Tyler while we're doin' this."

"She loves being with Tyler." Annie spritzes the pretty oval thrift shop mirror hangin' over my dresser. "Julia doesn't have a lot of friends, besides her buddy, Emma. She spends too much time alone for a girl her age. Being with Tyler is good for her."

Loneliness is the worst. Wish I could do something to fix that for her. "I don't get it. She's real nice, and real smart, too."

"That's part of the problem. Her high IQ and fascination with all things science make her different." Annie attacks a stubborn smudge along the beveled edge of the mirror. "Unfortunately, kids shy away from kids who are different."

Memories drift into my head. Parties I wasn't invited to, endless years of wishin' I had a best friend. It changed a little when I got settled in with the Howells. Girls liked coming over there. Everyone loved Mr. Howell with his corny jokes and Mrs. Howell with her smiles and homemade cookies. "I know. Bein' a foster kid made me different. Everybody at school had moms and dads, or at least a grandma or someone." I put my new shampoo and conditioner side by side on my dresser. Full size bottles, not samples. And they smell like jasmine. "Doesn't Shilo ever hang out with her?"

"Not much, but it's hard to blame her. She's got tons of friends, a boyfriend, soccer, homework. Her life is pretty full."

"It was real nice of her to offer to make dinner today." I turn my back to her as I hang the shirts from Shilo. Lucky for me they didn't fit her anymore. They're *beautiful.*

Annie laughs. "*Offer* is a bit of an overstatement. Let's just say I was glad she kept the complaining to a minimum. Well, I think everything's pretty clean now." I hear Annie ruffling through my suitcase. "Where do you want this, Misty?"

I turn around and catch my breath. She's holdin' the yellow box I've kept for almost three years. There are daisies on the lid, with fancy gold lettering that spells s-t-a-t-i-o-n-a-r-y. Inside, there's a yellow pen, ten stamps with a heart design, and a stack of pastel paper. The top sheet is covered in Mrs. Howell's beautiful, scripty handwriting. I don't have to see it to recite the words in my head.

Dear Misty,

You know I never got the hang of using a computer or tex-
ting, so I hope you don't mind communicating the old fashioned
way. I will be missing you each moment we're apart, and I'll call
every day. It breaks my heart to leave you, but it won't be for long.
We'll be back for you before you know it.

We love you, Bunny — more than you know. Write every
day, and we'll do the same. We'll see you soon.

Love,

Mom and Dad

Only they weren't Mom and Dad; something I forgot when those walls around my heart finally crumbled
and I let them in. It took two years before I called them
that, and just when it started to feel comfortable, they
took off. Guess the joke was on me, as usual. They left
me with Mrs. Howell's sister, sayin' they had to get some
things in order in North Carolina, and we'd all be together again soon. I get it that they wanted to retire in
and live near their son and grandkids, but they didn't
have to go and pretend they were comin' back for me.
Two weeks with that woman were more than I could
stand. I never used that box of stationary. Never replied
to her letters. And when two days went by without a
call, I knew they'd left me for good. A lump forms in
my throat, and I shove it back down.

"Misty?" Annie looks at me, brow wrinkled. "Are
you all right?"

It hits me that I've been letting those walls start to
cave in lately, after building them up nice and strong
these past few years. Better not make that mistake again.
"Yeah, fine. You can just stash it in the closet. Up high.
I don't need it."

"Are you sure? It's so pretty. You might want to
send somebody a letter."

"Well I *don't*." It comes out harsher than I mean it to. The words leave a taste of guilt in my mouth. "I mean, I just don't think I'll need it for awhile."

Annie stretches on tip-toes and starts to slide the box onto the closet shelf, but loses her balance and steps back. The box topples, it's lid flying off along the way. "Oh! Sorry." She bends to pick it up.

"Hey, are you Misty?" One of the other residents appears in my doorway, her Pebbles ponytail bobbing on top of her head.

"Yeah."

"Pat sent me to get you. Said you need to sign a couple of papers. It'll just take five minutes."

Annie sits on the bed, smiling and shooing me away. "Go, go. I'll put your sheets on while you're gone.

"Okay, thanks." I turn and leave her sitting there with that yellow box in her lap, wishing I could throw it away. Knowing I won't.

CHAPTER TWENTY-EIGHT

Shilo

The house phone rings just as one of the last two chefs is about to get the boot on "Chopped." Great. Now I won't know who wins the ten-thousand-dollar prize. Hopefully it's the girl with the tri-colored hair. Her caramel dessert looked awesome. I sprint to the phone, glance at the caller ID, and catch my breath. Kenji. But why would it be from his house to mine, instead of cell to cell? Maybe his phone died. Still...

"Hello?"

"Hello, Shilo. This is Mrs. Hiyama. How are you?"

"Um, fine." Confused, definitely disappointed, but fine.

"May I speak to your father, please?"

My father? "Sure, but...is everything okay?" Something happened to Kenji, I just know it.

"Well..." She pauses for a lifetime. "I really think I should discuss this with your father."

My heart thumps my chest. "Hold on; I'll get him."

I run back to the family room, where Dad's ignoring "Chopped" and reading the newspaper, and hold out the phone. "It's for you. Kenji's mom."

His eyes ask "what does she want?" as he takes the phone. "Hello."

I sit next to him, straining to hear Mrs. Hiyama's end of the conversation, but her words aren't clear enough.

"I see," Dad says. "That's not good. I was afraid this would happen."

"What?" I whisper, but he silences me with finger to lips. More listening, then, "Okay. I'm glad you called. The kids are leaving for Kentucky in two days, so they should be safe for awhile. Just keep him away from public places. I need time to figure this out." More indecipherable talking comes from Mrs. Hiyama while Dad listens. "You're very welcome." He looks at me, shakes his head. "Take care, and call me if anything else comes up. I'll be in touch. Bye."

"What? What happened? Tell me!"

He sighs. Not a good sign. "Calm down. Thanks to you and your boyfriend, we've got a situation. Kenji's mom sent him over to Econo Mart for milk, and a couple of Warriors came in. One of them recognized Kenji from your little wrestling match at Dukes."

My hands clench and unclench, fearing the end to this story.

"Apparently, things got ugly," he continues. "Just as it was getting physical, one of my guys pulled up. He detained them while Kenji went home, so they weren't able to follow. But Shilo, they know he lives in the neighborhood. And here's something else that makes me *very* happy; one of them said 'where's your little girlfriend? I got some unfinished business with her.'"

Oh, my gosh. Kenji. My spinning brain tries to process the story, imagining what would have happened if a squad hadn't pulled up. My Kenji. "Is he alright?"

"Yes. Were you listening?"

I nod. "Just wanted to make sure."

He glares at me. "Are you grasping this? It didn't end when you walked out of Dukes. These guys are mad, and they want payback. This means until you go to Kentucky, you're not going anywhere without Mom or me along."

The spinning jars to a halt. "You've *got* to be kidding!"

"Dead serious."

"Come *on!* S, school just let out last week. I've barely had a chance to do *anything* yet. I never even see those gang guys. We don't exactly hang out in the same circles."

"There's no arguing this case, Shilo. What's done is done, and now I have to figure out the best way to keep you and your boyfriend safe."

"For the record, he's *not* my boyfriend, so please stop saying that." I know I'm pushing it. His eyes harden even more than before. Might have been best to leave that out.

"Forgive me for not keeping up with your social life." The sarcasm cuts deep. "You seem to be awfully concerned about someone who's *not* your boyfriend."

Knocks at the door halt the escalating argument. I run upstairs to open it, and Julia bounds into the room with Emma on her tail. They are oblivious to the tension thunderhead hovering over the family room.

"Guess what, you guys! I traded my epidote for Emma's celestine!"

I'm guessing my face is as blank as Dad's. We stare at the miniature geologist, who turns to the one friend who shares her obsession with all things rock. "They don't know the scientific terms like we do."

Emma giggles. Julia says she actually speaks, but I

haven't witnessed that miracle yet.

"We'll have to show them." Julia sighs her exasperation. She and Emma reach into their pockets and flaunt the treasures in their open palms.

"Look!" Julia glows brighter than the white and gold crystals shimmering along the surface of her rock, which appears to be a far better acquisition than Emma's lump of brown crystal.

What does one say to a rock exchange? "Wow. Beautiful." I hold the Celestine, pretending to examine it. "Good trade." It's no easy task to feign interest while reeling from the devastating loss of my freedom. I grab my guitar and head out to the back porch.

By evening, the realization hits me that I might possibly survive the next two days. Shortly after I took to the porch, Lauren invited me to the grand opening of her new backyard pool. Dad caved in to my begging and okayed it, long as I stayed in Lauren's backyard. My joy was short-lived, though, when I remembered I'd promised to make dinner while Mom and Misty were at Sonrise. Still, it was a nice little break.

Brown rice simmers while I slice cucumbers, red onions, and tomatoes for salad. Everything should be ready by the time Misty and Mom return. Out back, Julia and Tyler play among the growing collection of toddler toys. The bright orange and yellow cozy coupe rumbles across the porch as I toss the veggies with some vinaigrette and feta cheese. No sauces, no butter, nothing breaded. Will our bodies survive the shock?

I glance again at Tyler, who hardly resembles the fragile, pale little thing I first saw in the hospital bed. Tan and smiling, he runs across the porch in clothes that actually fit him. His lungs belt out the ABC song loud enough for the neighbors to hear. It is one of many he recently learned and sings repeatedly. Nobody minds, though; it's just good to see him happy, especially after a lifetime in that gloomy little apartment with crazy Jake. Fear, hunger, tension, abuse. The image shudders through my body. Has it really been only a month since the day I prayed for him?

Car doors slam, announcing Mom and Misty's return. They walk in full of Sonrise House stories—Misty's new accommodations, the other residents, the great daycare center. I listen while dropping fish fillets into hot oil, which sizzles in protest, shooting fiery droplets at my unprotected hand. "Ouch!" I jerk away.

"Careful, Honey." Mom runs the cold water. "Want me to take over?"

"No. I got this far. I want full credit if it actually turns out good." I hold my slightly cooked fingers under the tap, which is conveniently located next to the open window. "Hey, you guys!" Jules and Tyler freeze in place and look my way. "Dinner's ready. Time to come in."

"No, Sheebo. We play!" Tyler yells.

Yeah, right. He won't be saying that when I tell him who just got home. "Mommy's here!"

Tyler tornadoes his way through the door, nearly knocking Misty down. "Mommy! Mommy!" Mother and son hug as though they've been separated for weeks.

"Hey, Tiger, there's some kids your age at our new house. You'll have playmates!"

"Boys?"

"Boys *and* girls. And you can go to preschool and learn a bunch of things while Mommy works at the library."

"Really?"

"Really!"

Mom walks over to inspect the cooking progress, adding a dash of lemon pepper to the sautéing fish. "Oh, Misty. This is going to be so good for the two of you. I just know it."

"Yeah. I think you're right. Who woulda thought?"

Wheels seem to be turning in Misty's head as she grabs Tyler's hand. "Come on, Tiger, let's get washed up for Shilo's special dinner." Misty and Tyler walk off to the bathroom, and in a heartbeat, Mom sidles up to me, grinning like a kid with a double scoop ice cream cone.

I try to read the message in her eyes. "What?"

"Two things. First, I found something." She pulls a scrap of paper out of her pocket. "The address for the Howells was in a box of stationary in Misty's suitcase. Look."

My eyes scan the address. "Huh. North Carolina, just like Aunt Shannon. Maybe she knows them." Mom's best friend isn't really my aunt, but we've never called her anything else.

"It's a big state, Honey. We'll have check Google Maps to see if their towns are near each other."

I hand the paper back to her. "What are you going to do with it?"

"I'm going to find them. Talk to them. I want to hear their side of the story. What if they're missing her, too?"

"What if they're not and you start a bunch of trouble?"

"No, I saw a letter from Mrs. Howell. Something went terribly wrong."

I'm not so sure about this. If someone's gone from my life for awhile, it's usually because I'm fine with it being that way. The one time I contacted an old friend from fifth grade, she turned out to be obsessed with astrology. Emphasis on *obsessed*. It took six months to get her back out of my life. "And you're going to make it right? Mom, it's been almost three years."

"Love has no statute of limitations. Maybe you can help me find their phone number on the Internet."

"Seriously? You're going to call total strangers?" The woman is tenacious. I can't decide whether this trait

is admirable or hints of stalker. Either way, her mission
to reunite Misty with the Howells has her glowing from
head to fuzzy slipper.

"The worst that could happen is they don't want to
connect with her. Misty will never know, and no harm
done. But if it goes the other way..." Mom's eyes sparkle at the thought. "Think of the possibilities!"

And I do. I picture Misty reunited with the mysterious Howells. Smiling. Feeling loved. It's definitely worth
a phone call, but I'm glad I'm not the one making it.
Talking to strangers is not my thing. Guess we all have
our gifts. "Go for it, Mom. If anyone can do this..."

"And now for part two." She cuts me off, her smile
even bigger now. "You should have seen Pat. Oh, my
goodness, she was vibrant and energetic. Smiling, talking. Full of life. It worked, Honey. Your prayer."

The prayer you didn't want me to pray. I don't say
it, though. No point in ruining the moment. A minute
ago, my main concern was preventing the fish from
burning. Now I am blown away. Unable to respond because of a miracle so wondrous, it is beyond comprehension. And I was part of it. Literally. I still miss Kenji
so much it hurts, but I wouldn't trade this moment for
anything.

Mom hugs me, careful to avoid the hot spatula.
"Pat's adding rooms so she can help more girls. Not only are you healing the people *you* touch, you're healing
the people *they* touch. Even the dog from years ago.
Those kids were grieving over their daddy's death. The
dog brought them much-needed joy. So you see, if the
dog had died that day, it would have been devastating."
Mom brushes my cheek with her fingertips. "That's not
something I thought about with Nonna Marie. Guess I
was too young. But now I see it."

"So no more wanting me to promise I won't use
it?" Never intended to make that promise anyway, but it

would be nice not to deal with her asking.

Wistful eyes meet mine. "You will never fully understand my fears for you. But no, I won't ask anymore. Instead, I will say this. Be very careful, extremely discreet, and humble. *Never* forget it's not your power. Will you promise those things?"

I nod. "Absolutely." I hold up my right hand. "On my honor, I do solemnly swear to be careful, discreet, humble, etcetera."

Hands on hips, she admonishes me with a "Shilo Marie, I'm serious."

"Me, too, Mom. All kidding aside, I really do promise all those things."

I am part of a miracle. A plain, ordinary girl like me with faults and fears and a serious lack of amazing accomplishments. I don't understand it. I definitely don't deserve it. But I'm going to do what needs to be done…whatever the consequences.

CHAPTER TWENTY-NINE

Misty

I wish Annie had never found that stupid station-ary. Everything was going so well, but now I can't stop thinkin' about the Howells. I'm sure they're doin' fine with their retired life in North Carolina. Bet they love living by their son and grandkids. Bet they never think of the foster girl that lived with them for three years.

Tyler stares at a furry caterpillar on a leaf as we sit on the front stairs of Sonrise House. "Where Sheebo?"

"She's comin' soon, Tiger. Then we'll have a nice dinner, and you can play with Julia."

"And truck? And rocks?"

Hopeful eyes make me smile. I see kids with all kinds of fancy toys and electronic things, but give my boy a toy truck and some dirt, and he's in paradise. "Definitely."

He goes back to his caterpillar, while I go back to wonderin' about the "surprise" Annie said she has in store. She said to dress nice, so maybe she's having another guest, too. I hope not, though. I'm not so great with strangers.

Shilo honks as she pulls to the curb in Annie's car. While I get Tyler settled in his car seat, she's talkin' fast, but not making eye contact. Seems like this surprise has everyone a little edgy.

"So what's goin' on tonight?" Might as well ask her up front. I'm dying to know.

"Sorry, Misty. It's a secret. Mom would kill me if I told."

"Will I like it?"

"It will be interesting; I promise you that."

"Interesting" can go either way. I want to trust Annie, but trusting doesn't always work so well. "Really? That's the best you can do? At least tell me *when* it's goin' to happen."

"After dinner."

She offers nothing more, so I give up.

When Annie says "dinner's ready," we sit down to a table filled with chicken enchiladas, refried beans, Mexican rice, and pineapple wedges. Tyler's eyes widen to the size of his plate, but he doesn't touch a thing. He knows the drill. His little hands come together, and he bows his head as Nick says grace.

Once everyone starts passing plates, my curiosity starts killin' me again. "So what's goin' on, guys?" I blow on Tyler's steaming enchilada. "Everyone seems a little weird today."

Julia nearly chokes on her milk, and Annie reaches for the Tabasco sauce, knockin' it over.

"Don't look at *me*," Nick says. "This one's all Annie."

"Oh, it's just a surprise." Annie rights the Tabasco and twists off the cover. "A good one, I think."

"Can I get a hint?"

"No, but it won't be long. It's happening at seven."

All eyes, except Tyler's, glance at the clock. Forty minutes to go.

"Hmm. I can't imagine what it could be."

Shilo coughs. "You got that right."

"Shilo!" Annie's raised eyebrows accentuate her sharp tone.

"What?"

Washin' and dryin' the dishes with Shilo and Jules leaves ten minutes to go. As each one of those minutes clicks by, the air grows heavier. The delicious enchiladas don't seem as happy in my stomach as they did goin' down. At Annie's suggestion, an unhappy Julia takes Tyler outside to play with the truck, which usually makes Julia smile. Not today, though. Whatever's about to happen, they won't be part of it. I know Julia well enough by now—she's got to be hating that.

Two car doors slam outside, and Annie hustles me to the lower level family room, where the front door is out of sight. Shilo sits with me in silence. This room has been a comfort zone for me the past month. We watch cartoons here, play board games, and make plans for my new future. In this room, I'm safe and happy and free from the tyranny of life with Jake. But tonight is different. Fear has found it's way into my safe harbor. Change hovers in the air. Apprehension creeps along my spine and down my neck. Whatever it is, good or bad, I just want to be done with it.

"Don't worry," Shilo must sense my anxiety. "You won't have to wait much longer."

The front door squeaks open, and I look at Shi, but she doesn't look back. Hushed voices drift down to us. A man and woman. Annie calls us to come up.

Tan skin, graying hair, warm smiles. I gaze into Mrs. Howell's hazel eyes—eyes I haven't seen in almost three years. Eyes that could always see past the stone walls around my heart. Her hand flies to her mouth. Mr.

Howell stares, too, runs his fingers through thinning hair that's nearly all gray now. I stop breathin' as fog fills my brain. Is this real? Nothing but silence fills the space between us. Like a science fiction movie, everyone turns to statues. It's gotta be another dream. I can hardly feel my legs.

Mr. Howell clears his throat, then clears it again. "Misty. Our Misty. You can't imagine how worried we've been."

"Look at you." Mrs. Howell's voice cracks. "My beautiful girl. My Bunny. All grown up."

My mouth opens, but nothin' comes out. Shilo steps closer as if ready to catch me. She might have to, at that. What are they doin' here? This doesn't make sense.

"We searched and searched for you, Misty." But whatever else Mrs. Howell wants to say gets swallowed up in emotion.

Silence again. They should've warned me. I wasn't ready. Not for this. What did she just say? They searched for me? I force my voice to surface. "You did?"

Mrs. Howell nods, lips pressed tight.

"We did, Honey; we sure did." Mr. Howell jumps in. "We looked for you for two years. We called the police every week, and hired one of those private detective guys. Heck, we even had our son trying to find you on the Internet. You disappeared into the mist, just like your name."

"Maybe we should go," Annie says. "Leave you three to talk in private."

"No." I grab her hand and grip it like I'm dangling from a cliff. "No, Annie, I want you to stay." I look into her eyes, searchin' for answers. "Why didn't you tell me? I don't understand."

Small crinkles form at the edges of Annie's eyes—eyes that see into me like Mrs. Howell always did. Like she's doin' now.

Annie brushes a wayward strand of hair from my face. "I wasn't sure how to handle this. The Howells have important things to tell you. If I asked you to meet with them, you might have turned tail and never learned the truth."

"They left me." The words slip out in a little girl voice I'd swore I left behind. "That's all the truth that matters."

"No, Sweetheart, no. We never meant to leave you." Mrs. Howell takes a small step forward, speaking through her tears. "We had a plan. We had all the adoption papers filled out. Everything approved. All we needed was your signature, but then we had that damned accident, and by the time we called my sister…"

"Accident?" It's all I can manage to get out. What are they talking about?

"A man on a cell phone ran the red light and crashed into us," she says. "We were both bad for a few days, but we called as soon as we could. That's when we found out you ran away."

I stop breathing. Could their story be true? Those couple of days when they didn't call…they were in the *hospital*? Her sister just said they were probably too busy to call, but my brain said they didn't want me anymore. I'm an idiot. Worse than an idiot.

Mr. Howell pats her hand like I'd seen him do a thousand times. "We checked ourselves out, bandages and all, and caught the first plane back. But Misty, you did a darn good job of disappearing. We tried everything. Police detectives, private investigators, everything we could think of. After a month, we came back, but we kept trying to find you even from North Carolina."

"Mrs. Howell swipes a tear from her cheek and forces a little smile. "We fixed your room in your favorite color, sky blue, and bought a matching curtain and bedspread. And one of those big, furry pillows you liked, too. Remember?"

Yeah, I remember. We'd seen them at the bedroom store, and they were soft as a bunny. I wanted one more than anything. But that was a lifetime ago. I fling the memory away, but it boomerangs right back.

Mr. Howell wrings his hands, tanner now than last time I saw him. "Never changed it, either. We just kept hoping and praying someday a miracle would happen, and you would come back to us. We still have those adoption papers, too."

A battle rages in my head. *It's true; they love me. They're lying; it's a trick.* Could this all be real? My insides start flippin' around, like I might lose that enchilada after all. I'd gotten past all that pain. Left it behind, just like they left me.

I let go of Annie's hand. "Adoption papers?"

"Oh, Misty, we were so foolish. We should have just taken you with us in the first place. Can you ever forgive us? Please. Come back to us. Let us make it up to you." An endless stream rains down her face, but she never stops looking at me. It's like there's so much love in her eyes, it's just spillin' out.

Hug her.

It's not a command, not a voice, but I hear it from deep in my soul. I step away from Annie and fall into Mrs. Howell's open arms. They wrap around me, soft and warm, and I know the truth. I'm home again.

Mr. Howell kisses the top of my head, like he used to do every night at bedtime. "It's a miracle," he whispers. "A real miracle."

And I know he's right.

"Mom." Shilo says the word quietly, but I hear it all the same. "What about Tyler?"

"They don't know," Annie whispers back. "I wanted Misty to tell them herself."

She's right;, I need to tell them. But there's one thing I have to say first. I try to separate from Mrs. Howell, so I can say it to her face, but she holds tight. "I'm sorry I ran away," I say into her shoulder. She strokes my hair, silently crying, so I figure I should just continue. "Something happened after that. Well, a lot of things, really."

"You're here with us, Misty," she murmurs. "It's all that matters."

I pull back, just enough so we can look in each other's eyes, then turn to Shilo. "Could you please get you-know-who?"

She flies to the back door and yells, "Come in, you guys" through the screen.

Tyler gallops into the living room shouting "Mommy, look!" With a grin fillin' his face and his hand caked in dirt, he holds up the biggest, squirmiest night crawler I've ever seen. Mrs. Howell squeals, Annie lets out an "ewww!" and I jump back. Then dead silence, until Nick erupts in a rumbling laugh from the bottom of his belly, followed by Julia, then Mr. Howell and the rest of us. All that tension and emotion just goes flyin' out the window. Tyler glows, lovin' the attention, so proud he scared us. He just stands there dangling that thing until Annie shoos him out and tells Julia to get a jar for it and wash Tyler's hands.

"Oh!" Mrs. Howell's face scrunches in a mix of tears and laughter. "He's beautiful, so beautiful. Just like his mommy."

She doesn't ask about his daddy, and for that I'm thankful. That part can come later.

Annie turns to Shilo. "Why don't you and Julia help me get coffee and dessert set up?" She tells Nick to get two more chairs for the table, then gives me a wink. "We'll leave Misty and the Howells to get reacquainted."

Mr. Howell settles into the couch and motions for us to do the same. They sandwich me, each taking a hand like I might bolt any minute. It's kind of funny, us sittin' there like that, but corny as it might look, I'm lovin' it. Still afraid it might be a dream, but lovin' it.

Mr. Howell retells the story of how they looked for me, this time in more detail. I partly listen, more focused on his face than his words. Weathered skin crinkles around green eyes that peer over silver-rimmed glasses. A lot more of his forehead shows—a lot more scalp, too. He still stands straight, though. Always was proud of his military posture. His hands gesture this way and that as he talks about the detective's reports and his son's efforts in searchin' the Internet. All of it leadin' nowhere, 'til he got the call from Annie. His eyes mist up again at that part, and Mrs. Howell squeezes my hand even tighter.

Annie peeks her head in the living room. "Would you like to come in for coffee and Strawberry Delight?"

"Oh, now, you didn't have to go through all that trouble." Mr. Howell stands as he speaks. That man sure does love his desserts, just like Nick. If he didn't walk a mile every day, he'd probably have a paunch like most men his age.

"Thank you so much, Annie." Mrs. Howell stands, too, finally releasing my hand. "I just don't know how we're ever going to thank you."

Annie laughs. "Are you kidding? This night just may go down as one of the highlights of my life."

Knowin' Annie, I'm pretty sure she means it.

Tyler snuggles in Mrs. Howell's lap, belly full of strawberry dessert and eyes half closed. He leans his head against the soft cushion of her arm and yawns. The roles of grandma and grandson came as natural as breathin' to them both. I touch his velvet cheek, where no trace of that cut is visible. "My Tiger's gettin' tired." I wish I had a camera to take a picture of the two of them. But it don't matter—it's in my head forever.

Mrs. Howell kisses the top of his head for the hundredth time. "Don't leave us tonight, Misty. I couldn't bear it. Not after all this time. Come stay at our hotel. There are two double beds and plenty of room." Sincerity pervades her words. She really does want us to come. "There's even a kiddie pool. We could take Tyler swimming in the morning."

Tyler's eyes fly open at the sound of the magic word. "Yay, a pool! A pool! Just like the Wiggles have."

I remember how excited he got when he saw the episode where the Wiggles went swimming. He asked if we could have a pool. The simple request broke my heart. "We don't have swimsuits or nothin' like that."

"You can borrow mine," Shilo says. She stands up, ready to get it. I still think she's a princess—grew up with *everything*—but as princesses go, she's pretty cool. She woulda made a great sister.

Mrs. Howell pats my arm. "Now, you don't worry about that, Bunny. T, there's a nice shop at the hotel, and we'll get swimsuits for both of you first thing in the morning."

Mr. Howell shakes his head. "Oh, boy. Let the shopping begin."

"Might as well kiss your bank account goodbye." Nick laughs his contagious laugh, and everyone joins in.

"Now you know I'm kidding, Misty." Mr. Howell's eyes twinkle like he's so proud of me, but I ain't done nothin' to be proud of. Fact is, he'd have a heart attack if he knew about that stuff I stole from the grocery store. But I'm not ready to tell them that, yet. Not ready for them to be buyin' me stuff, either. I sure wouldn't mind staying in that hotel room, though.

"It's okay, Mrs. Howell. We don't need swimsuits.

Tyler's got shorts, and I'll borrow Shilo's suit." Me in a bathin' suit—now there's a weird image. When was the last time? The memory sweeps into my brain like a warm summer breeze. It was my fourteenth birthday, and Mrs. Howell gave me a beach party. Took me and five girlfriends to one of the Chicago beaches for the day. We had the best time, splashin' around, playin' Frisbee, eatin' those drippy ice cream cones. A lifetime ago.

"Please, sweetie. Don't call me Mrs. Howell. It breaks my heart. We were Mom and Dad before...before everything fell apart. We want to be that again. Permanently, if you'll have us. You don't have to answer now. Just promise you'll think about it."

My heart is too afraid to believe her words. They still want to adopt me? What if I misunderstood? The best way to figure it all out is to spend more time with them. "I will. Think about it. We'll come with you tonight, too. If you're sure it's okay."

Her smile tells me it is.

"Come on." Shilo grabs my hand and pulls me up. "Let's go see which suit you want. I've got three."

"Of course you do."

She laughs. "Misty thinks I'm spoiled."

"You totally are."

"But you love me anyway."

I roll my eyes and shake my head. But yeah...I totally do. Ditto for Annie, Nick, and Julia. And after three years, buckets of tears, and a vow to hate them forever, I totally love the Howells, too.

How is that possible?

CHAPTER THIRTY

Shilo

The doorbell rings, and I open the front door to what must be an apparition—Melody. She stands there grinning her gorgeous grin, melting away all my resentment for her chronic unavailability. We shriek and hug and laugh like we just stepped out of a "Legally Blond" movie. I forget how much I hate ballet because it stole my best friend. She is here.

We pull apart, and Mel just keeps smiling. "I'm skipping practice."

"You're what? No way."

"I know you're leaving tomorrow, and we haven't been together in sooo long, Shi. I really miss you. I told coach I had a family commitment. Not really a lie, right? You're my soul sister."

Soul sister. The two words make everything else disappear—the resentment, the hurt, the feeling that our bond had stretched beyond its limits. "I can't believe you did that."

"Please tell me you've got time. We could just go walk by the river and…"

"Yes! Are you kidding? Of course I have time. You're really skipping practice?"

"Yeah. I wanted to see you before you left."

"Everything okay?"

"*Better* than okay. Grab your jacket, and we'll do some major catching up."

Mel asks about Kenji as we walk the two blocks to the riverwalk in Pioneer Park. I tell her about the break up, avoiding anything about The Gift. No easy task. Without that element, my reason for breaking up sounds shallow, despite my attempt to justify it. A question forms in her eyes, but she keeps it to herself. It isn't hard to figure out she's wondering why I didn't fight to hold onto a relationship worth fighting for. But I can't tell her the healing power has become a thread in my tapestry, weaving through every aspect of my life. Instead, I tell her about Misty and Tyler coming to live with us, about missing Aunt Rita, and life getting so crazy I hardly had time for Kenji.

"I don't know, Shi. It just doesn't feel right. You guys had something, you know? Something special. Bet you get back together."

I want that hope she's handing out. Crave it like an addict. "You think?"

"I think."

We reach the path, stopping simultaneously to stare at the sunlight shimmering the river. I take a breath before saying something I hope won't ruin our little reunion. "I'm really glad you came over. I wasn't sure you still wanted to hang out. Know what I mean? Kinda felt like I didn't fit into your world."

"You mean, you thought we weren't friends anymore?" Melody's voice reflects the same hurt I'd been harboring for months.

"Not like we used to be." Silence descends in the wake of my words. Did I start something I should have let go? A breeze flutters through the nearby crab apple trees, and some pale pink blossoms float down like spring snow.

Melody clears her throat. "I didn't know you felt that way. I mean, we've been through, like, *everything* together."

"I don't want to feel that way;, it's just you're always busy. Too busy to notice if something's bothering me. Too busy to hang out after school, catch a movie, *anything*."

Her gaze sweeps the river before landing back on me. "I know, but I thought you understood. The only way for me to make it in ballet is to work my buns off…literally. My feet hurt;, my muscles ache. And it's hard being different than everyone else at school, Shi. You have no idea."

A trio of girls our age walk past, giggling loud enough for the whole park to hear. The middle one links arms with the other two as they continue down the river walk. Melody's eyes follow them until they round the bend, and still she stares. "You're into everything with all your other friends, but that's not *my* life. No parties, no going out for pizza after school, no football games. My life is the dance studio."

Across the water, the girls come back into view and Melody continues her fixation. Longing shades her eyes. I never knew. Never thought about all that.

"At school, I'm always alone because I don't have time to make friends," she continues. "You're my best friend, Shilo. At least, I thought so. You're my connection to the real world."

Mom had been right. Hearing it from Mel makes it all clear. We're getting older, with amazing changes taking place in our lives. But one thing doesn't have to change. I hold up my right hand, with my little finger extended, the way we've done for eight years. "Pinky swear we're best friends forever and always?"

The glorious grin returns. She hooks her pinky into mine. "Forever and always."

We start walking again, and it hits me that I've been so focused on wanting to tell her everything going on in my life, I don't even know what's new in hers. But I remember what she said on the doorstep, so it's time to find out what's going on. "So what's '*better* than okay?'"

She laughs, mocha cheeks glowing from something more than the cool breeze. "I hope you don't mind me saying it, considering your break-up and everything."

"Tell me now, or I'll pound you."

More laughter. Man, she looks happier than I've seen her in a long time. It can only mean one thing.

"Well, I sort of have a boyfriend."

"What?! You let me talk and talk, and you didn't tell me?"

She nods, eyes sparkling brighter than the water.

"Remember I told you about the cute guy on the production crew? Blake? I guess he thought I was kinda cute, too. So after about three weeks of flirts between dances, he finally asked me out."

"And?"

"I like him, Shi. *Really* like him."

"Yes! This is awesome."

Mel tells me all about Blake, his hair, his smile, how smart and nice and funny he is. For the first time in ages, we are giggling like we did that first day in the park. She stops to pick a huge dandelion and tucks it behind her ear. "Maybe you can meet him when you come to the show. You *are* coming, right?"

Little does she know I've never wanted to attend the ballet so badly in my life. "Wouldn't miss it for the world."

"Good. It's going to be amazing, Shi. You'll love it."

The sparkle in her eyes when she talked about Blake was nothing compared to the glow she has now. This dance thing…it's who she is. It's lodged deep in her heart, runs through her veins, courses through her soul. Why didn't I see it before?

Because I was just looking at *me*.

I get it, and I need to let her know. "It's going to be awesome, Mel. I can't wait. And listen…I'm sorry I never realized how tough this is. It just always seemed to get in the way of us hanging out."

"Totally! I hate that. But it's the only way to reach my goal. And when I get that amazing call from the Joffrey Ballet Academy, I want to celebrate with my best friend. I want you to be happy for me."

And so I will. Even if I only see her once a year, I will truly be happy for her. And I hate the little part of me that hopes that call never comes. Wish I could drop kick it into oblivion.

"Are you kidding? When you get that call, *and you will*, we're gonna…well, I don't know what we're gonna do, but it'll be *huge*! And I'll be more than happy, Mel. I'll be president of your fan club!"

Mom sits in the living room, looking through a booklet titled "American Mensa." She sets it down as I walk in. "I'm trying to figure out what to do with your little sister."

I glance out the window to where Julia is watering the vegetable garden. "Leave her in an open field. Maybe her mother ship will beam her up."

"I'm serious, Shilo. She needs friends just like anybody else. Kids she can relate to on her level."

"So what's with the Mensa book?" I'd heard of Mensa before—some sort of organization for genius types.

"I'm just checking it out, seeing what they have for kids her age. First she has to take the test to see if she qualifies, but I have a feeling she will. You have to have an IQ in the top *two percent* of the population. If she gets in, I might splurge and send her to one of their camps this summer. I want to get her a special gift, too. She got straight As again, even with taking those high school classes."

"What does she want?"

"Fulgurite. That's what she wants more than anything."

Only Julia. I shake my head. "Well hey, who doesn't? It was always my greatest wish to have my own fulgurite. More than a pony, more than a shopping spree at the mall. Every night I would lie in bed dreaming of
…."

"Okay, funny girl. I get it. Yes, it's a little different than what most girls her age ask for, but Julia's unique. Do you even know what it is?"

"It ends in 'ite,' so it's got to be of the rock or mineral persuasion."

"It's what happens when lightning hits sand. It melts into a part glass, part rock sculpture. Sort of a tube thing."

"Huh. That's borderline cool. Are you getting it?"

She shrugs. "Digs doesn't have any. I'll probably have to resort to the Internet, but haven't had time to check it out. I've got to plan my next class, look into this Mensa thing, bring some food over to Misty and…"

"Chill. I just have to figure out what I'm taking on the trip. I'll help you order a chunk-o-fudgerite."

"Fulgurite."

"Whatever."

"Don't you normally pack about eight minutes before you leave?"

I laugh. It's an exaggeration, but only slight. Choosing clothes two days in advance is definitely not my norm. "Guess I'm more anxious than usual. Where's my suitcase? Basement?"

"Check your room. I think Dad brought it up."

The bright orange suitcase had been one of my prize possessions…when I was eight. Now the obnoxious color, marred with years of scratches and a broken handle, makes me seriously consider taking the bag I always used for sleepovers at Mel's. I climb the stairs with images of Pastor Frank's slideshow filling me head. Next time I open this suitcase, I'll be part of that world. And if the pictures broke my heart, what's going to happen when I'm face to face with the real thing?

Lost in thought, I nearly bang into my bedroom door. My *closed* bedroom door, which isn't the way I left it. Julia better not have been snooping around in there. If she was, she won't live long enough to add fulgurite to her precious collection. I turn the knob, open the door, and freeze in midstep. Tied in bright purple ribbon, a brand new suitcase lays on my bed. Bands of brown leather trim tan canvas. An extendable handle and wheels means no more lugging it the old-fashioned way. Yes! A note on top reads, "With love from your family," signed with Mom's fancy script, Dad's totally illegible scribble, and lastly, Julia's precision formed cursive. Stairs creak, and I turn to see Mom and Jules coming up behind me.

"Surprise!"

"Do you like it? Look, Shi, it has these cool pockets on the side." Julia flips it over, demonstrating the smooth zipper action. "And the handle pulls out so you can roll it!" She sounds remarkably like a TV commercial.

I laugh; trying to push aside the guilt of thinking she'd been messing with my stuff. "I love it. It's wonderful. Thanks, guys."

"I think that's worthy of a hug; don't you?" Mom holds out her arms, and I comply, hoping she lets go before I turn blue.

"We're so proud of you, Honey. You just be careful out there, okay?"

The emotion in her voice caresses my heart. I breathe deep before responding. "I'll be fine, Mom. What can happen?"

But Mom doesn't answer. She just holds me tighter.

CHAPTER THIRTY-ONE

Misty

All these decisions are hurtin' my brain. For years, I didn't have much say in anything. Now there's choices at every turn. Big ones. Counselors askin' what I want to study in college. The Howells askin' me to come back with them to North Carolina. And me, askin' myself what I believe. Where to put my hope. Shilo says I'm overwhelmed because I'm tryin' to figure out everything at once. "One breath at a time," she says. "Focus on one thing and figure it out. Follow your heart."

I think it's the move to North Carolina. Seems like that will affect a lot of other decisions. But followin' my heart ain't all that easy, especially when it's at war with my mind. That's what I've been trying to tell Shi as she sits on her bed, strummin' her guitar. She's pretty good at it, too. Even though she's just messing around – not playin' a real song or anything—it sounds nice. Kinda calms me. I grab her big stuffed rhino and plop down next to her.

"Here's the thing. Your mom jumped through hoops to get me a place at Sonrise. My librarian friends helped me get a GED *and* the shelver job. Your dad made sure I could live here without Jake messin' with me no more. Seems like I'd be betraying everybody if I just picked up and left."

I stare at the rhino and pet its fuzzy snout, not sure how to word this next part. Maybe it's time for one of those heart-to-hearts, like on those Hallmark movies Annie likes so much. Not exactly my strong suit, but I'll give it a try. "You're my friend, Shilo. That might not seem momentous to you, but for the past few years I only had Jake and Tyler in my life. Me and you, we're totally different, but you still care about me and listen to me. And you got me hopin' for things I gave up on a long time ago. Leaving you would be so …"

"You're crazy."

"Excuse me?"

Those star blue eyes gaze into mine, with just a hint of sadness. "You're crazy."

I just laid my heart out, and that's not the response I expected. Or wanted. Guess I thought she'd miss me a little if I went, but maybe friendships in books and movies don't reflect real life. That's probably why people like fiction so much. You can get lost in a world where people act the way they should in real life. I thought me and Shilo were getting pretty close. I need to quit makin' that mistake.

"My mom wanted you to reunite with the Howells. Why do you think she called them? The librarians helped you with the GED to get you on a path to a better life, no matter where that might lead. And Dad…he was thrilled to put Jake and those other guys behind bars. They belong there. He cares about you a lot, but let's face it, he was doing his job. Don't you see? They all want you and Tyler to be happy." She strums a few more times, like she wants to say something else but it's coming out in music. "And as for me…"

She stops dead, just starin' down at her guitar. The air thickens around us, and I think maybe there's a chance I was right after all. Maybe she's not sayin' anything because me leaving would be hard for her, too. Or maybe that's just wishful thinkin'.

"I'll miss you a lot, Misty. Saying goodbye to you is going to be a killer, but truth is, I want you to go. You belong with the Howells. They love you so much. You'll have the family you always wanted. You'll be happy, and that's what I really want for you." She squeezes my hand, just like her mom would have done. Bet she'd take it back if I made that comparison. "Make choices that make you happy. We'll keep being friends, no matter where you live."

Words that beautiful never came my way before, except from the Howells. It's the kind of thing those girls in *The Sisterhood of the Traveling Pants* would say. There's just no reply good enough.

I scrunch up my knees, hugging the rhino to my chest. If everything Shilo says is true, then maybe me and Ty should go to North Carolina. Start fresh. I close my eyes and picture us at the ocean, like I did a million times after fights with Jake. Images fill my head. The Howells settled into beach chairs next to Tyler, who's happily scooping sand into a bucket. Warm sand beneath my feet falling away as the cool Atlantic flows over me. I venture into the water with the sea air blowin' my hair back and gulls soarin' overhead. Just as I get waist deep, I fall forward and sink down, down, letting the salty water swallow me.

And then I rise.

I walk back to shore, where I stand on solid ground and let the sun pour over me, knowing I've left my past behind in that water. Knowing there's a new life ahead.

Pat hugs me for the third time as me and Ty get ready to leave. I thought she might be mad or disappointed when I told her we were movin' to North Carolina, but she was cool about it. Even said she had a girl on the wait list who'd be really happy to get the room. Annie was even cooler. Kinda misty-eyed, but she said that was the best plan for me. Even promised they'd visit next summer, and we'd all go visit her friend, Shannon. She owns a bakery, so that would be pretty cool.

Shilo's face lit up. "You'll love Aunt Shannon. She makes pies that come straight from heaven. She's a riot. Plus I am way overdue for a beach vacation." That girl is so funny sometimes. I get it though; there's somethin' about the ocean. At least, I think so. Just imagining it is wonderful, so the real thing just *has* to be amazing.

Man, I still can't believe it. North Carolina. College. A home and my own real family. By next week, it'll be totally official. Julia thinks I'm crazy, but I'm taking their name and everything. Tyler, too. We'll be Misty and Tyler Howell, and if I ever get married, I'll do one of those hyphen things so I can keep it. No more Misty Morning, even if Julia thinks it's the "awesomist name ever." No, there's a new Misty in town, and this one is stronger, smarter, and not about to be bullied ever again. I've made my choice, just like that girl Ruth in the Bible. I'm choosin' to leave behind everything familiar to be with my family.

My family.

And to think it all began in a trench so dark and bleak, I thought I'd never be able to crawl out.

CHAPTER THIRTY-TWO

Shilo

Shorts, tees, tanks, and a pair of jeans lay neatly in the new suitcase. Pastor Frank said to keep it simple and light, considering Kentucky's summer temperatures. No favorites. N; nothing that would cause a wardrobe crisis if it got torn or stained. I lower the suitcase to the floor and lay back on my bed. A heartbeat later, Julia bursts through my bedroom door.

"Hey, Shi. We went to Blossom's to buy flowers for Auntie's grave, and guess what? Kenji was there."

Her words stomp my heart, and I have to suck in a breath before answering with forced nonchalance. "What was he doing?" Maybe he was applying for a job. Or buying something non-floral. I strain to remember what else they sell at Blossom's. Greeting cards. That could be it.

"He was buying roses. Three. This really cool peach color and they were tied with a matching ribbon."

Good, my brain shouts to my heart. That's good.

He's got a girlfriend, and he's buying her flowers. He's got a girlfriend who won't involve him in a life that might get crazy and weird and out of control.

He's got a girlfriend. And she's a long-legged, short-skirted, prissy...

"Shi? You okay?"

"Yeah. Why wouldn't I be? Kenji and I are over. People move on, Jules." I smile, hoping to express the sheer joy of knowing Kenji and Miniskirt are an item. "I'm glad for him."

"Really? Cause that's a pretty phony baloney smile if you ask me."

The kid memorized the periodic table of elements in half a day, but can't remember to occasionally keep her thoughts to herself. I lose the "phony baloney" smile that doesn't even fool an adolescent. "I'm fine." Jules rolls her eyes and heads for her room, leaving me alone with images I don't want in my head.

My cell goes off, and Brittany covers the plans for who's bringing what to Kentucky, who's sitting with who, and so on. Ten minutes later, Lauren calls, and we have the same conversation. As dusk darkens the summer sky, my group leader from church calls to remind me about the five-thirty arrival time tomorrow morning. Working in the hot sun for a week is little sacrifice compared to getting up at four-thirty to board the bus. Ugh. I toss the last few items into my suitcase, happy the orange one is outside with the garbage. Just one last thing to do before calling it a night.

I knock on the Yellowstone poster, noticing for the first time how the Prismatic Spring is really pretty amazing. Might be cool to see it someday. "Hey, Jules."

Julia's door opens to a view of rocks in all sizes, some dull, many multicolored, several that sparkle. They are spread across an old folded sheet on her floor. Placed neatly in groupings of like kinds, they appear ready for display at an international rock convention. The girl is crazy, no doubt about it. But…in a good way.

"Man, Julia, how many do you have?"

"Two hundred and twenty-three now. These are just about half. The rest are in boxes."

"Pretty soon there's not going to be room for *you* in here."

She beams. Somehow, it's a compliment.

I pick up the nearest rock and examine it. She likes when people seem interested. "Anyway, I figured you'd be going to bed soon, so I just wanted to say goodbye. I'll be leaving super early tomorrow, and you'll still be asleep."

"Wait, not yet." Julia reaches under her pillow. "I have something for you." She hands me a chunky little package wrapped in metallic blue paper. "It's a goodbye, good luck present. I know we gave you the suitcase, but this one's just from me. You know, to remind you of me while you're gone."

"You didn't have to do that, Rockhound. I'll think of you every time I see a rock…or a star."

"Open it. It's really special. Well, I mean, *I* think it is."

I tear open the pretty wrapping to reveal a familiar looking combination of white and gold crystal. The lump forming in my throat is far bigger than the one in my hand. This is silly, getting all choked up over one of Julia's rocks. And yet, it is so much more.

"This is the rock you traded with Emma. I can't take this."

"You have to. It's a present, so you can't give it back. Anyway, I really, really want you to have it. Just take good care of it."

"I will. I promise."

"Remember, it's celestine. Just in case anyone asks."

I smile. "Celestine. Got it." I hug my sister, suddenly wishing I could bring her along. Knowing I will always remember the name of this rock. "When I get back, we'll take a walk to Seven-Eleven and get a slushie, and I'll tell you all about the trip."

"Really?"

"Really.

Jules scoops up a geode, dull gray on the outside, sparkling blue and white crystals on the inside. "I heard you crying in your room the other day." She talks to the rock, without making eye contact. "Was it because of Kenji?"

"Yeah, kiddo." Not much point in trying to deny it. "It was."

"I hope you guys get back together on the mission trip."

"I don't know, Jules. I'm not counting on it."

"But there's a chance, right?"

"Umm...pretty small." My hand clenches around the Celestine. In my head, an echo bounces off the corners of my brain. Would I take the chance if it presented itself? Wouldn't that put us back where we were, with me afraid to tell him anything? Worried he'd find out or become part of something that could mess up his life?

"But you want to, right?"

"It's complicated."

"If you want to, then you will. You always find a way to get what you want."

I look behind me to see if she's talking to someone else. "Me?"

Julia laughs. "Yeah. Mom says you're like a bulldog when you want something. You always make it happen. Like soccer. She said you kind of stunk at it when you first started..."

"Gee, thanks, Mom."

"But then you practiced all the time in the backyard until you got great."

"I got okay at it, Jules. 'Great' is a stretch."

"You're in club soccer, Shi. That's pretty great. So if you can do that, you can figure out how to get back with Kenji. I know he loves you. It's in his eyes."

Clearly she's watched too many romantic movies, but it's sweet of her to say it. "We'll see. Right now, you better get some sleep. It's getting late." I kiss her head. "A bulldog, huh?"

"Totally."

I laugh. "*Ti voglio bene*, Jules." She doesn't know much Italian, but she knows *that*.

"I love you, too, Shi."

"Take good care of Mom while I'm gone. I think she'd *love* to look at the gems book you were going to show me the other day."

"Really? Cool. I'll show it to her tomorrow."

"*Ciao.*"

Back in my room, I set the alarm and groan, remembering it will go off while the world is still dark. Nothing to do now but sleep and awaken to whatever adventures await in Greenwood, Kentucky. I imagine giving the kids the food we're bringing, telling them Bible stories, fixing their school. Should be a pretty remarkable experience. It will be fun, too, with Brittany and Lauren along.

But what about Kenji? Ten-thousand watts of pain jolt my heart at the thought of him. Could Jules be right? Is there still a chance? The reasons we broke up are fading from my memory. Maybe all I had to do was talk to him, like Mel said. Tell him I had a lot of crazy things going on. Tell him about Misty and Tyler, without the healing part. If I can keep my friends and relatives without revealing the secret, why not Kenji? God never asked me to sacrifice him—that was all *me*. Is there still a chance for us? Now that the plastic beauty queen is in the picture, I'll have tough competition. But that's never stopped me before.

From somewhere deep inside, I hear the growl of a bulldog. And it makes me smile.

CHAPTER THIRTY-THREE

Shilo

A crescent moon still hangs in the morning sky as my Maple Creek church group boards a southbound bus. Suitcases and backpacks cram the luggage compartment. Parents hug and wave as thirty-one teens, a ten-year-old, and six adults prepare to head south. I slide in next to Lauren— not what I envisioned when Kenji talked me into this little journey. He was supposed to be at my side, holding my hand, making stupid jokes, and mapping out plans for the summer. Not three rows back, sitting with his buddies.

But he's here. And I'm here. And Miniskirt isn't.

"Hey, you want to play cards?" Lauren's hand disappears into her backpack, emerging with a new deck. "Figured it would help pass the time."

"Yeah, but hold on a sec. Gotta do something first." I fish out my cell and find the name that sends my heart into overdrive. My thumbs fly over the letters.

Hi. Can we talk?

Now to see if I've even got a prayer.

"Who's going to see your text at this ridiculous hour?" Lauren yawns. "All the normal people are sleeping."

"Kenji."

Lauren's half-closed eyes fly open. "Seriously?"

"Yeah." My hand holds my cell in a death grip as seconds drag by.

"Good. And don't worry. You always manage to get what you want."

Deja vu. Am I the only one who never knew that? The cell vibrates, and I nearly drop it. Lauren smiles and turns toward the window. "Go ahead. I won't spy. Long as you promise to tell me *everything*."

"Promise." I look down at his response. *Why?*

My fingers fly. *There are things that need to be said.* I'm not getting into this in text. No way. Without the persuasive power of eye contact, it's never going to work. My phone remains painfully silent as my heart prepares for a crash landing. I'm not sure which would be worse, a "no" or nothing at all. The screen flicks on with a simultaneous vibration.

Let's leave it alone for now…see how the week goes.

I sigh loud enough for Lauren to turn from the window with sympathetic eyes. I show her the text. "Not what I wanted, but could have been worse."

"He just needs to think about it, Shi. Considering everything you've put him through, I think that's fair."

Maybe. But I wasn't looking for "fair." Still, the socially correct thing to do would be to answer with an "Okay" or "I understand" and let it go, like he asked. I send my response, clearly oblivious to the socially acceptable way of handling things. *Five minutes. Then I'll drop it. Promise.*

Lauren sighs, and I glance up to see she's staring at my phone.

"Hey, what happened to giving me privacy?"

"Sorry. It was a battle, and curiosity won."

"Short battle."

"Don't expect anything, Shilo. Kenji sounds like he needs a break. Maybe he'll talk to you in a few days."

The cell vibrates in my hand. Kenji's text says he'll switch seats with Lauren after Pastor Frank's announcements. He ends it with *Five minutes.* I no sooner finish reading it than the bus rumbles forward, beginning what I hope will be more than a mission trip.

Lauren once again eavesdrops on my text conversation. "Unbelievable. That never would have worked for me." She begins shuffling the cards, then stops and drops them in her lap. "Hey, if Kenji's coming up here, where am I supposed to go?"

"With Nico. You and Kenji are switching seats."

"Um, I don't think so. I hardly know him. Plus he's cute, in a band, and I look like crap. You're out of your mind. Not happening."

Lauren's blush tells me it won't be that tough to get her cooperation.

"Hmmm. Interesting."

"What? Don't give me that look, Giannelli. There's nothing interesting."

"Come on. Just say yes. Please? The next five minutes could change everything. And who knows? This bus ride might be full of possibilities."

She sighs, narrowing her eyes at me. "Fine, but you owe me."

A comb, mascara, and lip gloss come flying out of Lauren's backpack as Pastor Frank stands to speak. He jokes about how quiet we are, saying it inspires him to schedule more predawn events. He introduces the leaders, including Angela, my favorite, and her little sister Rebecca, the youngest member of our troop. Blonde and blue-eyed, the ten-year-old looks like a mini version of her big sister. Pastor Frank says he'll go over the schedule later, "after everyone's brains gear up."

Soon enough, the world is a little brighter, the noise level in the bus increases, and suburban streets give way to green and gold fields of corn, beans, and wheat. Finally, my cell vibrates.

Ready?

I nudge Lauren, who sighs and stands. "You owe me," she says again. "Major."

Ready. If only that were true. I pushed for this little encounter, and now I have no clue what to say. But that doesn't stop Kenji from scooting next to me with his soapy fresh scent. And that shaggy hair. And a tight-lipped grimace replacing what used to be a killer smile. My heart and brain race simultaneously, knowing there's a lot to accomplish in the next five minutes. I hope for a miracle, that he'll take my hand and tell me nothing needs to be said. We're fine. Let's start fresh. Instead, there is only awkward silence as I strain to find words.

"So, I'm here," he says. "And before you say anything, I've got just one word to say to you."

"And that is…?"

"Indiana."

Not exactly the word I was expecting. Not that I had one in mind, but if I had to come up with fifty, Indiana would not have made the list. "Indiana?"

His dark eyes bore into mine. "Farnsworth, Indiana, to be more specific. Population twenty-two hundred. Location: a thousand miles from nowhere."

"And you're telling me this because…"

"Because that's where I've been exiled to for the summer, thanks to you. When we get back from Kentucky, my parents are shipping me off to Farnsworth until August fifteenth." His words are monotone. Coldly matter of fact. Far worse than if he were yelling at me. "I will spend practically the *entire* summer living on a farm with my aunt, uncle, and eight-year old cousin. All my summer plans are trashed – my lifeguard job, soccer camp, hanging out with my friends, everything.

"Because of the gang? Kenji, I'm sor…"

"Don't even say it, Shilo. It really doesn't matter. Just tell me what's so important that you had to say it now."

My hand, the one he can't see, clenches the bus seat. "I didn't rehearse anything. This is harder than I thought."

"Good. I'm really tired of mixed messages and cryptic answers. Tell me why you wanted me here. Don't stop to think."

"I messed up." The words pour out before I have time to ponder them. "Things were happening in my life. Kinda stressful. I should have talked to you, but I didn't. I was afraid, so I kept things secret and ruined everything between us."

"Afraid of what?"

"Losing you."

"Huh." He turns and gazes out the window. We drive past an awesome field of sunflowers that would have stolen my full attention if it weren't already zeroed in on Kenji. "And then you did."

"Yeah."

"Pretty stupid."

"Yeah."

He turns back toward me. "Your five minutes is almost up. Anything else?"

He's not going to make this easy for me. Guess I don't blame him. "Where do you stand on the issue of second chances?"

He laughs a little. Very little, but I'll take it.

"Interesting question. I'll have to think about it."

"Okay." My voice cracks, and I know he hears the emotion. It just blew in from nowhere halfway through the word. "Because I was kind of thinking of giving you one."

"Funny."

I stare at the seatback in front of me, until Kenji's fingers lift my chin. Our eyes meet, and my insides go limp.

"If we got back together, I'd have to know there'd by no more mysteries and secrets."

"Every girl needs a little mystery."

"I'm serious."

Little does he realize I am, too. And much as I want this to work, I won't make promises I can't keep. "If we got back together, I'd be more open and less secretive, but Kenji, everyone has their private stuff. It's just that I was keeping way too many things to myself. Pretty sure I could improve on that."

"Fair enough." His voice softens. "I liked the way you were in the beginning. What changed?"

I stop breathing while my mind races around the philosophical question of whether semi-honesty is simply a lesser form of honesty or a deception. Problem is, a long pause isn't appropriate now. At least, not if I want him back. Which I do. But answering with "I acquired a miraculous healing power" probably isn't appropriate either.

Kenji starts to get up. "You know what? Maybe this isn't such a good…"

"It started with the boy." Something had to come out fast. I was just about to lose him again before I even got him back. Now to figure out where to go from here.

He settles back in his seat. "The one the rumors were about? They said you healed him. Like a miracle or magic."

I shake my head, unsure of how to proceed, but knowing I can't risk another pause. I dive in with the story of meeting Misty and Tyler, praying for him, and the circumstances that led to Misty becoming a friend. Kenji takes the healing in stride, saying he believes in the power of prayer, but also thinks there might have been a mix up with the X-rays, or a fanatical nurse that exaggerated the story.

"On top of Misty's problems, I was dealing with Aunt Rita being so sick. That was hard, Kenji. So hard. Helping Misty, running back and forth to the hospital, trying to keep up with soccer and school. I was exhausted and stressed. Then she died." The painful memory thickens my throat.

"I could have helped with that, you know. Maybe not fixed anything, but we could have talked. Isn't that what couples do?"

"Stop being right. It's annoying."

His grimace morphs into the smile I've been longing to see. It gives me courage to ask the question that's been plaguing me since talking to Julia the Spy.

"What about Butt...I mean, your girlfriend?"

"My what?"

"The girl from your Language Arts class."

"Olivia? Not my type. Kinda plastic, know what I mean? I hang out with her brother, though, which is why I saw you take that graceful mud dive at the Redbirds' game."

So far, so good, but there's still the mystery flowers that are driving me crazy. "What about the roses? Peach."

"Roses? Oh, roses." Kenji laughs. Then he laughs some more. "You jealous?"

"Nope."

"Good, then you don't need to know peach roses are my mom's favorite, and I buy them every year for her birthday."

My whole body sighs, and for the moment, all is right with the world.

"Did you know the area we're going to has a forty-five percent poverty level?" Lauren settles back into the seat next to mine, her face glowing like she just found a fifty on the street.

"You come back after an hour with Nico, and that's what you've got to say?"

"Well…he's the one who told me. It's unbelievable. The people there are so incredibly poor. You just don't think about that kind of poverty here in our country."

"You're right. I hope we can do some good."

"And by the way, 'five minutes' ended about fifty-five minutes ago."

"Yeah, about that. Things turned out pretty good. Took a little while, but…"

"Your grin speaks volumes. And so did his."

Despite wanting to tell her every detail of our conversation, I hold back, knowing she wants to do the same. "So, how's Nico?"

Instead of answering, Lauren nods toward the front of the bus, where Pastor Frank is standing once again. This time he has to cup his hands around his mouth and shout "Listen up!" to get everyone's attention. He explains we'll be working side by side with kids from Bethel Baptist who attended plumbing workshops while we were learning carpentry.

"By ten each night its lights out, and I'm serious about this. You'll be rising at six-thirty, having breakfast at seven, and heading to our work site at eight."

After the groans die down, Pastor Frank covers a few more details and explains we'll be running Sunday School for the local children. As for the rest of the week, each adult leader will have a team of five. Kenji and I land on Angela's team. Divine intervention? I don't know, but whatever the reason, it makes me very, very happy.

"Angela's team has Rebecca," Pastor Frank added. "She may only be ten, but she's a whiz with a hammer. Remember to stick with your team for work, meals, and the rafting trip on Saturday."

Mention of the rafting trip immediately accelerates the noise level. Yes, we were there to accomplish good things, but who wouldn't get excited about whitewater rafting?

Pastor Frank holds up his hand and continues. "Alright, ladies and gentlemen, just one more thing, then I'll stop talking." He pauses to silence the low mumbling. "I am incredibly proud of you. You have chosen, of your own free will, to use ten days of summer vacation to serve those in need. The Bible says, 'let your light shine before men, that they may see your good deeds and praise your Father in heaven.' This is what it's all about – what you are doing right here, right now. Let your lights shine. God bless all of you."

Pastor Frank sits down, but his lingering words momentarily hush the group. Lauren and I stare out the window, watching two girls on horseback gallop in the distance. Up ahead, a herd of cows amble around a pasture. They munch grass, oblivious to the line of storm clouds off to the west. I hadn't noticed the darkening sky until now, and can't explain why it makes prickles creep along my neck. In books and movies, it's always the symbol of something bad on the horizon. But this is real life. Storms are just water falling from the sky. They nourish the earth, make things grow and give the air a fresh, clean, wonderful scent. Without the rain, we would die.

But none of that makes the prickles go away.

CHAPTER THIRTY-FOUR

Shilo

Those storm clouds never came our way. Not even a remnant. One puff now and then would have been a joy to behold. But no, that sun blasted from clear skies for seven days, giving us temps in the nineties and, as an added delight, enough humidity to cause a sweat fest as we hammered, sawed, and painted. Nope, not one single cloud.

Until tonight.

Gale force winds blast hail and rain against the church windows. A blinding flash of light produces a boom that makes Lauren's hands fly to her ears. "We're going to die here," she says.

I nod. "Probably."

She slinks down into her sleeping bag and disappears.

Even sheer exhaustion from a week of hard labor can't lull me to sleep. If this ruins tomorrow's rafting trip, there's going to be a lot of disappointed people. Me included.

I shift and turn for the millionth time, trying to get comfortable, but that's so not going to happen. Just two nights left, plus two days on the bus. And then...my bed. My lovely, wondrous, previously under appreciated bed.

Maybe mentally rehashing the week's events will help me drift off. I imagine trying to explain this trip to everyone at home, and having them stare at me like I'm crazy. It's been nothing short of amazing, but it won't sound that way. Long hot days followed by five-minute showers and dinner. Or what qualified as dinner. Then a little chill time before unrolling our sleeping bags. If I wasn't completely wiped out every night, I could have never fallen asleep on this rock-hard floor. I smile as I imagine Jules saying, "I don't think you quite grasp the definition of 'amazing.'"

But the people we helped, now they were something else. Those wide-eyed kids never stopped grinning as they gobbled the lunches we made for them. Their smiles stretched even broader when they got their take-home goody bags. Watching them jump and dance as they sang with us made my heart nearly explode. Their parents handed out cold water and a thousand thank-yous and bless-yous. So happy, despite their desperate need for health care and jobs. Despite their lack of computers and video games and cell phones.

Stuff.

Stuff that used to matter. That seems so meaningless now. Because what I loved most of all was the purity of their faith. The spiritual aura that permeated the church during Sunday's service. The way their hymns poured from the depths of their hearts and flowed up to Heaven. And in response, Heaven infused that church with a wave of love washing over the music and prayers, wrapping around us like angel wings.

And it was amazing.

Then there was Kenji. Conversations were stiff the first couple of days, like maybe he didn't trust me anymore. Until Wednesday, when we brought our dinners out to a shady bench in the courtyard. Just the two of us. I set my cookie on the bench and sipped the sweet iced tea that accompanied our nightly meals.

"Um, Shi?"

"Yeah?"

"Were you planning to eat that cookie, 'cause..." He pointed to my right, where a squirrel was racing away with the best part of my dinner.

"Come back here!" I rose, ready to give chase. "Give me that!"

Kenji grabbed my hand. "Now think about this. Do you *really* want it back?"

The squirrel stopped at the base of a tree, turned to face us, and started munching. Clearly an intentional move.

"Do you see the defiance in his face? He's mocking me." I faked an attempt to pull away, but he pulled me closer and stood.

"You're crazy, girl. You know that?" He kissed me then, long and sweet. And we became "us" again.

I would have happily given that squirrel my entire dinner.

The week replays over and over, until I realize the room is quiet, the booms are distant, and I am becoming one with my sleeping bag.

My eyes open to sunlight pouring through windows that somehow survived last night's onslaught. Minutes later, Angela walks in, followed by her shadow, Rebecca, to announce the trip is on. We dress and eat before heading out to a bus that looks suspiciously like its been repaired with duct tape. Its tires thwack thwack as they ramble along the muddy road, then out to a highway and back to the woods before stopping in a small gravel parking lot. A hand painted wooden sign, faded from years of baking in the southern sun, reads "Tanger River Rafting."

"Yes!" Kenji shouts from the seat behind me. "Finally!"

Sunlight glimmers on the river's surface, where inflated red rafts are tied securely to a pier. Faded orange life jackets are piled next to a small shack. Calm water promises a pleasant and scenic trip ahead. But exciting? I'm thinking "no." One glance at Kenji's disgusted expression tells me his thoughts mirror mine. Too bad. He's been obsessing about this rafting trip all week. All month, in fact. A grandma style ride wasn't on the radar.

A guy in faded jeans and a sleeveless t-shirt ambles out of the shack to greet us. He shakes hands with Pastor Frank and turns toward the rest of us. "Thank ya'll for coming to Tanger River Rafting. I'm Jay, and this here's a class three or five ride, dependin' on which fork you take. You church people will be takin' the south fork, that's the class three, since most of you don't have experience." Jay stops to jot something on his clipboard, then turns his attention back to us. "Another group will be comin' any minute now. Some of them will go with your group, while the experienced ones will take the class five route. River's runnin' rough today on account of the storms last night, so be careful and hang tight."

A large blue van approaches, its side painted with the words Kentucky River Rats over a background of whitewater rapids. Jay trots over to the driver shouting "Hey, Charlie! Where ya been the past two weeks?" They talk as Charlie and his people gather in front of the bus.

"Welcome back, River Rats. Your newbies can go with these church kids here on the class three," Jay yells.

Charlie talks to his rafters, then he and Jay divide everyone into groups. They place Angela and the rest of our team with two of the River Rat "newbies." Each raft holds eight, Jay explains, which includes a guide. He tells us about the "top quality" rafts with self-bailing floor systems and demonstrates the proper way to secure the life vests and helmets.

"These are *not* life jackets;, they are personal floatation devices. PFDs. They're not as buoyant as a life jacket and will not turn your face up if you fall out. They will, however, bring you to the surface so we can locate you and rescue you."

Kenji glances my way and rolls his eyes. Yes, Kenji, I know you just want to *go*. Finishing his rehearsed speech, Jay places his finger and thumb to his lips. A shrill whistle splits the quiet country morning, producing six guides from the shed. After introducing them, he assigns each group a guide and tells us to grab PFDs from the pile.

Chaos ensues. Our Maple Creek and Bethel Baptist groups mix in with the River Rats, grabbing the vests until the orange heap disappears. Angela tightens the straps on Rebecca's vest and helmet.

Rebecca immediately unhooks her helmet strap. "This thing's choking me."

"Too bad." Angela hooks it again. "You need it. That's the rules. Anyway, it could save your life."

Rebecca rolls her eyes, mumbling "I hate it."

I secure my jacket and turn to Angela. "Which Rats go with us?"

She surveys the mass of people, all wearing the helmets and PFDs, and shrugs. "No idea."

Kenji points to two guys heading our way. "Them?"

Judging from the mass confusion around us, it's clear we aren't the only ones who lost track of our rafting partners. Eventually groups form, with us getting the two guys Kenji had pointed to moments ago.

"I don't think these are the guys," I whisper to Kenji.

"It doesn't matter, Shi. If you say anything, it will take forever before we get all arranged again."

I let it go. He's probably right;, it isn't that important. We follow the River Rats over to a guide named Tom. I'm pretty sure our guy was Tim, but like Kenji, I just want to hit the water. Tom offers a few paddling tips before we cautiously step into the raft. One by one, the bright red inflatables float down the river.

Thick forest lines both sides of the river as we drift along watching hawks soar overhead. To my right, a doe and her fawn guardedly step out of the woods for a drink. Mama keeps a lookout as the little one sips, then lowers her head to the water after determining we pose no danger. In this moment, there is no ugliness in the world. No anger or greed or hate. Peace lives here. And yeah, it's not the wild ride I'd wanted, but as I breathe in pine-scented air, I feel like one with the earth. Angela smiles at me, both of us immersed in a joy too pure for words. We continue floating, paddling occasionally to avert boulders. Ten minutes into the trip, white streams of bubbles appear in the water. We move faster, heading toward a fork in the distance.

Tom hollers from the back of the raft. "Okay, Rats, we'll be followin' the left fork. I hear it's pretty crazy today in the rapids, so do *exactly* what I tell you. And whatever happens, *don't* fall out. Not today."

Angela's eyes widen. This time, the glance we exchange holds an entirely different meaning.

"Excuse me, Tom." Angela strains to overcome the increasing volume of the water. "There's five of us here from the church group. My sister is only ten. We've never done this before."

"Well, what the heck!" Tom shakes his head. "This

ain't right. How did you folks get on here?"

Panic knits Angela's brow. "I don't know, but I think we better get off!"

Flashes of sun tap-dance wildly on the whooshing water, which grows louder as we close in on the fork. I wedge my feet in tighter, like they showed us. One under the seat in front of me, the other in the crease between my seat and the raft's side.

"We can't get off." Tom strains to make his voice reach Angela. "This ain't no bus, ma'am. We're in for the ride now." A boulder looms up ahead. "Forward four!" We all plunge our paddles into the water and give it all we've got.

"Back two! Back two!" Tom shouts over the increasing volume of the water. "Forward two! Forward two more!"

We follow orders and veer away just in time.

"Hold on tight, ladies and gents. She's runnin' rough."

"Rebecca!" Angela yells across the raft. "Your feet wedged in tight?"

"I'm fine. This is fun." Rebecca's grin covers half her face.

We enter the north fork, splitting from the rest of our group. The peaceful river has morphed from kitten to wildcat. It bubbles and churns, rushing around boulders and drowning out words. Kenji turns and shoots me a glance, his smile as wide as Rebecca's. I share his excitement...but something dark hovers beneath the surface. Something like fear.

Angela's elbow nudges mine to get my attention. "I'm worried about my sister."

The words "me, too" are about to slip off my tongue, until it hits me that's not what she needs to hear. "She'll be fine." I have to shout, even though she's inches away from me. "These guys are experts. They take people on this river all the time."

She nods, but is clearly unconvinced.

We race, splash, and bump along in a whirlwind of water. Laughs and shrieks erupt constantly as the cold river sprays us and the wind whips our faces. Rebecca's smile widens to Grand Canyon proportions. No doubt the same is true for Kenji, who's getting soaked in his front row seat. I force away my fear, loving the craziness. What a story to tell when I get home! This is just what I needed after the stress and sadness of the past two months. I let go of it all, happy to live in this wet and wild moment.

Tom screams something that gets swallowed by the river's roar. He tries again. "Forward four! Back one!" He points toward the right side of the river. Like the rest of the passengers, my eyes follow his motions to a huge cluster of boulders jutting from the river. Suddenly we are the Titanic. Collision isn't just a possibility;, it is inevitable. But in that moment, something scares me more than the boulders.

Rebecca's helmet strap dangles next to her chin. Unhooked. Useless.

My shouts to her disappear amidst the screams of terror and rushing water. Tom continues to yell orders, his expertise no match for the angry river. We veer slightly. It is not enough. I suck in a breath;, my stomach crunches. Silent pleas fly up to Heaven.

Impact! Bodies fly out and crash into whirling water. A wave swallows Rebecca. Her helmet sails downstream like a miniature boat. It is the last thing I see before the rapids swallow me, too.

Water. Everywhere. Above and below, though I can't tell which way is up. My body twists and turns chaotically at the river's command. Every direction is a green blur. I have to get up. Get air. Get Rebecca. Fight the panic screaming in my head, telling me I'll never breathe again. Rebecca's going to die. It's over.

But the life vest accomplishes its mission. My face breaks the surface for one joyous gulp of warm air before I'm slapped by another icy wave. When I can finally whip around to search for her, I see our raft heading downstream, void of life. Our guide must have hit the river, too. The rescue guides scramble to pull people and paddles from the water, shouting instructions that blend into nothing but noise. Straight ahead, a trio of rocks lay directly in my path. But it's something else that makes my blood run colder than the river - Rebecca thrashing crazily in front of me, pulled toward the same set of killer boulders.

And no way to reach her in time.

She hits head first. I suck in air and kick with all I've got. Each glance ahead shows Rebecca's motionless body riding the current. I'm closing in, then smack! Pain shoots through my arm as I hit the first one. No time to check for damage. This is a race against death.

"Shilo!"

I turn toward the voice and see Angela struggling to fight a different current pulling her further away from her little sister. Her efforts are futile.

"Get Rebecca!" she screams. "Save my sister!"

Trying is not an option. I have to reach that girl.

Movement catches my eye. Kenji battles the rapids, heading for a huge branch that must have broken off during the storm. Cracked and jagged, it juts out of the water like a spear. He raises his arm to protect his face from the deadly point. Struggling to reach Rebecca prevents me from seeing what happens next. I hear a yell, but there's no time to stop and check it out.

My lungs plead for air, but every time I open my mouth, I am deluged by the angry river. It is forever before I can maneuver behind Rebecca's head, keeping her face above water as I force my legs to kick through the current. Kenji closes the distance between us and grabs her feet, kicking forward while I swim backward toward shore. We give all we've got to our mission until we reach calmer water. When I feel like one more kick will kill me, the riverbed rises to meet my feet. Kenji sees me stand and does the same. Heaving, we continue to hold Rebecca. But when I look down at her, my ragged breath catches in my throat.

We are standing in a cloud of crimson water.

Blood gushes from Rebecca's head while b. Blood spurts like a macabre fountain from Kenji's wrist. It runs down my arm where I hit the rock, but my wound is by far the least significant. As we gently lift Rebecca onto the riverbank, distant shouts reach me from the opposite shore. An overfilled raft sails past, it's occupants staring at our horrific scene. They gesture wildly, and I faintly hear "stay there!" and "ambulance" over the river's roar. But we are in a place with no roads, where dense mountain forest veils the land beyond the river's edge. Paramedics will never make it here in time.

But I am here.

There's no time to ponder the consequences. If my secret gets out…so be it. Images of Yahoo headlines and paparazzi rise like invisible walls between me and whatever happens next, but one glance at my bloodied friends crumbles those walls to rubble. Cold, aching, and exhausted, I ready myself to become a vessel for a miracle. But it's not up to me, and that's the hardest part. The One who created everything from amoebas to great blue whales knows what's best. When to heal…and when not. I shudder, praying it will not be the latter today. Terrified and hopeful of what the next few minutes will bring.

I peel off the soaked t-shirt covering my swimsuit and place it on the sand, careful to leave one sleeve extended. Using his good arm, Kenji lays Rebecca's head on it with shaky hands. He kneels next to her, his dull eyes peering at me from a pasty face. His wrist spurting like a bloody Old Faithful.

"Quick, give me your arm." I grab it before he can respond. His blood flows over my hand, and I force back the bile rising in my throat. He says nothing as I tie the outstretched sleeve around his wound.

"I don't." He sways, but continue to kneel. "I don't feel so good."

Oh, God. Please.

"Kenji, listen to me. Do as I say. Don't ask questions. Got it?"

He nods. Sways again. He's fading fast, and Rebecca looks even worse.

"Above all, don't tell anyone, ever, what you are about to see." I take a breath and place his hand in Rebecca's. It worked with Misty. She felt the warmth when I prayed for Tyler. I have to give it a shot. "Hold her hand. Do not speak, and do not let go." I wish I had more time to make him understand the desperate need for secrecy. I kneel on the opposite side of Rebecca, my back to the river.

And lay my hands on her wounded head.

Sticky blood warms my cold fingers. I close my eyes and picture Rebecca. Pretty little Rebecca, vibrant, feisty, full of life and love. Rebecca dancing in the sunlight with the Appalachian children. Singing as she hammered nails and painted shutters. Screaming as she fell into the cold, churning river.

Warmth.

The miracle begins.

Thank you, Lord.

It emanates from my heart, filling me with a power both strong and gentle. Heat waves radiate through my body, outward toward my arms. The world fades away. No roar from the river rapids. No more panic or chattering teeth. Silence and tranquility descend upon me like a soft morning fog, blue and hazy and magnificent.

Please, God, help Rebecca and Kenji. Use Your awesome power to heal them.

The mystical warmth slips into my shoulders and flows down, down, past my elbows, into my wrists. My hands. Muddled images grow clear. The gash is deep. Her skull, cracked by the impact with the boulder, presses against her swelling brain, catapulting Rebecca toward permanent damage. Or death.

Warmth flows from palm to fingers, intensifying in my fingertips, heating more and more until it bursts forth into Rebecca. Invisible rays radiate from me and permeate her injured head. Unseen wounds begin to heal. Blood ceases to flow. Her swollen brain fills with peace and returns to its healthy, normal state.

All things are possible with You, Lord. Thank You for grace. For love. For healing Rebecca. Please, God, I pray with all my heart, heal Kenji, too.

Serenity embraces me, lifting me up on soft summer breezes, away from the river, into the clouds. Golden rays light my way. In this holy place, lions and lambs rest at my side. Flowers in colors I've never seen bloom all around me. And there in the hazy blue tranquility, I am enveloped in an everlasting, unconditional love. My spirit soars. It is beyond comprehension. But I don't need to understand. It is there. And that is enough.

If only I could stay forever.

CHAPTER THIRTY-FIVE

Shilo

Shrill sirens jar me from the depths of a sweet, delicious sleep. A strong, loving hand clasps mine as I regain consciousness. Assaulted by the sounds and sunlight, my eyes strain to open, finally managing a squint. Kenji appears in my slit of vision—gritty, windblown, and blood-smeared. He looks a mess, but the most wonderful mess I've ever seen. Kenji is alive. The joy of it dances inside me, and I send up thanks to the One who made it possible.

"Shilo." The word escapes his lips like a lullaby. Kenji lets go of my hand and brushes sand from my arm. "You have to wake up now. They're here."

His eyes are vibrant again. Only a faint red line marks the place where blood flowed a short while ago. Just like Tyler's cheek in the hospital. I squeeze his hand. "You okay?"

"Yeah. Really confused, but fine."

The ambulance must have parked in a clearing a

short distance away. Doors open and slam. Leaves and sticks crackle as paramedics rush through the woods. Even with my foggy brain, I realize the potential for disaster.

"Don't tell." I whisper. "Please, Kenji, for me. Don't lie, but don't tell."

Rebecca leans over me, wet hair dripping on my cheek. "Don't tell what?"

"It's nothing." So tired. Just want to sleep here on this riverbank. But the rescuers are getting closer. "You okay?"

"Uh huh." She smiles at me. "You?"

I smile back, knowing this moment could have been grief beyond measure. "I am now. Just tired."

Another drop hits my cheek and slides down.

"Why is your hair dripping?"

She tilts her head and squeezes water from a handful of hair. "I must have scraped my head a little. It was all sticky and bloody, so I rinsed it out."

Another miracle: she doesn't know. I breathe deep, close my eyes, and soak in the joy of this moment. But my peace is short-lived. Rescuers race up to us with stretchers and medical bags. A burly man kneels down, the space between his eyebrows creased in a V-shape. His name badge reads G. Wilson.

"Okay, ya'll. Help is here now. We're gonna take care of ya." His casual air of authority tells me he's in charge. "Who's hurt the worst?"

"She is." Kenji points to Rebecca, who sits up and smiles prettily at the paramedic. "Well, she *was*."

"I'm not so bad," she says. "My head hurts a little, but I think I'll be okay."

G. Wilson tells the other paramedics to check Kenji and Rebecca before turning to me. "How about you, young lady?"

"Tired." I yawn, completely lacking the strength to

say anything more.

"Let's take a look at your arm."

I turn my head and discover the t-shirt tied around my gash. Kenji must have done it while I was sleeping. G. Wilson unties it and opens his bag. "This is going to sting a bit." He wipes the blood and dirt away with antiseptic. He wasn't kidding. It stings. A lot.

"Sorry about that. I'm gonna wrap this and get you over to the ER for stitches. Not to worry; it's not serious. Five or six should do it." He reaches back in, pulls out a sterile packet of gauze, and begins winding. "Now tell me somethin'. If you're the only one injured, why is your friend's arm all bloody?"

His question catches me off guard. I mentally thank Rebecca for rinsing out her hair. If he'd seen all that blood, he'd really dish out the questions.

"It could have gotten on me when we were helping each other out of the water." Kenji winks at me, knowing I'll pick up on his carefully chosen words. Not a lie. It could have. Wilson doesn't have to know it didn't. He secures the gauze with medical tape and helps me up. Oh, what I'd give to lie down and sleep out here till tomorrow morning. I sigh, forcing myself to mask the after affects of the healing. It's going to take an Emmy award-winning performance.

"Is this everyone?" Wilson asks.

My pulse quickens, remembering Angela heading downstream. "Another girl fell out, but she headed off that way." I point in the direction she was floating. "We have to find her. We have to ..."

"Don't you worry, Miss." G. Wilson cuts me off. "The rafting guides got everyone but ya'll. Some are a little banged up, but all things considered, they could have fared worse." He grabs his radio and calls in an update, saying he's bringing all of us to the ER to get checked out. "Your pastor's gonna meet us there."

Fresh white gauze covers four Frankenstein stitches on my arm. They really need to make these things more attractive. And waterproof. Trying to shower while keeping one arm dry was a challenge I could have happily lived without. After all the dust settled, Kenji texted me to meet him in the courtyard.

He stands before me, those mahogany eyes locked on mine. There is no playfulness in those eyes tonight. No mischief. Just an intensity that reduces my insides to slush.

"Come on." We walk without speaking, following a dirt path into the woods until trees and more trees are the only things in sight. I breathe in the primal scent of the earth, letting it fill my senses. Damp leaves, wildflowers, pine needles. It doesn't matter that a million questions are coming my way, or how long he takes to speak. I could walk this forest with him until the end of time. A glimmer catches my eye, and I scoot down to pick up a green rock. Possibly some kind of crystal. The details are lost in the darkening woods, but there's no denying the prettiness. It seems interesting enough for Jules, so I pocket it, and we continue walking.

Kenji stops at a fallen tree, and we sit, fingers entwined, listening to the melodic pitches of a cardinal and the rustle of leaves in the breeze. "We almost lost each other." He caresses my cheek with his free hand. "For real."

This is a Kenji I've never seen. Cautious. Guarded. Almost afraid to let go. But with all that's happened today, I hadn't stopped to consider what he'd been through. The life flowed out of him on that riverbank until he was facing death head on. Close enough to touch it. I've never been in that tenuous place, hovering between this world and the next, but it's got to have a powerful impact on a person's perspective.

"I know." Enveloped by the twilight, we hold onto each other as the sun descends beyond trees and hills. The country sky deepens to royal blue. One by one, stars sparkle around a waning moon, as unseen woodland creatures rustle through the underbrush. And still we hold on.

Until he pulls away, and I see a look in his eyes I've never seen before. The questions are coming, but I'm not ready. Not now. Why can't we just have this moment?

"I don't know what happened today, Shi. We need to talk about it."

Words elude me, so I nod. It may be time to keep that promise about no more games or secrets. But this...this wasn't part of the plan.

"Not tonight, though." His words come to me like an unexpected gift. "Tonight I brought you here to say one thing."

I dare not hope. It might be a thanks for saving his life. Or even a "let's be friends." Oh please, anything but that.

He stares at the pine covered forest floor until I think my heart will burst, then finally meets my eyes again. "I love you."

Instead of bursting, my heart catches in my throat, but it is no match for the words that long to break free. "I love you, too, Kenji. I have for a long time." I thought it would be so awkward, but in this blissful moment, it's just free and easy and right.

The darkness can't cloak his smile – a smile that draws closer until I feel his warm breath on my skin. The sensation unravels me. Let us never be farther apart than this. My hand reaches up toward shaggy hair, my fingers curling around it then releasing to settle on the back of his neck. Lips touch. Soft and tentative gives way to bold and hungry, both of us feasting after weeks of starvation. His arms wrap me in a bear hold I could not escaped if I wanted to.

And I most definitely do not.

The primordial forest and everything that lies beyond it disappears. For all I care, the sun can set and rise a thousand times, and I will be content to stand in these woods forever, lost in Kenji's kisses. Feeling our hearts entwine. Knowing he is mine, and I am his. In this moment, it is all that matters, and I cannot imagine any moment when that wouldn't be true.

But in the distance, twigs snap, breaking the silence and stealing the passion from our midnight rendezvous. We pull apart, still holding tight to each other. Padded footsteps draw closer.

"Shilo! Kenji!" Pastor Frank's voice bellows through the trees. "Where are you? Shiloooo! Kenjiii!"

"Shilo! Kenji!" Another voice. Probably belongs to one of the leaders. We turn toward the sound, where beams of light sweep the trees. The search party closes in.

"We better answer." I whisper the words, desperately wishing I didn't have to say them. "Pretty sure we're in trouble."

"Probably." Kenji squeezes my hand. "But at least we're in trouble together, right?" He turns toward the lights. "We're here, pastor!"

Seconds later, Pastor Frank appears, closely followed by Angela and another leader.

"What's going on here?" Not a yell, exactly, but loud enough to convey his anger. It's a rare thing to hear Pastor Frank's words heated to the point of boiling, and not a pretty one. I open my mouth to respond, but Kenji steps forward.

"It's not what you think. A lot happened today. We just wanted some time to talk about it. Sorry if we worried you."

"Yeah, really sorry." I echo his words. Not much else to say.

Pastor Frank shakes his head. My hopes for a smile to emerge vanish as his lips form a grimace, an expression never before seen on the man. At least, not by me. And I hate that I put it there.

"What were you thinking? After the chaos and worry of this afternoon, you had to pull this little stunt? You both know the rule about walking into the woods at night. I should make the two of you walk back to Cedarcrest!"

Only the trees respond, softly rustling their leaves in the language of the earth. I hope that was the end of it, that we can toss out another apology and head back. Slipping inside my sleeping bag seems mighty appealing right now. Closing my eyes, remembering those kisses, replaying his "I love you" over and over again until I fall asleep and dream of Kenji holding me under the night sky.

Pastor's eyes zero in on me. "Your mother called, Shilo. She already heard about the river disaster from Lauren's mom, who heard about it from Angela's father."

I cringe, knowing Annieconda must have freaked. Julia probably tried to comfort her with statistics on rafting accidents, which would've made her freak even more.

"Bad news zips through the church grapevine at an amazing pace," he continues. "If God's word spread half that fast, I'd be out of a job. Imagine my embarrassment when she asked for you, and I couldn't find you. Where's your cell?"

"Dead. Charging. I'm really sorry, Pastor. Seriously." I try to think of more words to emphasize the sincerity of my apology, but a "really" and a "seriously" are all I've got. My eyes stay focused on the darkness around my feet.

"Yes, so you've said. And I accept your apology, but I'm disappointed in both of you. Just didn't expect this."

Ouch. This is a man I respect, admire, and trust. A man I most definitely do not want to disappoint. "It won't happen again." I look up, hoping my eyes convey the sincerity of my words.

"I trust it won't. We're leaving day after tomorrow. See that no more rules get broken between now and then. Are we clear?"

"Yes sir." We answer in unison.

He reaches in his pocket and hands me his cell. "Call your mother. And be extra nice. She's worried sick."

We head down the path, flashlights lighting the way, as I assure Mom I'm fine. Since she doesn't know Kenji and Rebecca were three-quarters dead, she doesn't ask about me using The Gift, and I sure don't bring it up. By the time our conversation ends, the stress has slipped out of her voice.

Kenji holds my hand as we follow Pastor Frank and the leaders. Despite the trauma of this afternoon, and the embarrassment of the past few minutes, I walk with lighter steps and a happier heart than I've had in weeks. Me and Kenji. I can breathe again. My heart can beat again. No need to worry about what might happen if he discovers the truth about me. For now, our love is enough. He gives my hand a squeeze.

"I'm sure going to miss you this summer," he whispers. "I can't believe we'll be a million miles apart."

I don't want to think about him going to Indiana. I'll go insane. "We have to figure out something. We can't just…" And then it hits me, the plan of the century. "Wait! In three weeks I've got soccer camp at Notre Dame." Indiana's a long state, but maybe, just maybe, this will go the way I'm hoping. "Is South Bend near

Farnsworth? Can you visit me at the campus?"

Kenji cocks his head and stares at me like I sprouted a third eye. "Did you forget? You're leaving way before then. You'll be splashing around in the Mediterranean while I'm sitting on fences, staring at cows."

My feet freeze. We fall back from the search party. Has he lost his mind? "What are you talking about?"

"You leave next week."

We stare at each other through the darkness. I can't breathe. Can't respond. Something's wrong. He must be confused, and yet, conviction weights his words. The question hovers on my lips, but fear blocks it from emerging. If I don't ask, and he doesn't answer, maybe this will all fade away and I'll be happy again.

"Blue...you knew right? Tell me you knew."

Still can't find my voice.

"Oh, man." Kenji speaks slowly, realizing his mistake. "You didn't know about Sicily?"

Why couldn't we just stay in that perfect moment, where everything felt right? Why did it have to crash and burn before I'd hardly had a chance to savor it? No soccer camp. No summer job at Frosty Freeze. No Kenji. Instead, they are sending me to Sicily.

They are sending me to Nonna Marie.

No. I shake my head, and mentally repeat the word again. No. They *think* they are sending me to Nonna Marie.

CHAPTER THIRTY-SIX

Shilo

Pink wisps of dawn streak the sky as our group piles sleeping bags and suitcases into the bus. Only eight days have passed since this same bus pulled out of the church parking lot. Eight days, and a lifetime of drama and emotion. The shock of Kenji's news still ricochets around my sleep-deprived brain. As we continued walking toward the church last night, he kept apologizing for breaking the news. He had talked to his Mom earlier in the day after she'd heard about the accident, called my parents, then called Pastor Frank.

"Your dad told her you'd be in Sicily while I was at my uncle's farm. Said it was the safest way to deal with the Warriors."

If all he wanted was my safety, he could have sent me to my cousins in New Mexico or California, but I didn't say so. No point, when the strategy was clear. Keep me safe and get me trained in the ways of a healer.

"Earth to Shilo."

I mean, I get it. Only Nonna Marie can understand my unique circumstances and answer my questions. Only Nonna Marie can teach me, from experience, the right and wrong way to handle The Gift. But Sicily? It's too far. Too foreign. Too much for me to comprehend, though I tried all night.

"Hey," Kenji nudges me. "You still with me?"

"Yeah, sorry."

"Good, because when we get settled on the bus, I really want to talk about yesterday. The accident." His eyes look beyond me, like he's journeying back to the bloody scene. He shakes his head. "Everything that happened."

Oh, God. My fuzzy brain can hardly wrap around Sicily, much less engage in a conversation that requires clarity and carefully-worded answers. Everything in me wants to run into the woods and disappear. Maybe fall asleep under a tree until summer is over. My perfect summer. How did it veer so far off course? And I don't even have time to process that because Kenji wants to know "everything," which is way more than I can tell him. How on Earth do I dance around the issue of a spiritual power when he was smack in the middle of it? The sun has barely risen, and my brain is already on overdrive.

This is going to be one very long bus ride.

Once we get seated, Pastor Frank announces next year's trip will be to El Salvador, where much of the water is contaminated. "Think wells, you guys. Deep wells. That's what we'll be working on. It won't be easy, but it'll be great." He goes on to say some nice things about how much we helped the residents of Greenwood, then prays for God's protection as we head home. It's the first time I've ever wanted him to keep talking, but he sits right after the "amen." Naturally.

Kenji's face tells me he's going to dive right in. It's a

wonder he's waited this long. And how can I blame him? Unlike Rebecca, he was fully conscious when blood was gushing from his wrist. He probably remembers feeling like he was about to pass out. The only thing I don't know for sure is if he felt the warmth and consciously experienced the miracle. He was a heartbeat from death. Maybe that clouded his memory.

He turns to me with a thousand questions burning in his eyes. "So."

And here we go.

"I've been over it a million times. Me and Rebecca, we were in bad shape, as in fatally bad." He talks low, but everyone is half asleep and not paying attention to us. "It was all I could do to follow your instructions. And then you went into this trance or something. Your hands moved real slow. This is gonna sound weird, but warmth was flowing from Rebecca's hand into mine. Up my arms and through my whole body. *Warmth*, Blue." His lips get closer to my ear as his voice gets even softer. "Flowing through my veins, toward my heart. It was like…well, it wasn't like anything else in this world. It was incredible. What *was* that?"

I'm on my own, here. No Mom to jump in with an answer or cleverly redirect the conversation. Just me and Kenji, who's always listened to me better than any of my friends. Who cares enough to insist we're honest with each other. Who stood at the edge of death and experienced a miraculous, intense, life-changing experience with me that few others could even imagine. And suddenly I want, *need*, to tell him everything, because it feels right. So very right.

I take a deep breath. "It started with the boy."

"That's the same thing you said on the way up."

"Yeah, but this time I'm going to fill in the blanks, so hold on tight."

I begin with the dog, then Tyler in the hospital and

the late-night talk with my parents when I learned about The Gift. From there I tell him about Nonna Marie, Aunt Rita, Pat Nicholls, and Misty. And through it all, the dreaded risk weaves its way through every word. If he were to ever share my secret, life as I know it would be rocked to its core. Possibly forever. Worse, I risk losing *him*, because this whole thing is probably too weird to believe. But my story flows like that wild river, rushing and bubbling over fears, doubts, and the indescribable joy of pulling someone from the clutches of death.

I try to describe the elation I feel during a healing, how it lifts my soul to places beyond this world, but the words are paper effigies compared to the real thing. Kenji listens. Occasionally, there's a shake of his head, a comment, but mostly he listens. I finish talking, and we sit in silence for the longest minute of my life. And still he says nothing; just turns his head to stare out the window. Unlike me, who sits frozen, so afraid that a breath, a blink, will break whatever spell is keeping him silent. And terrified of what might happen when the silence ends.

"You're a faith healer."

The quiet statement leaves me wondering how to respond. I nod.

"I didn't think they really existed. At least, not in modern times."

"I didn't either."

"You're nothing like those people on TV."

Not this again. "No. They just con people for money. This is real, Kenji. I don't know how else to say it. It's real. Please don't think I'm crazy."

He turns away from the window, dark eyes peering into mine. Is he looking for The Gift inside the girl? "I might have, if you'd told me before. But I've *seen* it, Blue. Felt it. The warmth … it was supernatural. Spiritual. I don't know how else to say it." He takes my hand, entwining his fingers in mine. "I felt it pouring into my wrist, my heart…my soul. The bleeding stopped, and when I looked at the gash, it was a faded red line. Then I looked at you, Shi. Your eyes were clear blue gems. Your face, white as winter. You looked like an angel."

I inhale deeply, pretty certain I haven't taken a breath since I bared my secret. He believes me. He gets it. My frozen self begins to melt.

"And then you passed out." Kenji squeezes my hand, gently rubbing it with his thumb. "That was the scariest part of all. Worse than all the blood. I didn't even know if you were alive until I checked your pulse, which I kept doing every five minutes until you woke up."

The sweetness of that gesture forms a lump in my throat. He thought I was going to die. That particular terror is not lost on me. I thought the same thing of him when there was more of his blood on the ground than in his body. "It's weird hearing about it from someone else. I know about the warmth, of course, but the rest is kind of a blur to me."

"So that's why they're sending you to Sicily, to be with the mysterious Nonna Marie."

"Yeah."

His face lights up. "It's kinda like when Luke Sky-walker had to go to that Dega Ba planet to train with Yoda. I mean, he *had* his Jedi powers; he just needed to learn how to control them and use them the right way."

He's dead serious. Not even a hint of a smile on his face. If there's such a thing as a Jedi death glare, I'm do-ing it now. "Yeah Kenj, it's *exactly* like that."

"What? What did I say?"

So not worth a response.

Greens and golds of Illinois' farmland line both sides of the two-lane highway as we near home. Up ahead in the aisle, Kenji hovers over Nico and Lauren, who laugh at whatever he just said. He turns and smiles at me, a gesture that will dissolve my heart til the day I die. How I hope we are together even then.

As we close in on Cedarcrest, the bus's volume rises with the shuffling of backpacks, snack bags, and promises to call newly made friends. We head up the church's driveway, and three familiar faces stand out in the crowd of waiting families. I have so much to tell them, especially the part about Kenji knowing my secret, but anger over the Sicily trip will likely preclude that conversation.

As the bus doors open, Kenji grabs my hand, and we inch our way down the jam-packed aisle, parting ways with a kiss before heading to our families. In less than a heartbeat, Annieconda is squeezing the life out of me. I stand with arms at my sides, refusing to return the affection.

"Mom!" Julia tugs at her arm. "Let go. You're killing her."

Mom loosens her death-grip and holds me at arm's length. "Look at you, so tan. Your eyes look tired. And I see you and Kenji are back together." She finally stops talking long enough to contemplate my glare. "What's wrong?"

"Sicily." The word widens her eyes. Dad's and Julia's as well. Clearly they were not expecting me to find out until I came home. "I'm not going. I start my job tomorrow, and I'm definitely not missing soccer camp."

"How did you find out?"

"Kenji told me. He thought I knew. Funny, his parents told him, yet my parents somehow neglected to mention it to *me*. How do you not tell me you're sending me to a foreign country? How do you make a decision like that—about *me*— without including me?"

Dad wraps his arm around my shoulder. "You weren't here, and we had to figure out something. Simple as that. Pastor Frank didn't want the parents calling you guys unless it was a dire emergency. And yes, Sicily is a bit drastic, but I think you know why we chose that location."

"It's so you can meet Nonna Marie." Julia lowers her voice to an exaggerated whisper. "It's so you can learn more about you-know-what."

"Yeah, I get it. But I'm not going."

"You're going, Shilo." Dad drops his arm from my shoulder and turns so we're face to face. "It's all arranged and paid for, and it's necessary for multiple reasons. We'll finish this discussion at home, not here surrounded by people."

We squeeze between reunited families to find my suitcase in the pile next to the bus, then head home in silence. The sight of our house takes the edge off my anger. Even though the trip was great—hard work, heat, accident and all—I'm glad to be home. Now all I have to do is find a way to stay here for the rest of the summer.

As Dad opens the front door, the unmistakable scent of baked peaches and cinnamon envelopes me. In the kitchen, a pie is cooling on the counter. In a glass bowl, shrimp marinates in a bath of olive oil, lemon, and crushed garlic. Mom made my favorites to welcome me back, a gesture that washes away some of my anger. But only some.

"Smells good." It doesn't completely close the gap between us, but at least it's an acknowledgement of the love that went into her efforts.

"Thanks. How was the food?"

"Fine."

"Quite an eye opener, wasn't it?" Mom tears lettuce leaves over the salad bowl. "Those people live a challenging life." She's not fooling me with her strategy to small-talk me out of my anger before we move on to the real issue. But the combination of my ten-day absence and knowing she made all this food softens my heart.

"No kidding." She can have this win. I'm still not going to Sicily. "One little girl was excited because her brother bagged a squirrel for dinner."

Julia scrunched up her face. "Ewww. Disgusting!"

"Not really, Rockhound." I tug on her ponytail, even though she pretends to hate it. "Not when you're starving."

Her face unscrunches as she contemplates my words. "Oh. Oh, gosh. You think you'll eat that kind of stuff at the convent? Or just bread and water?"

I want to tell her it doesn't matter because I'm not going, but decide to hang on to our moment of peace a little longer. "Pretty sure the nuns don't live on bread and water, Jules." Since I don't want to continue with anything about Sicily, I quickly come up with a redirect. "Which reminds me, wasn't there something in the news about finding water on Mars?"

"Yeah! Researchers found clues there might be saltwater flows. There's no conclusive evidence yet, but wouldn't be exciting?"

Project Manipulate Julia works again. If only it were that easy with the other two members of my family.

After a dinner that probably added forty pounds to my body, I stand at Julia's door and face a new poster: Rocks and Minerals of the World. I knock on amethyst. "Open up;, I've got something for you."

She swings open the door and gazes at the closed hand I'm holding in front of her.

"Is it rocks? From Kentucky?"

"Just one, but it's pretty good, I think. Hope you like it." My fingers unclench to reveal a small chunk of green crystal. Julia gasps.

"You okay, Rockhound?"

Eyes wide, mouth open, she looks like she's a breath away from fainting.

"What?" I look at the rock, then back at her. "Is this toxic or something?"

"Oh my gosh, oh my gosh!"

"Deep breaths, Jules."

"Do you know what that is?" She carefully transfers the crystal to her open palm. "I think its pyromorphite!"

I refrain from rolling my eyes, even though I can't believe this little rock caused all that drama. "Just what I was thinking. Pyromorphite."

My sister grins. "Really? You thought it was….oh." The smile disappears faster than a magician's rabbit. "You're making fun of me."

"No, I'm not. I'm just trying to be funny. In fact, if anything, I'm making fun of myself."

"I don't get it." She sets her translucent green treasure down on the nightstand.

For someone who's such a brain, she can sure be dense when it comes to humor. "I saw that and thought it was special. Right away I thought of you."

"Honest?"

"Yes. But the word pyro-whatever would never even come to mind because I don't have your brains. You have something very cool. I don't know how you do it. Wish I did."

"You're not just teasing? You don't wish I was different? You know, normal?"

"No way. If you weren't different, you wouldn't be you. Anyway, let's face it;, normal doesn't seem to run in our family."

The smile returns, and she picks up the pyromorphite. "Thanks, Shi. And thanks for this. It's a rare lead phosphate. Did you know pyromorphite is very similar to apetite?"

And here we go. "No. It's still taking everything I've got to remember the rock you gave me is Celestine. If I try to add another one, my head will explode."

This time she laughs.

A few hours later, Julia is sound asleep, and I pull out the box of orange spice tea.

Mom pours a cup of decaf as I microwave my water. "Aren't you tired?"

More than she could possibly know. My body is limp, aching to sleep til Tuesday, and my brain is fried from lack of sleep and more thoughts than it can hold. Which is precisely why I need to let some of those thoughts escape into a conversation. Better than having them ramble around in my head all night. "No, I feel like talking, but not about Sicily. Not tonight. Things happened on the trip. Maybe Dad should hear this, too."

"Already in bed. Got a crack-o-dawn sergeants' meeting, so it's just me and you."

I cup my hands around the hot mug and quickly run through the Shilo-Kenji reunited saga, then move on to the rafting trip. All the gory details are included, the crimson water, blood gushing from Rebecca, from Kenji. Watching the life drain from both of them, and knowing only a miracle could save them. Mom's face turns the color of her snowball cookies. Whether it's from the horror of what could have been, or fear over revealing my secret…I do not know.

"Shilo, what did you do?"

"What I had to."

Her eyes get glassy. She leans her elbows on the table, placing her face in both hands. Emotions batter me from every angle as I watch her deflate from the Mom of moments ago. I understand her fears for me, and love knowing someone loves me that much. Not everyone has that. I shove away thoughts of her wanting me to do nothing, just to protect myself from unwanted notoriety.

"There was no choice, Mom. And please don't say 'there's always a choice.' Letting them bleed to death was not an option."

She sighs, lowering her hands. "I know, Honey. I know." The pain in her eyes hurts my heart. "I would have expected and wanted nothing less. But that doesn't make this any easier."

I nod. The fear she feels is mutual, only mine is for *her*, knowing she's been through this before. Knowing it will destroy her if anything happens to me. "So, Kenji knows. He witnessed it. We talked about it, and I told him everything." I wait for the freak out, but none comes.

"What about the little girl?"

"Rebecca just thinks she bumped her head and passed out for awhile."

"That's a relief. But Kenji knows." She sips her coffee. "Now it's Kenji and Julia. And Misty, of course, who doesn't fully know, but definitely suspects something."

"I trust Kenji, you know. I really do."

"Yes, but Shilo, you and Kenji may part ways someday, and then what? It's very hard to keep such a remarkable secret."

"It was the right thing. That's all I know. I figure, if God gave me the power to heal people, He'll give me a way to handle whatever comes next. And right now, the only thing coming next is Sicily. *That's* the thing I can't handle."

"You'll handle it just fine. Right now your head is wrapped around all the things you'll miss. But it will be exciting, I promise. And incredibly beautiful." She sets down her cup and yawns. "The mountains, the sea, the vineyards. Ruins of ancient temples built thousands of years ago. And the view from the convent will take your breath away."

"A family visit is one thing. But not this...I'm not spending the summer there."

"Tomorrow's another day, Sweetheart. I'm all talked out." She yawns again, stands, and kisses the top of my head. "We'll continue this after Dad's meeting tomorrow."

This day had begun forever ago, and despite a head full of questions, I crave the soft, cozy warmth of my bed. I crawl in and lay beneath the covers, sleepily thinking of Greenwood's tall coffee trees and pretty little white teaberry flowers. The rich, earthy scent of the woods as Kenji and I walked in the dark the night he said he loved me. It is the last image I remember before my room fills with morning light.

A glance at my iPod shows the morning is nearly gone. Amazingly, no one woke me for French crepes or egg cassulettes. I shower, dress, and start to head downstairs before the sound of my cell draws me back to my room. I grab it without checking the caller ID.

"Hey stranger, welcome back."

I smile. How I missed her voice. "Hey, Mel. What's going on?"

"You tell me. I want to hear every detail. How were the kids? What was Kentucky like? Did you and Kenji just ignore each other or what? Start talkin'."

I struggle to begin what will likely be a lifetime of challenging conversations. The first part is easy—me and Kenji's first talk on the bus, the week of working and teaching the Sunday School kids. But the second part...not so much. I have to tell her about the rafting accident because she's bound to hear it from someone else. The creative part is doing it without the miracle and without starting a pattern of lies. And therein lies the problem.

I *want* to tell her the miracle. Want it so bad I could burst. She's been there for me since we were pigtail girls playing at the park. She knows my heart. My dreams. And I want her to know about this amazing thing that happened. But it's been revealed to too many people already, and much as I trust Mel, I can't fight statistics. The more people who know, the more chance of my secret getting out. I inhale the words that long to come out and give her the version I rehearsed.

We hang up, and I head downstairs, where I hope to settle this ridiculous Sicily fiasco. Silence fills the house. Outside the glass patio doors, Mom, Dad, and Julia attack the earth with hoes and trowels. Dad concentrates on weeding the vegetable garden, already abundant with young tomatoes, green beans, and cucumber plants. The veggies are unaware they are destined for fame in one of Mom's upcoming foodie presentations. Mom and Jules brighten the fence line with orange and yellow marigolds. I step out into a perfect blue-sky day.

Dad stops weeding and glances up. "Hey, lazybones! Ready to work?"

"Um…sure?"

"Good. You can help with weeds. Why is it they grow ten times faster than the vegetables?" He hands me a trowel and points to the other side of his tomato patch.

I dig in and prepare to launch my anti-Sicily argument, when Jules starts a detail-rich story about her recent acquisition of Hawaiian lava. I dig and pull, dig and pull, not so patiently listening to her endless story.

"And then Emma said she wasn't sure she wanted to do a trade, so then I said…"

Finally she gets to the part where her friend agrees to the trade and puts the lava in her hand. Time to jump in before she drifts into a new story, or worse, an extension of this one.

"What a cool addition to your collection. Maybe we can drive to Starved Rock State Park this summer and find more."

Dad stops pulling and brushes dirt off his hands. "The trip is on, Shilo. You can say what you want, but we're going through with this plan. We'll all be together for the first week, though. Mom didn't want you going alone." He attacks another weed that seems to have roots down to China. "Now, me, I thought we should just box you up at the Fed Ex place, but she wouldn't go for it."

My summer is going down the tubes, and he's making jokes. "Hilarious."

"Do you remember what I said that first night we talked about The Gift?" I open my mouth to respond, but he continues. "I said we're all in this *together*, and I meant it. We'll stay for a week, visit with the cousins and Nonna Marie, then me, Mom, and Julia will have to leave."

"But you'll be in safe hands there with Nonna Marie and the nuns," Mom chimes in.

"How long? Not the whole summer, right? A week? Ten days?" I look at Mom, silently imploring her to give the right response, but she says nothing. "Mom. Please. It's so far. They're so old."

"It's a beautiful place, Shilo." She speaks calmly. Much too calmly. "And not all the nuns are old."

Dad grabs his cell and pulls up a calendar. "We leave here," he points to a Sunday, and you come back here," his finger moves to another square on the calendar. "The cousins will take you to the airport a week before school starts." He places the cell in my hand. "It's not that bad; we're already almost three weeks into summer break."

I stare at the calendar, sliding my finger over the

dates he indicated. "Five weeks?"

Mom launches into verbiage like "incredible adventure" and "the opportunity to grow and learn," but it bounces off my head and into oblivion. "Do you realize how many people would love to have this opportunity?"

"Let me think. Zero?"

She expounds the benefits of spending time with one of the few people who have experienced The Gift. "Honey, you've had so many questions about it. Here's your chance to get answers from someone who knows, someone who's been there."

One valid point does not make this a trip worth taking.

A long day of trying to change their minds, shopping for the trip, and catching up with friends has me wiped out. I flop into bed, and precisely eight seconds later, there's an obnoxious rapping at my door.

"Shi, you awake?" Julia enters without waiting for a response.

"Not really."

"That rock really is pyromorphite! Me and Emma checked it out." She plops herself down on the side of my bed.

"That's great news." I mumble the words into my pillow, hoping she'll get the message.

"I think it's awesome you can heal people." Julia's voice morphs into adult mode, like when she discusses world events most kids her age don't even understand. Obviously in the mood to talk, she fails to notice the sleep in my voice. "Guess this kind of changes the trajectory of your life."

I yawn, with no effort to hide it. "Yep. There goes my trajectory."

"I'm happy for you, but I was kind of jealous at first." She plucks a stuffed polar bear from the floor and fluffs out its fur. "Well, I guess the truth is, I'm still kind of jealous."

"Don't be. I'm getting sent to Sicily for the summer, remember? Nuns and all that?"

"I know, that's what I'm *most* jealous of. You're going to learn stuff from Nonna Marie. It's just like when Harry Potter went to Hogwarts to learn wizardry from Professor Dumbledore."

And just like Kenji with his Star Wars stuff, she is ridiculously serious. "Yeah, Julia. It's *exactly* like that."

She nods without the hint of a smile. Sarcasm often escapes Julia. Tonight is no exception. She sets the bear back on the floor. "Anyway, I was just wondering if maybe…"

"Yes, I'll find Sicilian rocks for you, and some shells from the Mediterranean beaches."

"Actually Bella Costa is on the *Ionian* Sea. Didn't you look at the map?"

"Right. Ionian Sea. Goodnight."

"You'll be right by Mount Etna, you know. Europe's highest active volcano. It still spews steam and ash from time to time. Lava, too, but that's more of a rarity."

"How do you know this stuff, Rockhound?"

"Geez, Shi, who doesn't know *that*?"

"Just me, I guess. Can I go to sleep now?" I scrunch my pillow and lay my head back down.

"Oh, are you tired?"

Seriously?

"Goodnight. It's so weird that pretty soon you won't even be here for me to talk to at night. I'll miss you. Emma's leaving for a couple of weeks, so it's going to be pretty boring around here."

Guilt washes over me, clearing away the debris that prevented me from seeing my little sister. I look at her elfin face and imagine her having no one to hang around

with once Emma leaves. She will spend countless hours
in her room or at the library. Take walks by herself. Ask
mom to take her to a movie now and then.

"Send me letters, okay? They might be the only
thing keeping me sane."

She smiles, happily anticipating her summer assignment, then leaves. I close my eyes and ponder nights
without Julia's interruptions, but the view does not make
me happy.

I wake to a hum of activity. Feet moving quicker
than usual for a Saturday morning. Drawers sliding open
and shut. Jules thudding her suitcase on each step and
dragging it into her room. Twenty-four hours from now
we'll be boarding the flight to Sicily, a place I'll call
"home" for the next five weeks. And before this day is
out, I have to pack, see Kenji and Mel, and call Misty.

So far, sounds like she and Tyler are adjusting fine
to life in North Carolina. The beach is half an hour
from their house, Tyler made friends with a neighbor
boy, and Misty enrolled in two classes at the local college. She's also planning to volunteer with an anti-
human trafficking group. I miss her…but I'm glad she
left. Her new life is better than just about anything she's
ever had. I pray for her and Tyler before getting up to
start a crazy-busy day.

My new suitcase lies empty and ready on the floor.
It was the perfect size for Kentucky, but for what's coming next, I'll definitely need reinforcements. I grab another from the basement and start packing, completely
bewildered about what to bring. It's going to be Africa
hot over there—that much I know. Shorts aren't allowed
in the convent, which doesn't leave me with many options. At least I can wear them when I'm with the cousins. My plan is to endear myself to the relatives so they'll
come often to rescue me from the nuns. I toss in my

bikini – definitely a convent "no-no," but there's *got* to be beach days. A couple of sundresses go in as Mom enters my room. She plucks them right back out.

"Your knees have to be covered, Honey. Shoulders, too. Wear these, and they'll banish you forever."

"That's the plan."

She shakes her head. "You haven't gotten very far with packing."

"This may come as a shock, Mom, but I don't own convent clothes."

In the end, I pack some capris, jeans, and a few shirts that may or may not be acceptable, with a plan to buy "modest clothing" when we get there. It is not the kind of shopping I imagined doing on my first trip to Europe. The torture of packing comes to a welcome end with the ring of the doorbell.

Mel stands on the doorstep, trying to smile but failing miserably. "I've only got an hour before practice." She hands me a book shaped package, wrapped in bright paper and topped with a purple bow. "It's a going away gift. Open it."

I tear off the paper to unveil the prettiest journal I've ever seen. Yellow and purple silk flowers frame its satin cover. "It's beautiful."

"Look inside."

Mel's pretty script writing fills the first page.

To Shilo, My Best Friend,

Fill these blank pages with your hopes and dreams, thoughts and adventures, joys and sorrows. May you live life to the fullest, and may I always be part of it.

Your Friend Always,

Mel

I want to thank her for the journal, tell her how perfect it is. I want to say how much I'll miss her. But my voice betrays me. Instead, I pull an Annieconda and hug the guts out of her.

"Remember, Shi, when you get back, I want to hear every detail. And I want letters and postcards and…just anything."

We head to Pioneer Park, walking aimlessly along the cobblestone path that parallels the sparkling river. Moms push strollers, kids fish off the bridge, and couples walked hand in hand as we talk about her new boyfriend, her upcoming show, and Sicily. She thinks my parents are sending me there because of the gang situation, which is all the truth she needs to know. A couple of guys around our age keep glancing our way in a futile attempt at being inconspicuous. I look at Melody, her caramel skin glistening in the sun, her black wavy hair pulled back, exposing ebony eyes and high cheekbones. No doubt she's the topic of their conversation.

Melody glances at her watch and gasps. "My coach is going to kill me!" She grabs my arm, and we take off running and laughing. The boys look at us like we're insane, which makes us laugh harder and run slower. The moment we reach the house, the carefree moment slams shut like a broken window. This is it. Through hugs and tears, Melody promises to tape her ballet so I can see it when I return from Nunville.

Half an hour later, the doorbell rings again. Kenji stands in the spot Melody occupied earlier, and like her, clutches a wrapped package. Elation and heartbreak battle inside my heart. My happiness at seeing him is destined to be crushed by a goodbye kiss that will have to last the rest of the summer. We retreat to the backyard deck, where he places the small gift-wrapped box in my hands.

"This is for you, Blue. I picked it out. Hope you like it. It's sort of a going away and happy birthday present, since we won't be together when you turn seventeen."

His uneasiness is contagious. I fumble with the wrapping paper, avoiding his gaze. The black velvet ring box oozes elegance. Beautiful…and intimidating. No more putting off the big moment. I slowly open the lid.

Blue topaz sparkles like a drop of the Mediterranean Sea. I hadn't known what to expect, but this was beyond anything I'd imagined.

Kenji tilts the stone to reflect the sunlight. "See? It's the color of your eyes. It reminds me of how they looked that day on the riverbank. You know, after you…after everything happened. Try it on. Your mom told me your size."

"This is amazing."

"*You're* amazing. I always thought you were pretty special, but now that I know your secret, 'amazing' definitely seems like a better word. Anyway, you deserve something special. Turning seventeen is a pretty big deal."

The ring fits perfectly. Which is good, because I am never, ever, taking it off. "Kenji, this is way too expensive."

"My aunt and uncle own a jewelry shop. Family discount." He grins.

"Lucky for me."

"Happy birthday." He leans over and kisses me, then brushes the hair back from my face and kisses me again. "How are we going to survive this summer?"

A question with no good answer. I shake my head and lean against him. "I don't know. It's so hard to leave, but I'm starting to feel like it's important that I go. Mom said there are things about this healing power only Nonna Marie can explain. Even a dark side." I realize my mistake the moment the last word slips out.

"Dark side?" His face lights up. "I told you. It *is* just like…"

My hand flies up and covers his mouth. "Stop. Do not mention the name of a Jedi or wizard unless you want to get hurt. And while we're at it, vampires are off limits, too."

He licks my palm, and I jerk it away with an "Ewww," before wiping it on his shirt.

"Fine. I promise."

We sit and talk, both dreading the moment when this backyard scene dissipates into a memory to savor until we meet again. A memory I will cling to heart and soul. He talks about his farm relatives and the little cousin he'll be sharing a room with. "They're really great, Shi; you would like them. But it's going to be a killer. We're talking corn and cows and endless miles of dirt roads with pure nothingness on either side. I'll go insane."

I give him an eye roll, wishing small town USA was my biggest challenge. "I've got nuns, Kenji. I'll be living in a convent that's been around since Adam and Eve. Pretty sure I've got you beat."

He types his Indiana address into my cell, a simple act that drops my heart to the ground. We walk hand in hand to the street as I silently curse each step that brings us closer to his car. A breeze sweeps up a cluster of fallen petals, and they dance in midair before floating back to the sidewalk. It is the kind of nature thing that, under normal circumstances, would make me smile. But I don't remember how.

Kenji cups my face in his hands. "Don't go falling for any hot Italian guys out there, okay?"

"Don't go following any hot farm girls into the barn." My voice cracks on "barn," and I feel warm drops sliding down my cheeks.

"Hey, it's not forever." He holds me tight. "Let's make a date for your first night back. Dinner at Freddy's Rib Shack and a walk along the river. Sound good?"

I nod. It's the best I can do.

"You still love me?"

Another nod.

"Not good enough, Miss Giannelli. I need more than that to get me all the way to August fifteenth."

I take a breath, determined to say it without a sob stealing the words. "I love you."

"I love you, too."

More warm, sweet kisses, until without warning, he stops and pulls out his keys. Neither of us speaks as he starts the car. Frozen to the sidewalk, I watch him drive to the end of the street and left turn into oblivion, wondering what in the world happened to my life.

Sunrise. Dawn eases into daybreak as I stand at my window surveying my little corner of the world. My heart is still heavy over leaving Kenji, but at some point during the restless night, an unexplainable peace settled on me. My friends will be here when I return. Mel and I are closer than we've been in months. Kenji loves me. *Loves* me. And somewhere in Sicily, in a remote little mountainside convent, lives an old woman with the key to unlocking the mysteries of a gift so powerful it can alter people's lives. A gift that, for reasons far beyond my understanding, God gave to me.

Turning away from the window, I pause to check my pocket for the chunk of celestine, then lock my suitcase and head downstairs. What comes next on this journey is anyone's guess. One thing I know for sure, I don't want to crash and burn like Nonna Marie. And if spending time with her prevents that from happening, then bring on Sicily.

ABOUT THE AUTHOR

Susan loves to wander. Beaches, mountains, deserts, caves, and canyons...it doesn't matter, as long as she's surrounded by God's amazing creation. When wandering isn't an option, she's an author, travel presenter, public relations professional, and photographer. A native of the Chicago suburbs, Susan graduated from Northern Illinois University with a degree in journalism and a determination to become a reporter. From a newsroom in Berwyn, Illinois to a television station in Albuquerque, New Mexico, her dream became a reality. Back in her home state, she now works in public relations for a library and is a member of Willow Creek Community Church and the American Christian Fiction Writers. Susan is happily married and the mom of a daughter, son, stepdaughter, and one incredibly adorable Cleo cat.

Find out more about Susan and her books on her website at: www.susanmiura.com.

ACKNOWLEDGEMENTS

Years ago, when HEALER was in its infancy, a brilliant, accomplished author graciously critiqued it for me. Thank you, Lisa Samson, for sharing your gift and experience with someone who clearly had a lot to learn.

Fast forward a few years, when another gifted author and friend, Patti Lacy, read through the somewhat improved version and provided valuable suggestions and editing to help me take it up a few notches.

In the years to follow, comments from family, friends, editors, and fellow authors aided in nudging HEALER toward publication.

Nearly there, I turned to my daughter, Kasie (a budding psychologist with the heart of an author and the eyes of an editor) to give it a hard-core proofing...after having already done so several times throughout the years. As she finished chapters, she handed them off to my husband, Gary, for yet another round of proofing.

When all was said and done, my son and favorite musician, Nico, enriched this book further by writing a beautiful song from Kenji to Shilo.

In addition to everyone mentioned above, huge thanks also go to my sister, Patt, who loved Healer from the start; Amy Cattapan, for connecting me with Vinspire Publishing; The American Christian Fiction Writers-Chicago Chapter, for support, friendship, and valuable workshops; and most of all, to Willow Creek Community Church, where under the bold and challenging leadership of Pastors Bill Hybels and Steve Carter, my faith has soared, and my armor has been secured.

TRADEMARK ACKNOWLEDGMENTS

Frosty Freeze—Gold Medal Products Co. CORPORATION OHIO 10700 Medallion Drive Cincinnati OHIO 452414807

M&Ms—Mars, Incorporated CORPORATION DELAWARE 6885 Elm Street McLean VIRGINIA 221013883

Bloomingdale's—(REGISTRANT)FEDERATED DEPT. STORES, INC. CORPORATION DELAWARE LEXINGTON AVE. AT 59TH ST. NEW YORK NEW YORK 10022 (LAST LISTED OWNER) MACY'S WEST STORES, INC. CORPORATION OHIO 50 O'FARRELL STREET SAN FRANCISCO CALIFORNIA 94102

Disney—(REGISTRANT) Walt Disney Production, 500 S. Buena Vista St., Burbank, CA 91505

Girls Gone Wild—(REGISTRANT) GGW Marketing, LLC LIMITED LIABILITY COMPANY DELAWARE 1601 Cloverfield Blvd., Suite 420 South Santa Monica CALIFORNIA 90404

Harry Potter—(REGISTRANT) Time Warner Entertainment Company, L.P. Composed of Nils Victor Montan, Assistant Secretary of Warner Communications Inc., a general partner of Time Warner Entertainment Company. L.P. LIMITED PARTNERSHIP DELAWARE 75 Rockefeller Plaza New York NEW YORK 10019

Nordstrom's—REGISTRANT) Nordstrom, Inc. CORPORATION WASHINGTON 1501 5th Ave. Seattle WASHINGTON 98111(LAST LISTED OWNER) NIHC, Inc. CORPORATION COLORADO 701 S.W. Broadway, 4th Floor Portland OREGON 972053398

Peace Corps—Peace Corps Organization, United States

Popsicle— (APPLICANT) Conopco, Inc., 700 Sylvan Ave., Englewood Cliffs, NY 07632

Mini Wheats—(REGISTRANT) KELLOGG COMPANY CORPORATION DELAWARE PO BOX 3599 ONE KELLEGG SQ BATTLE CREEK MICHIGAN 490163599

Bon Appetit—(REGISTRANT) Advance Magazine Publishers, Inc., Four Times Square, New York, NY 10036

Walmart—(REGISTRANT) Wal-Mart Stores, Inc. CORPORATION DELAWARE MS 0215 702 SW 8th Street, Bentonville, AR 72716

GED—(REGISTRANT) American Council on Education, One Dupont Circle, N.W. Washington, D.C. 20036

The Wiggles—(REGISTRANT) Wiggles Touring Pty. Limited, The Limited Company, Australia, 39 Young Street, Redfern East New South Wales, 2016 Australia

Kia—(REGISTRANT) Kia Motors Corporation, Republic of Korea, 12, Heolleungro, Seocho-gu Seoul REPUBLIC OF KOREA

Mensa—(REGISTRANT) American Mensa Limited Corp. New York, 1229 Corporate Drive West, Arlington, TX 76006

Target Corporation—(REGISTRANT) Target Systems Corporation, 14860 N. Cave Creek Road., Suite 5, Phoenix, AZ 85032

Barbie—(REGISTRANT) Mattel, Inc., 333 Continental Blvd., El Segundo, CA 90245

Star Wars—(REGISTRANT) Twentieth Century-Fox Film Corporation, 10201 W. Pico Blvd., Los Angeles, CA 90064. (Last Listed Owner) Lucasfilm Entertainment Company, Ltd., P.O. Box 29919, San Francisco, CA 94129

Walgreens—(REGISTRANT) Walgreen Co. CORPORATION ILLINOIS 200 Wilmot Road Deerfield ILLINOIS 60015

World Market—(REGISTRANT) Cost Plus Management Services, Inc. CORPORATION CALIFORNIA 200 4th Street Oakland CALIFORNIA 94607

Joffrey Ballett—(REGISTRANT) The Joffrey Ballet of Chicago, Inc. NOT-FOR-PROFIT CORPORATION ILLINOIS 70 East Lake Street, Suite 1300, Chicago, IL 60601

Legally Blonde—(REGISTRANT) Metro-Goldwyn-Mayer Studios, Inc. CORPORATION DELAWARE 245 N. Beverly Drive, Beverly Hills, CA 90210

Nike—(REGISTRANT) BRS, Inc. CORPORATION OREGON, One Bowerman Drive, Beaverton, OR 97005

Dear Reader,

If you enjoyed reading *Healer*, I would appreciate it if you would help others enjoy this book, too. Here are some of the ways you can help spread the word:

Lend it. This book is lending enabled so please share it with a friend.

Recommend it. Help other readers find this book by recommending it to friends, readers' groups, book clubs, and discussion forums.

Share it. Let other readers know you've read the book by positing a note to your social media account and/or your Goodreads account.

Review it. Please tell others why you liked this book by reviewing it on your favorite retailer.

Everything you do to help others learn about my book is greatly appreciated!

S usanM iura

PLAN YOUR NEXT ESCAPE! WHAT'S YOUR READING PLEASURE?

Whether it's captivating historical romance, intriguing mysteries, young adult romance, illustrated children's books, or uplifting love stories, Vinspire Publishing has the adventure for you!

For a complete listing of books available, visit our website at www.vinspirepublishing.com.

Like us on Facebook at
www.facebook.com/VinspirePublishing

Follow us on Twitter at
www.twitter.com/vinspire2004

and join our announcement group for details of our upcoming releases, giveaways, and more!
http://t.co/46UoTbVaWr

We are your travel guide to your next adventure!